ROAD
RASH

ROAD RASH

A SHEA STEVENS CRIME THRILLER

DHARMA KELLEHER

Dark Pariah Press

ROAD RASH: A SHEA STEVENS CRIME THRILLER

Ebook ISBN: 978-1-952128-18-9

Paperback ISBN: 978-1-952128-19-6

Hardcover ISBN: 978-1-952128-20-2

ACKNOWLEDGMENTS

This story was, in part, inspired by political events over the past few years that left me wondering how previously decent (or at least tolerable) human beings turn into people who buy into absurd conspiracy theories and turn a blind eye to other's suffering.

This question led me to research cults and make this the center of the story. Key to this research was Catherine Oxenberg's riveting memoir *Captive: A Mother's Crusade to Save Her Daughter from the Terrifying Cult NXIVM*.

This led to the documentary series on HBO, *The Vow*, which was also about the NXIVM cult. And finally, to a documentary about Scientology, *Going Clear: Scientology and the Prison of Belief*.

I want to thank the creators of all of these for shedding a light on the terrifying subtlety and ease with which people are manipulated, victimized, and even turn into victimizers themselves. The similarities to the cult of Trump are eerily similar.

I would also like to thank author Robyn Gigl for sharing her legal expertise with me for some of the story points. And if you're into legal thrillers, I highly recommend her Erin McCabe series.

Much appreciation goes to the members of the *Trauma Fiction* and *Cops and Writers* Facebook groups for sharing their experience and knowledge. Both are invaluable resources.

Thanks to Erin Wright and the members of the Wide Done Wright mastermind group. Erin is a treasure trove of information on how to get traction when you're an indie author who chooses not to be exclusive with Amazon. The mastermind group she created has helped me reach readers consistently.

I want to thank Lynn McNamee and her team of editors at Red Adept Editing. You make my words look good.

Last, but certainly not least, I want to thank my wife, Eileen, for her diligent support of my writing. I don't know how I lucked out to be with someone like you, but I am grateful beyond words. You are my hero.

I am truly grateful for all of these amazing people and for what they've contributed to this work and my author journey.

CONTENTS

CHAPTER 1
INAGUA'S HANDS

"QUIT CRYING AND GRAB HER LEGS."

Megan Thornton wiped her wet face and did as her mentor instructed. "Bethany was my friend, Linda."

"And now she's just heavy."

Together, they pulled the body out of the back of the van.

The night was alive with the ratcheting drone of katydids, punctuated by the hooting of a pair of owls perched on opposite sides of the truck.

The gibbous moon's argent light washed out the red rock landscape silhouetted by Capitol Butte, Coffee Pot Rock, and Sedona's other oft-photographed sandstone towers against a mandala of stars.

Under any other circumstances, Megan would have savored the breathtaking splendor of Sedona after hours. But this evening, her heart felt as heavy as the remains of her friend wrapped in a threadbare bedsheet.

Megan sobbed, straining to carry her end of the body up the narrow, dimly lit trail. Thorny palo verde branches scratched her face and arms, but she paid them little mind. She was being punished, though she didn't know why.

When they reached a small clearing, Linda set her end on the rocky ground. "This will do."

"I don't understand why we couldn't have called 911."

"Because NCB said so. That's why."

The words triggered a childhood memory in Megan's mind. Her mother, Nita, used the same nonreason for many of the crazy things she did prior to getting clean. "Because I said so."

Megan sat on a rock and cried heaving sobs, no longer caring what Linda told her. She wanted to understand, to know that she was a good person, changing the world for the better.

Linda's hands gently wrapped around hers, the older woman's breath a whisper next to Megan's ear.

"Sweetie, I understand you're grieving. It's understandable. No one wanted Bethany to die. I did everything I could to save her. But now she's gone. Leaving her here at this beautiful vortex is the most loving thing we can do to honor her memory, to pay tribute to all that she contributed to Luminos and the world."

"But shouldn't we bring her back to her family?"

"NCB has confirmed that laying her here is for the greater good. Taking her back to her family will only bring trouble. We don't need the government interfering with our work. They are part of the system we are trying to change. You've accomplished so much in your time with Luminos, rising faster than many of your peers. I know you understand that."

Megan didn't understand. But after reflecting on the lessons she'd learned over the past six months in Luminos, she figured that if NCB said it was true, then it must be so.

"Yeah," she mumbled.

"That's my girl. Doing this should earn you your orange slider. Now let's go."

"Shouldn't we... shouldn't we bury her or something?"

The thought of coyotes and other animals tearing apart

her friend's body horrified Megan. She shivered and wiped the tears from her face.

"She's in Inagua's hands now," Linda replied. "She'll be okay."

CHAPTER 2
UNDER PRESSURE

SHEA STEVENS'S custom 1300cc sport bike blazed up the switchbacks on Sycamore Mountain's south face. The wind roared in her ears. Yucca, cactus, and brittlebush blurred past her. Each hairpin turn was an exhilarating ballet as she whipped the bike around, leaning so hard in the corners that her foot pegs nearly scraped the pavement.

The August morning heat from the lower desert faded the higher she rode. By the time she reached the summit and cruised into town, the air was cool, with the promise of autumn just around the corner.

Olde Towne Sycamore Springs was a mile-long strip of businesses that included an antique shop, a pharmacy, a café popular with locals and tourists alike, and Iron Goddess Custom Cycles, Shea's destination.

She wheeled around back to the employee lot and cut the engine. When she stepped inside the service bay, the familiar scents of metal and oil enveloped her like a lover. This shop was as much her home as the house down at the bottom of the hill. The whine of a pneumatic torque wrench and the sizzle of a welder were a symphony to her ears.

Lakota, the woman welding an oil pan, stopped and

lifted her mask. "Morning, boss. Running late today, are we?"

Shea blushed. She and her girlfriend, Toni, had ignored the alarm and enjoyed a little morning lovemaking, taking advantage of the opportunity since Annie, Shea's niece, was on a sleepover at a friend's house.

"Slept through the alarm."

Lakota smirked and pulled a loose strand of her salt-and-pepper hair behind her ears. "Yeah, right. Can't fool me. You got some this morning."

"How could you possibly know that?"

"Ancient Oglala secret."

"Uh-huh. Where are we with the Cabello bike?" Shea asked, eager to change the subject.

"Fuel tank, frame, and fenders have been sanded and ready for paint. Fabricating the oil pan now. Gonna be a helluva bike. I think Ms. Cabello will love it when we're done."

"Glad to hear it. I'm hoping to have the design for the Jenkins bike by tomorrow. We can go over it then and see if we need to make any structural changes before getting started on the frame."

Lakota was a mechanical engineer by trade, but a substance abuse problem had sidelined her career many years back.

As ex-cons who had put their criminal pasts behind them, Shea and her business partner, Terrance Douglas, routinely hired second-chancers, including ex-cons, recovering addicts, and people rebuilding their lives after various traumas.

After Lakota joined the crew back in 2013, she and Shea developed a symbiotic relationship. Lakota's education and training made a perfect match for Shea's experience and creativity.

Shea waved at Digger and Kyle, the other mechanics

working in the service bay, and continued through to the shop's office. Terrance sat behind his desk, talking on the phone.

He was a big man with dark skin and a beard. Some people found his appearance intimidating, but Shea knew he was a total softie with a sharp mind for business and marketing.

Terrance made a show of looking at his watch then up at Shea with a shrug of his shoulders. "Yes, ma'am. Keep me posted if you get any likely candidates. Thanks."

"Morning."

"Oh? Is it still morning?"

"Hey, I'm on lesbian time. It's different from transgender time."

"Funny. Come up with a design for the Jenkins bike yet? We don't want to be incurring any late penalties by not meeting deadlines."

"Absolutely. Just gotta tweak a few things, and I'll go over it with Lakota. We still need to hire at least one, maybe two more builders. Preferably someone with electrical skills. Ever since Switch moved on…"

"I know. I'm trying. I was just talking with Ms. Jackson at Cortes County Probation and Parole. No likely candidates. Also been checking with the county labor department, the halfway houses, and the women's shelters in Ironwood and Bradshaw City. And of course, put help wanted ads online, as well as in the *Cortes Chronicle*, the *Arizona Republic*, and the *Daily Star*. There's a shortage of workers with mechanical experience now."

"What about that guy down at Goblin's shop in Ajo? Supposed to be a whiz with all things electrical. Even has experience with bikes."

"Arturo Fuentes? I've seen his resume. The man's got skills. Believe me, I'd love to hire him. But he's undocumented. If he can get a green card, I'll put him on the payroll in a heartbeat. Until then, I can't risk INS shutting us down."

"Shit."

"Also, we should discuss what kind of bike to enter into the competition at Tucson Bike Week."

"Why? We've already got more work than we can handle. And we'll be getting more business when temperatures cool down in the valley and the seasonal riders start hitting the roads."

"Our win last year in Bradshaw City gave us a nice boost in sales, but people soon forget. We could use another."

"I'll see what I can come up with." Shea started her computer and stared at the MotoCAD design window.

Despite what she'd told Terrance and Lakota, Shea had no idea what to build for the Jenkins job. The client was a relatively new rider with more cash than experience. She hadn't given them much direction, just asked for something unique.

She flipped through previous designs she'd created, but every approach or style had been done to death, either by her or their competition. Her muse had ghosted her with no forwarding address.

The Flying Tree bike she and Lakota had built the previous year, a powerful electric bike with a reclaimed wood fairing, was a bold move. It would be hard to top or even match.

Even radical designs needed to be practical with the horsepower and clearance of any mass production bike. A motorcycle without much torque or that couldn't take tight corners at speed might as well be a metal sculpture in a museum. Or a Harley.

She flipped through magazines and surfed the web for inspiration, ignoring the gnawing emptiness inside her. Her mind kept drifting to her niece, Annie.

Five years earlier, Annie's parents had been killed, and

she'd moved in with Shea. Now the girl was a teenager and blossoming from a preadolescent tomboy into a feminine young woman. Shea felt completely out of her depth. Maybe that was a part of being a parent.

In a few days, Annie would spend a month at Bold Women of Tomorrow, a sleepaway camp for girls who dreamed of becoming entrepreneurs and business executives. It seemed an odd theme for a summer camp, but Annie had begged to go.

Shea had approved only after some initial research to make sure the organization running the camp was legit. And yet, something about the camp nagged her. Nothing she could put her finger on. Maybe it was the idea of going a whole month without seeing her niece.

Shea found herself doomscrolling social media and feeling increasingly depressed. Nothing was coming. No grand ideas. Not so much as a spark of inspiration. Her brain felt like a cotton boll baking in the desert sun. Thoughts kept getting lost.

She drifted off to sleep at her desk. Then her phone rang, making her jump. Caller ID showed Toni was calling. "Hey, babe."

"You busy, chica?"

"Busy? No. What's going on?" She shot a glance at Terrance, hoping he wasn't listening in. But his focus was on his screen. Probably doing accounting or going through resumes.

"I may require your assistance with a case."

Until last year, Toni Rios had been a homicide detective with the Cortes County Sheriff's Department. After retiring, she began working as a private investigator, freelancing for a local law firm to locate evidence to exonerate their clients.

"You need my help? That's a first."

"You know where LezBeans Coffee and Books is, right?"

Memories flashed through her mind. She wasn't a

frequent visitor to the coffee shop in Ironwood's University District, but she was friends with the woman that owned it.

"Sure. I can be there in thirty minutes."

"Great. We'll see you then."

Shea shook the cobwebs from her mind and pulled on her leather jacket.

Terrance glanced up as she walked to the door. "Heading out somewhere? Not even lunchtime."

"Gee, Dad, didn't realize I needed your permission."

Terrance stared at her blankly but said nothing.

"Sorry, T," she said. "Just frustrated with trying to brainstorm this Jenkins bike."

"I thought you were almost done with the design."

"Still trying to work out a few details. I'll get it."

"And no, you don't need my permission. I was only curious."

"Toni needs my help with something."

"Everything all right?" The concern in Terrance's voice was genuine.

"I'm sure. Be back after a bit. A little wind therapy might do my creativity some good."

"*You* all right?" His expression conveyed more than casual concern. It was the look he gave her when she was getting herself into a dangerous situation. He'd given her that same look when she went after the gangbanger she suspected of robbing their shop. The same look he'd given her when she joined the Athena Sisterhood Motorcycle Club.

"I'm fine. Just meeting my girlfriend for coffee."

"Okay, then. Give Toni my love."

"Will do."

CHAPTER 3
A FRIEND IN NEED

SHEA ARRIVED at the coffee shop as a summer monsoon storm blew in from the east, unleashing its furious winds. Lightning slashed among the dark clouds. The air was heavy with the smells of ozone and approaching rain.

LezBeans Coffee and Books had once been a small house in Ironwood's University District. Despite the name, the coffee shop attracted a clientele of all sexualities and genders, mostly of the politically progressive variety. Many were students or faculty at the nearby Central Arizona University.

The shop had an open, airy feel to it. Many of the outer walls had been replaced with plate -glass windows. Among the labyrinth of tables stood shelves crammed with used books and tchotchkes for sale. Original artwork hung from columns and walls.

Toni waved her over from the front room overlooking the street. Nita Thornton, the owner of the shop, sat next to her. She was a Black woman in her fifties with a 1970s-style afro haircut and always a kind word on the rare occasion that Shea stopped in.

Nita's wife, Cat Hamilton, a white woman with a chestnut ponytail, sat beside her. Cat's sleeveless shirt revealed muscular arms that had been honed from years as a metal sculptor.

"I think you know Nita and Cat," Toni said when Shea sat down at the table.

"Good to see y'all again," Shea said.

Nita smiled warmly. "Likewise. Can I get you a coffee?"

"No thanks, I can't stay long. What's this about needing my help?"

Nita's cheerful expression dissolved like sugar in hot coffee. "It's our daughter, Megan."

Although Shea wasn't a regular at LezBeans, she knew Nita, Cat, and Megan through the tight-knit queer community. Shea had admired the vibrant young teen for her buoyant, generous personality and her aspirations of making the world safer for marginalized people. "She okay?"

"She's gotten messed up with a group in Sedona called Luminos," Cat replied.

"Never heard of them."

"They're a cult," Nita said sharply. "Brainwashing, gaslighting, abuse, the whole nine yards."

A rumble of thunder rattled the building. Rain pelted the windows like a power washer.

"We're worried something's happened," Cat explained. "We haven't heard from her in over a month. No calls. No texts. No social media posts. Nothing."

Shea glanced at Toni then back at the other women, unsure of what she was getting into and why Toni was expecting her to help. "Have you called the cops?"

Cat laughed darkly. "Nita and I talked with the Sedona police, the Coconino County Sheriff's Office, and the FBI. Sedona PD told us the Luminos campground was outside city limits, so not their jurisdiction. A deputy at the Coconino Sheriff took a missing persons report, but it seems he's written it off as a family spat. The feds referred us back to the sheriff. Megan's nineteen now, so legally an adult. Unless we have hard proof she's being held against her will or that she's being harmed, they claim there's nothing they can do."

"What makes you think this group she's with is a cult? Or that they're brainwashing or abusing her?"

"We didn't at first," Cat said. "We believed that Luminos was a nonprofit helping to train a new generation of progressive activists. But then…"

Nita let out an anguished sigh before picking up her wife's thread. "A woman in one of my NA meetings told me about her experiences with Luminos. The story she shared chilled my soul. People there are being physically, mentally, and sexually abused. This woman experienced things so horrific she wouldn't even tell me."

Cat's expression hardened at Nita's words. "We called Megan. She assured us that Luminos wasn't anything like what this woman described. She insisted she was having a wonderful time and learning a lot. Then she asked us for more money to attend the next level of training. We'd already given her a total of seven grand for classes at Luminos, each one more expensive than the last. Now she was asking for another twenty thousand. As much as we support Megan's goal of becoming an activist, we simply don't have it right now."

Nita wiped the tears from her face. "With most of the university students gone for the summer, business here at LezBeans has been way down. And we'd just paid her tuition for fall semester at U of A. We're running lean until classes start up in the fall. When we told her no, she begged and pleaded. When we still refused, she became hysterical, as if something terrible would happen if she didn't get the money."

"Something terrible like what?" Shea asked.

Another thunderclap shook the building. The lights flickered for a second.

"She didn't say. It was the desperation in her voice. As if her life depended on it. Like we were denying her air to breathe by not coughing up the money. We implored her to come home to discuss options. We were so worried about what my NA friend had shared. But Megan refused to leave, kept saying what she was learning and doing at Luminos was too important."

"What happened?"

Cat put an arm around Nita and said, "She stopped answering our calls and texts. When we left voicemail messages, she blocked our number. We sent emails. Nothing. We haven't heard a word from her since the end of June. She promised to come home for the Fourth of July weekend, but she never showed. Never called. At this point, we don't know if..."

Nita dissolved into heaving sobs. "My precious girl..."

"Last time I checked, the sheriff's office hadn't even talked to her," Cat continued. "The detective keeps giving us the runaround, saying it's an ongoing investigation and that he'll contact us when he knows something. That's when we called Toni."

"I researched the organization," Toni said. "There've been a few allegations over the years. Claims of sexual harassment and physical abuse. Cited for a few labor violations. A couple of former members filed complaints they were being stalked after leaving. But nothing stuck. Luminos is aggressively litigious and appears to be well funded. They've sued nearly every person who's spoken out, winning in most cases. No one has proved anything against them."

"Which doesn't mean the claims aren't true," Cat replied bitterly.

"Sí." Toni exchanged a glance with Cat. "It just means Luminos has covered their tracks well."

"And you want me to do an emergency extraction? Pull her out of there so you can deprogram her?"

"Not that simple, amor. Because she's an adult, we can't take her out of there against her will. That would be kidnapping. It was a legally gray area a few decades ago, but there has since been significant case law prohibiting any forced extraction and deprogramming."

"Whaddya need me to do?"

"Infiltrate the group, get close to Megan, and persuade her to come home voluntarily."

"Couldn't you do that, babe?" Shea asked. "Megan knows you, doesn't she?"

"Sí, she also knows I used to be a cop, which could compromise the entire operation. We need someone she trusts, but who has no obvious ties to law enforcement."

"Does she know we're dating?"

"As far as we know, she doesn't," Cat answered. "We've never mentioned it to her."

Shea considered the request. "What kinda place is it? An armed compound with razor-wire fences?"

Toni shook her head. "I've studied the photos Megan sent her moms early on and also pulled up satellite images from the web. The Luminos property is on private land inside the Coconino National Forest just off 89A, twelve miles north of downtown Sedona. No walls or fences. No one in the photos appears armed. My best guess, their primary weapons are psychological, not physical."

The desperation in Cat and Nita's eyes felt like an emotional black hole, and that terrified Shea. "I'm really tied up with deadlines at work right now. But I can talk with the Athena Sisterhood, see if a few of them are available."

Cat put a hand on hers. "Shea, we got no problem with your club, but we need you there. She knows you. We're sure she would trust you. You'd have a better chance of persuading her to leave Luminos than a stranger would."

"And you're smart and resourceful, querida," Toni added. "You rescued Annie when she was kidnapped. And you went undercover when the Sisterhood was suspected of dealing drugs. I can't think of anyone better qualified for this than you."

"Please, Shea. We'll pay you," Nita added. "We have a few thousand currently and can get you more if necessary. It will just take some time."

"You wouldn't have to leave until Sunday. That's when the next orientation session begins," Cat explained.

Shea considered the request. If Annie were the one in jeopardy, she'd do it without hesitation, no matter what deadlines she had at work or what dangers she'd face to get her back. Still, there were so many unknowns.

She turned to Toni. "I don't even know what I'd say to Megan. I'm not much good at talking folks into doing things. I can't even get Annie to clean her room."

"Tell her that her moms are worried about her and that they love her. They want her to come home for a visit. That's it. If nothing else, we need Megan to re-establish communication, not to coerce her or kidnap her. Unless, of course, she's being hurt or held against her will. We're hoping she's not, but if she is, she'll need your help. Bring another member of the Sisterhood with you, but any more than that may look suspicious."

Shea studied Nita's and Cat's faces. The anguish they felt for Megan was the same anguish Shea'd seen on her sister Wendy's face when Annie was kidnapped five years earlier.

The memory of the night she rescued Annie was seared into her brain. Creeping through the dark streets of Ironwood's barrio. Discovering a wounded Annie terrified in the trunk of a police cruiser. And then running away only to witness Wendy get cut down in the street by a bullet to the head.

She and Wendy weren't supposed to be there. Wendy's old man, Hunter, had expressly forbidden it. But Shea knew Hunter and his outlaw biker gang, the Confederate Thunder, would fuck things up, and they had.

If Shea hadn't shown up, Annie probably would've died too. But maybe Wendy would still be alive.

"How do I get in without drawing suspicion?"

Cat slid over a three-fold pamphlet. "Luminos's orientation program is called 'Change Yourself, Change the World,' supposedly a program that trains people to become activists. They target supporters of Black Lives Matter, MeToo, and the LGBTQ rights movements. Progressive idealists, especially young ones."

Shea studied the pamphlet. Photos of diverse young people smiling and holding hands covered the pages. The text talked about inclusion, meditation, attraction, manifestation, and compassion interspersed with quotes from Gandhi, Martin Luther King Jr., and other famous people. "It says the program costs three hundred dollars."

"It's five hundred now," Cat replied. "They apparently raised the price. But Nita and I will cover it. It's my understanding that Megan is now facilitating these classes or was when we last spoke. Should be the perfect opportunity to talk with her and persuade her to come home."

"All right, I'll do it. But not alone. I'll need to talk with the Sisterhood, see if someone else is available to join me. We'll go up there Sunday and bring Megan back."

"Thank you, Shea." Nita reached across the table and clasped her hand. Tears streamed down Nita's face. "This means the world to us."

"Happy to help."

Cat slid a stuffed envelope over to Shea. "This should cover your entrance fees and some basic expenses. We'll get you more once you've brought Megan back. I just need to go to the bank and pull it out of a CD."

Shea stuffed the envelope inside a pocket of her leather jacket. "What about this woman from your NA meeting who told you Luminos was a cult?"

"What about her?" Nita replied, her tone wary.

"I need to talk with her, find out more about this place."

"I don't know if that's possible. What she shared was under the blanket of NA's anonymity. She's keeping a low profile since leaving Luminos and is terrified of what they may do if they find out she's talking."

"I have to know what I'm up against. Getting this information secondhand doesn't cut it. I gotta speak with her if I'm going to do this."

Toni wore an expression that said, "Don't mess this up." At the same time, Shea knew Toni understood that getting accurate intel was crucial to an operation like this.

"Let me call her." Nita pulled out her phone and dialed. "Hey, it's Nita T. from the Friday night meetings. We found someone who's willing to bring my daughter back home. Her name is Shea Stevens. She needs to know more about Luminos." She glanced at Shea for a second. "She'll protect your identity. I trust her. Call me back when you get this message."

Nita put away her phone. "When she calls back and gives me permission, I can give you her number."

"Fair enough. I have to get back to the shop. I'll do what I can to get Megan back." Shea pulled herself to her feet.

Nita wrapped her in a hug. "Thank you."

"Really appreciate it, Shea." Cat gave her a quick hug and a slap on the back.

Shea did her best to give them an encouraging smile. "She's a smart kid. I'm sure it'll work out."

Toni said, "I'll walk you out."

Outside, the torrent had subsided to a light drizzle. The

dark clouds were now to the southwest over the Cortes National Forest. The temperature had dropped ten degrees, and the air smelled clean.

Toni pressed her forehead to Shea's while tiny raindrops dampened their hair. "Gracias, querida. I know this is a big ask, especially with all you have going on at work."

"Honestly, I'm not convinced I'm the right person for the job. Passing myself off as a touchy-feely idealist? Really? My idea of meditation involves shooting holes in paper targets or riding like a bat outta hell on my bike."

"You don't fool me, Shea Stevens. Underneath that butch exterior is a very gentle soul. You adopted Annie after her parents were killed. You've protected countless women with the Athena Sisterhood. Your compassion is what will persuade Megan to come home. You are a fierce warrior woman with heart."

"This fierce warrior woman just wants to get back to the shop and come up with an idea for a new custom bike."

Toni laughed. The sound eased Shea's trepidation.

"One other thing." Toni reached around and patted Shea's lower back, where her pistol was concealed. "Leave the hardware at home when you go to Sedona."

"Are you serious? What if things go sideways?"

"If they spot you carrying a gun, they'll know something's up. You're resourceful. If worst comes to worst, you'll figure out what to do. You always do." She tugged on the black bandana tied around her neck. "Might also leave the club colors at home too."

"Yeah, suppose so." But the whole thing seemed like a shot in the dark. Shea pulled on her helmet. "Well, I better get going."

"You're not going to take White Juniper Road, are you?"

Shea stared out at the storm that now hovered over her preferred route back to Sycamore Springs. "Guess not.

Probably not a good idea to be riding twisty mountain roads in a monsoon. I'll take the Thatcher Road to the interstate."

"Cuídate mucho, cariño. I promised Annie I'd pick her up from her friend's house and take her shopping for business attire for her Bold Women of Tomorrow camp."

"I should be the one taking her," Shea said, guilt poking at her.

Amusement twinkled in Toni's eyes. "Shea, when was the last time you went shopping for a business suit?"

"Ever?"

"Exactly. Relax. I got this. Go make amazing motorcycles."

"See ya tonight."

"Hasta luego, mi amor."

CHAPTER 4
ROAD RAGE JUSTICE

THE WIND ROARED in Shea's ears as her sport bike flew past the Ace Hardware and the Dairy Queen on the rain-slicked street heading out of the Ironwood. The lingering drizzle had left her soaked, cold, and eager to get back to the shop.

She whipped around an armored truck and a Buick with Oregon plates. She thought she was in the clear and began pouring on speed when a hulking white pickup truck pulled out in front of her from the Walmart shopping center. Shea braked hard, executing a panic stop.

The bike's back tire drifted sideways on the wet asphalt, threatening to slide out from under her. The distance between her and the truck evaporated quickly.

She eased off the back brake and turned in the direction of the slide. The motorcycle straightened out and slowed just enough to avoid a collision.

Fury blossomed in her chest from the close call. "Fucking cager!"

She laid on the bike's tinny horn and flipped on the high beams in an anemic gesture of anger.

Years earlier, she might've drawn her pistol and put a round or two into the truck's back tires. But now that she was raising Annie, she tried harder to act like a law-abiding citizen. At least most of the time.

The pickup's driver stuck his arm out the window and flipped her off, adding insult to near injury. As Shea considered pulling around him, the truck drifted into the left lane. A deeper horn bellowed a moment before the armored truck she'd passed earlier sideswiped the pickup.

In an instant, time simultaneously sped up and slowed down.

The pickup swerved hard right into a spin until it skidded to a stop, blocking Shea's path of travel. A passing RV prevented her from going around.

She braked hard again, but she didn't have enough stopping distance. Rather than T-bone the truck, she gritted her teeth and laid the sport bike down.

She tumbled and slid, ending up next to the truck's back tire. Her left leg was on fire. "Fuuuucck..."

Above her, blood painted the gleaming white truck's door a deep crimson. Despite the searing pain in her leg, her instincts kicked into high gear.

She forced herself to her feet and yanked open the blood-soaked door. The driver's left arm was gone below the elbow. She yanked him out of the cab and laid him on the warm, steamy pavement.

Shea tore off her bandana and tied it around what remained of the guy's arm. She fished a pocketknife from her cargo pants and used it as a windlass to tighten the makeshift tourniquet until blood stopped pouring from the ragged stump.

The asshole cried out in agony. His face was ghostly pale, but he was alive.

"You're welcome, dipshit," she muttered.

A man in a Vanguard Armored Transport uniform rushed toward her. He reminded her of a young Kevin Costner. "Holy shit! Are you all right, miss?"

Despite the increasing pain in her leg, she focused on keeping the tourniquet tight and periodically checking the guy's thready pulse. "I'll live."

She glanced over to where her sport bike lay on the pavement. The debris trail of shattered fairings stretched behind it. She'd put considerable work into building it and could only hope the damage was minor. Insuring a custom-built motorcycle wasn't cheap, so she had only liability on this one.

"He still alive?" Costner's younger twin asked in a shaky voice.

"Barely." Her body thrummed with the rush of adrenaline.

"Thank God! He came outta nowhere. My partner's calling 911. Hey, your leg's bleeding."

She glanced down. Her thigh was a gory mess of blood, torn flesh, and ragged denim. The wound burned as if her leg were on fire. A wave of nausea hit her, and the world wobbled. "Fuck."

A woman in a matching Vanguard uniform and a hijab walked up with a phone to her ear and a first aid kit in hand. "Ambulance and police are on the way. Is he alive, Phil?"

"So far, thanks to this brave lady." Phil knelt next to Shea and reached toward the improvised windlass. "You should lay down, ma'am. You don't look so good. I'll hold the tourniquet."

Shea grunted and hobbled over to the sidewalk. A wave of vertigo hit her. She ungracefully flopped onto her butt and took inventory of her injuries. "Fuck."

The road rash was bad, though with all the blood and dirt, it was hard to gauge how much of her skin the chipseal asphalt had eaten away. Her feet felt as if they belonged to someone else. The fingers on her left hand tingled painfully.

As the sun emerged from the clouds, the air inside her

helmet grew stifling. She opened the visor but resisted the urge to pull it off, in case she'd injured her neck.

Despite the growing warmth, her body shivered from chill. A sign she was in shock. She lay flat and focused on her breathing to keep her mind off the pain. Like meditation but with a stream of profanity when she exhaled.

"Cops are here. Ambulance too," the female armored truck guard called from nearby. "You probably saved this man's life, ma'am. You're a hero."

"Great." The sun once again ducked behind a cloud, cutting the glare.

A moment later, a uniformed Cortes County sheriff's deputy appeared in her field of view. A scowl marked his narrow, sunburned face. He spat on the ground next to her.

"Well, well, a member of the Athena Sisterhood biker gang. And the vice president, too, according to the patches on your jacket." Clearly not a fan of the club. "I guess that would make you Shea Stevens, right? You cause this accident, Stevens?"

"Huh?" Shea squinted up at him. *What the hell's this guy's deal?*

"Looks to me like you rear-ended the pickup and sent it into the path of the armored truck. Following too close and speeding, no doubt. Probably cost this poor gentleman his life. That's vehicular homicide in my book."

"No."

"No? No what?"

"Didn't cause the accident, dude." Her adrenaline rush was fading into agony and shock, which were becoming impossible to ignore.

"It's 'deputy,' not 'dude,' lady. Deputy Winters. You Athena bitches act as if you run this county now that the Confederate Thunder's gone, huh? Think you can do whatever the hell you want on my streets. Well, I'm here to tell you it's time for some accountability."

The Confederate Thunder was a one-percenter motorcycle club once run by her father then later by her sister Wendy's old man, Hunter.

When the Athena Sisterhood established a chapter in Cortes County, the Thunder pushed back hard. They refused to allow another MC, much less one run by women, to operate in their territory. Things got bloody for a while. Now most of the local Thundermen were dead or in prison.

"Need medical attention."

"You'll get medical attention when I say so. I've pulled your sheet, Stevens. Three counts of grand theft auto, wasn't it? How many years you serve in Perryville? Five years? Not nearly what you deserve."

Shea didn't bother answering. It was four counts. Seven years. And she served the whole seven because she refused to rat out the chop shop she was working for.

"Sisterhood's a law-abiding club." She took a deep breath to tamp down the burning in her leg. "We protect women."

"Bullshit. Your club's been implicated in multiple cases. Drugs, arson, murder. God knows what else. And yet here you are, free as a bird. Like someone…say, a certain Guate dyke detective…has been covering your ass all these years."

Shea didn't respond, though she had wanted to punch this guy's lights out for talking this way about her girlfriend.

"Only now the great Detective Antonia Rios has retired. Ain't no one left to protect you now, Stevens. Nailing you's gonna help me finally make sergeant."

She took in a ragged breath and flipped him off with a trembling hand. "Fuck. You."

He clamped onto her wrist with one hand and drew back the other for a punch.

"Deputy Winters, is there a problem here?" A woman in a navy blazer walked up.

"Detective Reynolds," Winters answered with derision, lowering his fist. "Just checking this woman's pulse."

"I see. Thank you for your assistance. I'll take it from here." The woman was familiar, but Shea couldn't place where they'd met. So many run-ins with sheriff's deputies over the years that it was hard to keep track sometimes.

"Whatever." Winters shot Shea a withering glance. "Free ride's over, Stevens. I'm gonna see to it." He strutted off in a huff.

"Can we get some medical help over here?" the detective called out then knelt over her. "Good morning, ma'am. I'm Detective Denise Reynolds, Vehicular Crimes Unit. How are you doing?"

"Had better days."

"I imagine so. What's your name?"

"Shea Stevens." Shea's mind swam in pain now.

"Well, hey! Didn't recognize you with your helmet on. We met at a Christmas party last year. You still dating Toni Rios?"

"Yeah." Shea ground her teeth, having no interest in small talk.

"She's a good woman and was a great mentor for me. I miss having her around."

A jolt of pain shot like a lightning bolt from Shea's leg to the rest of her body. She gasped.

"Hang in there, Shea. Medics will be here shortly. Can you tell me what happened?"

"Pickup. Cut me off." She struggled to re-create the timeline in her mind. "He swerved. Into next lane. Armored truck hit him."

"Is that how the driver of the pickup lost his arm?"

"Yeah." It came out more as a raven's croak.

"Did your bike hit either of the two trucks?"

"Not till after."

"After?"

"Pickup spun out."

A pair of EMTs appeared—a stocky woman carrying a

large case and a man with a swimmer's physique pushing a gurney.

Shea recognized the woman as Chelsea Tucker, also known as Savage, the sergeant at arms of the local chapter of the Athena Sisterhood. She was one of the kindest people Shea had ever met. The nickname Savage was a reference to the pulp fiction character Doc Savage, one she'd earned because of her blond buzz cut and muscular build.

"Shea, I'm going to let these nice people take care of you," Detective Reynolds said, "but I'll have more questions for you later, okay?"

"Yeah."

"Hey, stranger," Savage said, her face a mix of concern and encouragement. "D'you forget to keep the shiny side up and the rubber side down?"

"Apparently. Good to see ya."

"This here's my buddy, Casey. We're gonna take care of you. Okay?"

"Thanks." She took a deep breath and tried to blow out the pain. It didn't help.

"Can you tell me your full name?" Casey asked while he flashed a penlight in each of her eyes. "Pupil response normal."

"Shealene Eleanor Stevens."

Casey peppered her with more questions—asking where she was, the day of the week, and where she was experiencing pain or any other unusual sensations. Shea choked out answers while ignoring what felt like a puma gnawing at her left leg.

Meanwhile, Savage applied a dressing on her road rash and set up an IV in the back of her hand. "Shea, we need to remove your helmet and put you on a backboard because of the risk of spinal injury. But I don't want you to move. Let Casey and me do all the work. Got it?"

"Yeah."

With Casey kneeling above her head and Savage by her shoulders, they slipped off her helmet and replaced it with a cervical collar. They slid a backboard underneath her and lifted her onto a gurney.

"Doing okay?" Savage asked.

Shea grunted.

"Okay, big question. How fond are you of this jacket?"

"Why?" She'd spent considerable effort to get the jacket's leather as supple as a baby's bottom and hours painstakingly hand-sewing on all the MC patches.

"Afraid it's gotta come off too. And we don't want you jostling around. We'll need to cut it off. Same with your jeans, though they're trashed anyway."

"Fuck."

"Sorry, darlin'. Life before leathers. I promise not to cut any of the patches. And we'll put you in the truck before I remove them, so the world doesn't see you in nothing but your birthday suit."

"Yeah."

"We're taking you to Ironwood Regional," Savage explained. "They'll get you fixed up."

"Thanks, Savage."

CHAPTER 5

DOTS ON THE CEILING

INSIDE THE AMBULANCE, Savage and Casey sliced off Shea's jeans, jacket, and shirt with the efficiency of a chop shop stripping a boosted sports car. The experience left her feeling as exposed and raw as the chewed-up flesh along her leg.

"This should help with the pain," Savage said.

A wave of warmth flooded through Shea's body, dropping her pain level from exquisite agony to a dull burning sensation. "Oh, thank God."

She stared up at the ceiling, unable to turn her head. Her mind flitted erratically through the consequences of the accident.

No doubt the medical bills would be astronomical with her crappy insurance, especially if her injuries were serious. Would she require physical therapy? How long before she could return to work? Who would drive Annie to camp on Saturday? Who would rescue Megan from the cult?

She replayed the accident repeatedly in her mind, trying to imagine how she could have avoided it.

Driving fast on rain-slick streets hadn't been the smartest of moves, even for an experienced biker such as herself. Maybe if she'd taken the back roads out of town or just slowed down, she wouldn't have been there when the idiot pulled onto the street. Maybe he wouldn't have flipped her off and drifted into the other lane. Maybe he'd still have an arm, and she wouldn't have a nasty case of road rash.

"How's your pain level, Shea?"

"Okay."

"You sure? Your blood pressure's high. We'll be at the hospital in a few. Try to relax."

"Relax. Right."

At the hospital, Savage and Casey rushed her inside the emergency department.

"Hang in there, Havoc," Savage said, using Shea's street name. "You want me to call Toni and let her know what happened?"

"Please. Thanks, Savage."

"Anytime, sister. Keep us updated."

"Yeah."

Hospital personnel rushed her to medical imaging, where she endured a grueling X-ray photo shoot from head to toe and from multiple angles. The backboard she was strapped to felt like a medieval torture device. But the real torture was yet to come.

The personnel transported her to a room and cleaned the bits of asphalt and dirt from the long gaping wound running from her hip down to her knee. Despite another dose of the pain med du jour, her exposed nerves fired like an Ingram MAC-11 on full auto.

She clenched her jaw and tried to refocus her attention by counting the dots in the ceiling tile above her. By the time they bandaged her up and gave her another dose of whatever for the pain, she'd counted all the dots three times. Four thousand, six hundred and something. The count varied each time.

Afterward, Shea drifted off until the sliding glass door to her room whooshed open.

"Aunt Shea?" a teenager cried in a panic-stricken voice. Her niece, Annie, appeared standing above her, followed immediately by Toni.

"Ay, mi canche hermosa." Concern deepened the wrinkles in the corners of Toni's eyes.

Annie's eyes were wet, and her suntanned face flushed. "Is it bad? You're not gonna die, are you?"

A dark chuckle escaped Shea's throat. "No, kiddo, it's not too bad."

Toni kissed Shea gently on the lips. "You look as if you've been hit by a burra, my love."

"You've seen worse."

"Sí, I have. But usually in the morgue. Are these your clothes?" She held up a clear plastic bag containing what remained of her shirt, jeans, and jacket. The inside of the bag was smeared with a dark crimson. She set it down next to a similar bag containing her boots.

"Oh my God! Is that blood?" Annie exclaimed.

"Relax, kiddo. Most of it ain't mine."

"¿Qué le pasó, amor?"

"Asshole in a truck. Cut me off," Shea replied groggily. "Had to lay down my bike."

"Pobrecita, I'm so sorry."

"I'll live." Memories of blood and pain seeped into her consciousness. She tried to drift below them into the embrace of whatever pain meds they'd given her, but the backboard only pressed harder.

As if summoned by her thoughts, a man and a woman in cornflower-blue scrubs appeared.

"Good news," said the male nurse. "No spinal injury, so we can remove the neck brace and backboard."

"Yes, please!"

A few minutes later, when she could finally relax in the bed and turn her head, she breathed a sigh of relief. "Fuck, that feels good."

"Aunt Shea! That's a dollar in the curse jar," Annie quipped.

"Sorry. You find some clothes to wear to camp?"

Annie shrugged without speaking.

"We were just getting started when Savage called. We'll go again tomorrow. Just have to shuffle a few things on my schedule."

"Sorry," Shea muttered.

"No hay problema. You're okay. That's what's important. They get the guy who did this?" Toni asked.

"They got him." Shea opted not to elaborate as long as Annie was in the room.

"You still going to help Nita and Cat?"

Shea's gaze drifted to her niece, who was staring at her phone. If Annie was the one in trouble, Shea wouldn't let a minor case of road rash keep her from getting her out of harm's way. Hell, she'd walk through fire to rescue her.

"It's not for a few days yet. I'll be fine."

The sliding glass door whooshed open, and the privacy curtain clacked to the side.

A woman in a white lab coat walked in. "Shealene Stevens?"

"Yeah?"

"Doctor Choudry. Good news for you. No broken bones or concussion. Just a nasty case of road rash on your left leg," she said with a lilting accent. "The abrasion's deep. These chipseal roads really chew up the flesh. Personally, I'd recommend a skin graft, but I'm not sure how much of that your insurance will cover."

"Crap."

"I think you can get by without the graft. You may have some scarring, but it will heal. Just change the dressing and put antibiotic ointment on it three times a day for the next few weeks. I'll write you a prescription for the antibiotic and for something to help with the pain for a few days. Just take as needed every four to six hours. Follow up with your primary in the next week. Questions?"

"When can I get outta here?"

"I'll put in your release orders and print out your aftercare instructions. Should have you on your way in an hour."

"Thanks, doc."

"You need anything else for the pain?"

Shea met Toni's smiling gaze. A warm, relaxing sensation flowed throughout Shea's body. "Nah, I'm good."

Toni held up a canvas tote bag bearing a screen print of a large owl with outstretched wings, the emblem of the Sisterhood. "I brought you a change of clothes."

Shea rubbed her neck. "Wow! You think of everything. How'd you know I'd need them?"

"Twenty-five years in law enforcement. I've seen a ton of motorcycle accidents. Medical personnel are great at saving lives, but they can be brutal on clothes, especially biker gear."

"Thank goodness." Shea took the tote bag from her. "I'm so ready to get the hell outta here."

Shea pulled out a shirt, groaning as she wriggled into it. She was gingerly slipping a pair of loose shorts over her bandaged leg when someone knocked on the room's door.

"Must be the doctor with your Get Out of Jail Free card," Toni teased.

"Just a minute," Shea called.

The room swayed when she stood to pull up the shorts. She grabbed Toni for balance. "Come in."

The privacy curtain clacked to the side. Detective Reynolds stepped into the room. "Knock knock. How's our hero?"

Shea's hopes sank. Instead of her release, she now faced an interrogation.

CHAPTER 6

GOING HOME

"¡HOLA, COMPAÑERA!" Toni wrapped her former colleague in an embrace.

"Been a while. You look good. Civilian life suits you."

"You two need a room?" Shea joked, feeling a pang of jealousy but knowing she shouldn't. The two had served in the sheriff's office much longer than Shea and Toni had been dating.

"¡Cállate, payasa!" Toni's tan face flushed pink.

"And who's this lovely young woman?" Reynolds gestured toward Annie.

"My niece, Annie Wittmann. She lives with Toni and me. Annie, this is Detective Reynolds."

"Aunt Shea's a hero?"

"She didn't tell you? She saved the life of the driver who pulled out in front of her. Despite her own injuries, she put a tourniquet on his severed arm and kept him from bleeding out. That's a hero in my book."

"Ew, gross!"

"Mi heroína!" Toni kissed her forehead.

Shea squirmed with embarrassment. "Hero" was never a word she used to describe herself. Biker. Ex-con. Vigilante. Sure. But hero? Not so much.

"Who was that asshole deputy at the scene?" Shea asked.

"Deputy Winters? Yeah, he's a real charmer, isn't he?" Reynolds smirked.

"Winters?" Toni's face scrunched as if she'd bitten into something sour. "¡Que gilipollas!"

"What's his deal?" Shea asked. "Dude was giving me the third degree, acting like I caused the accident."

Reynolds shook her head. "Strictly between the three of us, that man has no business carrying a badge or gun. He was with Phoenix PD until he and his partner killed an unarmed Black civilian several years back. When the dust settled, Phoenix PD fired them, but no criminal charges were brought. So naturally, CCSO hired Winters."

"That pendejo is a menace to anyone who isn't straight, white, and male," Toni added.

Shea shook her head. "Sounds like a candidate for Sheriff Buzzkill's employee of the month. No offense to you two."

"None taken. Keeler may be my boss, but I work for the county, not him." Reynolds pulled out a notepad and pen. "Much as I enjoy shooting the breeze with you ladies, I need to get your statement."

Shea shared what little she could recall. Then she asked, "Will the pickup driver be charged with the accident?"

She hoped her visit to the ER and the repairs to her motorcycle would not cost her an arm and a leg. Though technically, they already cost the asshole his arm and nearly cost her a leg.

"Too early to say definitively. We still have to review the dashcam footage from the armored truck. The driver of the armored truck and his partner corroborate your account of events. Paul Hudson, the pickup driver, is still in surgery. Be a while before we talk to him. But I'd say the odds are in your favor."

"Good."

"I'll be in touch. Good seeing you again, Toni. Pleasure to meet you, Miss Annie. Take care of our hero."

Toni fist-bumped her. "Will do. Be safe out there, girl."

After Detective Reynolds left, Shea pulled on her boots and asked, "Any idea where my phone might be?"

"Probably in there." Annie made a face and pointed at the blood-smeared bag containing her sliced-up jacket and clothes. "And no, I am not digging it out."

Shea pulled on a pair of nitrile gloves before digging around in the bag. She found her phone in a pocket of what was left of her jacket. To her relief, the screen wasn't cracked.

Shea had two voicemail messages—one from Terrance, asking where she was, the other from Fuego, the chapter president of the Athena Sisterhood, saying that Savage had told her about the accident and asked her to call back.

Shea hit the redial button. "Hey, Prez."

"¿Qué pasa, VP?"

"I'm in the ER. Piece-of-shit cager cut me off and crashed my bike."

"Ay, ay, ay. You okay? Need anything?"

"Still in one piece. Toni and Annie are with me. I'm good."

"Bueno. Cuídate, amiga."

"You too, Fuego."

Shea hung up and texted Terrance that she'd been in a minor accident but should be back at the shop the next morning. It was wishful thinking, but she had to come up with some ideas for the Jenkins bike.

A moment later, Terrance texted back, "Sorry about the accident. Call me when you can. May have a lead on new employee."

She put away the phone, not wanting to think about motorcycle designs, employees, or deadlines.

Three hours later, a nurse provided her with her discharge papers and aftercare instructions, and someone transported Shea by wheelchair to the entrance, where Toni and Annie met her in Toni's SUV.

After a quick stop at the drugstore in Olde Towne Sycamore Springs to pick up prescriptions, they wound their way down the switchbacks on Sycamore Mountain and into the neighborhood at the base of the hill. Shea gritted her teeth and clung to the "oh shit" handle around every turn.

When they finally pulled into the driveway, Toni helped Shea limp inside and get settled on their bed, where Shea reclined against a stack of pillows. Annie hovered nervously.

"You want something to drink?" Annie asked. "Juice? Soda? Water?"

"Yeah, bring me the bottle of vodka from the freezer."

"Shea, you shouldn't be drinking liquor while on pain medication." Toni gingerly lifted Shea's leg to stuff a pillow under it.

"Fine. Annie, bring me a beer."

"Annie, don't. Your aunt shouldn't—"

"Don't listen to her. I'm the patient and your legal guardian. One beer's not gonna hurt." The meds from the hospital were wearing off. Every cell in her body ached, and the raw flesh on her leg burned.

Toni sighed. "¡Está bien! Bring her a beer."

A moment later, Annie brought her an ice-cold bottle glistening with condensation.

"Thanks, Doodlebug."

"You gonna be okay?"

"I'm fine. Just need a day to chill." She popped open the prescription bottle they'd picked up and chased down two hydrocodone with a long swig from her beer.

"Will you still be able to take me to Bold Women of Tomorrow on Saturday?" Annie asked, worry mixed with anticipation written across her face.

"I'll take you, mija," Toni said before Shea could answer.

"Thanks, tía Toni. Get some rest, Aunt Shea." Annie strolled out of the room, leaving the two of them alone.

"I can take her, Toni. I'm not an invalid," Shea said, more tersely than she intended.

Toni gave her a look but said nothing.

"Sorry. I'm grumpy and in pain. It's just that I promised to take her. This camp is a big deal for her. She's never been away from home for so long. And I..."

"And you're going to miss her. I understand." Toni lay beside her on the edge of the bed and gently took the amber pill bottle from her hand. "But so long as you're taking these, let me handle the chauffeuring."

"I'll be off the pills by Saturday. Doc only gave me enough for a few days."

"Okay. Let's see how it goes."

Shea leaned her head on Toni's shoulder and closed her eyes. "I'm glad I got you in my life."

"Likewise, querida," Toni whispered. "Anything else I can do for you?"

"Just need to sleep."

CHAPTER 7
V IS FOR VODKA

SHEA TOSSED and turned throughout the night. Even with the help of the Vicodin the ER doc had prescribed, she couldn't find a comfortable position. Her whole body ached, but the worst was the road rash. The feeling of raw, exposed flesh cut to the core of her being. Even when she drifted off, dreams of falling and crashing haunted her sleep.

The next morning, Toni and Annie pampered her with a brunch in bed fit for a queen. Eggs and chorizo, crispy bacon, an English muffin topped with blackberry preserves, and a bowl of fresh fruit, with black coffee to drink.

"Thanks, ladies," Shea said through a mouthful of eggs. "I should crash my bike more often if this is how I get treated."

Toni laughed. "I wouldn't recommend it. After breakfast, I'll take Annie shopping again, since we didn't find many business outfits for her yesterday. You going to be okay without us for a few hours?"

Before Shea could answer, her phone rang. The caller ID showed Terrance was calling. "Hey, T."

"How you doing, girl? Got worried when I didn't hear back."

"I'll live. Got some road rash, nothing broken. Gonna take today off, but I'll be in tomorrow."

"Glad you're okay. We really need to get started on the Jenkins bike."

"I know. I've got my laptop. I'll finish the designs and send them to Lakota to look over."

"Good. You need anything?"

"No, I'm all right. See you tomorrow, T."

"Take care yourself, sister girl."

A rumble of engines approached outside, followed by the doorbell. Shea didn't need to check the video feed on her phone for the porch camera. She knew who it was.

"You up for company?" Toni asked.

"Yeah, let them in."

"Okay. Annie, finish getting ready. We'll head out shortly."

"Yes, ma'am," Annie said from another room.

As Toni walked out of the bedroom to greet their guests, Shea downed a couple more Vicodin, changed the dressing on her thigh, and hurriedly threw on some clothes before hobbling out to the living room.

Several women wearing Athena Sisterhood cuts and jackets stood in the entryway, including Savage, the chapter's sergeant at arms. Her wife, Indigo, who served as club secretary, stood next to her. She was a tall woman with dark brown skin and braids that were a mix of black and indigo blue.

Fuego, the Cortes chapter president, strode forward and wrapped Shea in a quick hug. "Good to see you still alive, VP. The cops charge that vato for causing the accident?"

"Haven't heard definitively but sounds like they will. Whether his insurance company will pay for the damage to my bike is another story."

Fuego nodded. "Yeah, one downside of riding a custom bike."

"How you feeling, sister?" Savage asked. "Any fractures or concussion?"

"Doc says the road rash is the worst of it. Hurts like a motherf—" She cut herself off as she spotted Annie washing dishes in the nearby kitchen.

Raven, the club's treasurer, slapped the leather chaps she was wearing. "I keep telling you, girl. Get yourself a pair of chaps. They'll literally save your skin. And you can even wear them when you're not on the bike. My boyfriend really digs them." She elbowed Shea teasingly.

Shea put an arm around her girlfriend. "Eh, chicks dig scars. I just added to my collection."

The group laughed.

"I hate to be rude, chicas, but you'll have to excuse me," Toni said. "I promised to take a certain teenager shopping, since our time was cut short yesterday. Good to see you all."

Toni gave Shea a kiss then retrieved Annie from her bedroom. The two of them left with a flurry of goodbyes and hugs from the bikers.

Shea settled onto the couch as her fellow members of the club sat in nearby chairs. "I'm glad y'all are here. I need to ask a favor."

"What's going on?" Raven asked.

Shea explained the situation with Megan and Luminos. "I need someone to go with me and help persuade Megan to come home. Someone with better communication skills than me. Her moms are paying a few grand, so it's not entirely volunteer."

"I'll go with you," Indigo said, tucking a blue braid behind her ear. "As the liaison officer for the Lambda Resource Center, communication is my job description, including explaining things to those not amenable to my point of view. Plus, I've known Nita and Cat for years, though I've only met their daughter briefly. I think I can get her to trust me."

"What about the other women?" Fuego asked. "Shouldn't we help them?"

"Not sure what we can do if they choose to be there," Shea admitted solemnly. "According to Toni, if we force them out against their will, it's kidnapping."

"Even if they're being brainwashed and abused?"

Shea shrugged. "Right now, I don't even know for sure what's going on there. I'm hoping to get in touch with this friend of Nita's who was a member for several years. My goal is to persuade Megan to come home. If we can help anyone else there, I'll do it. But we gotta be careful. What I hear, they got a lawyer who likes to sue people. Don't need the Sisterhood getting caught up in some drawn-out legal battle."

"How long you think this will take?" Savage asked.

"I don't know for sure. Indigo and I'll head up there on Sunday. Hopefully won't take more than a day to convince Megan to come home, at least for a visit. From there, I leave it in her moms' hands."

An hour later, the group hugged Shea and said their goodbyes. The rumble of their engines vanishing into the distance left Shea feeling depressed and lonely, especially with Toni and Annie out shopping. For years she had lived here alone, perfectly content in her isolation. But now the place felt so empty.

She lay on the couch, opened her laptop, and again stared at the blank screen in MotoCAD, still unsure what direction to take for the Jenkins bike. She pulled up an older design, saved it as a new project, and began adjusting the frame based on Ms. Jenkins's measurements. But it just looked wrong. And the ache in her knee kept pulling her out of any creative flow.

Just as she was about ready to pitch her laptop across the room, her phone chimed. Nita had texted with her friend Robyn's phone number, saying that it was okay to call.

Shea dialed the number. It rang four times then rolled over to voicemail.

"This is Shea Stevens, Nita's friend. She wants me to rescue her daughter from the Luminos cult. Guess you used to be a member. We need to talk. Call me." She left her number and hung up.

Growing impatient with the ache in her leg, Shea decided to jump-start the pain relief. She grimaced as she pulled herself vertical again and limped to the kitchen area. From the freezer, she grabbed the vodka and a reusable ice pack then hobbled back to the couch.

With her leg propped up on pillows and the ice pack settled on her knee, she took a long pull on the icy liquid, enjoying the burn in her throat. She replaced the cap on the bottle and opened her sketchpad.

Years had passed since she'd transitioned from drawing designs by hand to using the MotoCAD software. As she flipped through her previous sketches, long-abandoned ideas, trickled through the fog of her mind. Pencil hit paper, and she began sketching out shapes for frames, fairings, fuel tanks, and fenders. Pausing occasionally to take another swig of vodka, she let ideas and notes spill onto the pages.

An hour later, a blanket of fatigue swept over her. She set the sketchbook aside and drifted off. Her phone rang at some point. Or maybe she dreamed it. She ignored it, preferring to slip deeper into the embrace of sleep. After all, the ER doctor had recommended rest as one of the key components of healing.

A torrent of dreams haunted her. She found herself on that dreadful night years ago, creeping through Ironwood's Barrio District with her sister, Wendy, desperately searching for Annie. No matter where they looked, they saw no sign of the girl. In the distance, she could hear crying. But neither she nor her sister could tell where it was coming from.

Wendy's eyes stared back at her, blazing in the dark,

dulled from the drugs she'd clung to for normalcy. And then staring blankly. But not from the drugs. Half her face was missing. She was lying in the street. More screaming. Annie clinging to her mother's lifeless body. Sirens wailing in the background.

"Wake up, Mommy!" Annie pleaded. "Please, wake up."

"She's gone, kid. We've gotta go. Cops are coming."

"Please, Shea! Wake her up. Shea, wake up. Come on, mi amor. Despiértate."

"What?" Shea's eyes fluttered open to see Toni gazing down at her.

"Hola, cariño. ¿Cómo dormiste?"

"Uh, I slept okay." Shea picked up the ice pack, which had fallen on the floor. "Figured icing it, keeping it elevated, and taking a nap might help my leg. Isn't there some acronym? RICE? Rest, ice, something that begins with C, and elevation."

Shea sat up, and the room spun. The swelling in her knee had gone down, but it still ached, especially the road rash.

"C is for compression. Though I doubt you'd want to wrap your knee in a compression bandage with the road rash running down your leg."

Shea shivered involuntarily at the thought of a compression bandage wrapped around her knee and pressing on the raw flesh. The gauze holding the nonstick pads in place was tight enough. "Guess I'll stick with the R, I, and E."

Toni smirked and raised the vodka bottle. "And V for vodka, apparently."

"Figured it might help loosen my creative blocks. Lubricate the gears, so to speak. I need to design a new custom motorcycle design before I go rescue Nita and Cat's daughter."

"Considering your injury, if you want to back out…"

"No, not changing my mind. Indigo agreed to join me. We'll get Megan back."

"Thanks for doing this. I hate getting you involved."

"It's not a problem. The Sisterhood protects women."

"You hungry for some dinner?" Toni carried the bottle back into the kitchen.

"Dinner?" Shea checked her watch. It was five thirty. She'd slept for six hours. "Yeah, that'd be good. Could use some food in my stomach. How was shopping?"

"Good. Annie's in her room, putting her new clothes away. We got two business suits and several outfits that she can mix and match."

"Where is she even going to wear these besides this camp? She's not even old enough to get a job for another year. She'll probably outgrow them by the time camp's done."

"Consider it an investment in her future. It's not about la ropa. It's about mentalidad, mindset. She'll be starting high school next year. Won't be long before she'll head off to college. Now's the ideal time for her to be thinking about what she wants to become and do with her life."

"A kid in high school? We're getting old, babe."

Toni laughed. The sound of it felt like the sun reappearing after a storm. "Querida, you and I have seen enough mierda for many lifetimes. But we're not old. Just wise and strong."

"Old." She picked up her pill bottle. Her supply was getting low, and her pain wasn't going down as fast as she would like. She'd have to call her doctor in the morning to get a new prescription. Especially if things got a little crazy up in Sedona.

While Toni made dinner, Annie treated her to a fashion

show of the outfits she'd bought with Toni the day before. At one point, Shea grew misty-eyed, realizing the little tomboy she'd spent the last five years raising was becoming a young woman. In a few months, she'd turn fourteen.

"What do you think?" Annie asked, showing off a gray pinstripe suit.

"I think you look great, kiddo. Like you're ready to kick ass and take names."

"I agree with your auntie, mija," Toni added. "Perhaps one day you'll run your own multimedia corporation, like Oprah."

"I don't know about that," Annie replied with a goofy, embarrassed grin, a glimpse of the child peeking through.

Shea checked her voice mailbox but saw no messages from this Robyn woman. Maybe she changed her mind and didn't feel safe talking to a stranger about what she'd been through. Maybe Shea had come on too abruptly in her voicemail. Subtlety wasn't her strong suit.

By the time Toni served dinner, Shea was feeling the closest she'd felt to normal in a while. The pain from the road rash was down to an annoying itch, and the throbbing in her knee was barely noticeable.

"Wow! What is this?" Shea asked through a mouth full of pasta and sauce. "It's fucking amazing."

"Tagliatelle with Bolognese sauce. Saw it on the Food Network and thought it'd be good."

"There's baloney in here?" Annie asked, making a disgusted face.

Toni nearly choked and covered her mouth. "No, mija. It's a dish from Bologna, Italy. No American-style baloney. It's ground pork, onions, carrots, tomato, and some other ingredients."

"I suppose it's good," Annie said.

"Real good." Shea stuffed another forkful into her mouth.

"Have you heard from Nita's friend Robyn?" Toni asked.

"Left her a message before my nap. Haven't heard back. Maybe she's busy or didn't feel safe calling me back."

The doorbell rang. Shea stood, but Toni put a hand on her arm.

"I got it. You sit and enjoy your meal. Probably a delivery or a landscaper looking for work."

Shea watched as Toni opened the front door.

"Are you Shea?" asked the woman outside.

"No, I'm her girlfriend, Toni. Can I say who's asking?" The wary tone in Toni's voice was palpable. They rarely got unexpected guests. Particularly strangers.

"Robyn. I'm a friend of Nita's. Shea's expecting me."

CHAPTER 8

FRIGHTENED RABBIT

THE WOMAN LOOKED to be a few years younger than Shea, with a pixie cut and bangs that swept across her forehead. No makeup. Pale skin. A hazy memory of a phone conversation surfaced in Shea's mind. Had she talked with this woman and invited her over?

"Oh, of course," Toni replied, her tone instantly more welcoming. "Come on in. Are you hungry? We were just having dinner, and there's plenty."

"Oh, no thanks. I'm fine." The woman's eyes flitted about the room. She held her purse to her chest with both arms. The woman reminded Shea of a frightened rabbit hiding under a prickly pear patch, hoping not to be noticed by prowling coyotes.

"Anything to drink? Water? Tea? Soda?"

"No thanks. I have to be at work at Walmart up in Ironwood at eight. I can answer a few of Ms. Stevens's questions but then must be on my way."

Shea shuffled over to the living room area, where Toni directed Robyn to the couch.

"I'm Shea." She shook Robyn's hand and sat next to her. "Thanks for, uh, coming by." She struggled to remember talking to her over the phone, but her memory was a complete blank.

"What all did you want to know?"

Shea grabbed her sketchbook and pencil to take notes. "I need to know what I'm walking into in trying to rescue Megan. Layout of the camp, what threats Megan is facing and which I might face when I go try to bring her home. Everything you can think of."

Robyn took a deep breath and released it. "Maybe I will take you up on that glass of water."

"Sure." Toni strolled to the kitchen. "Annie, why don't you finish your dinner in your room while Shea and our guest talk."

"Oh, all right."

"So, what can you tell me?" Shea pressed.

Robyn met Shea's eyes for a fraction of a second then gazed down at the coffee table. "I joined Luminos seven years ago. I was newly divorced and working as a literature professor at CAU. There was a lot of office politics in the department. The dean of humanities was an ass, and most of my students couldn't care less about what I was teaching. I was getting burned out and a long way from tenure."

"I get feeling burned out," Shea said. Terrance's voice nagging her about meeting deadlines echoed in her mind.

Toni returned with a glass of ice water and handed it to their guest. "I worked for the sheriff's office for twenty-five years. There was a lot I wanted to change about it but couldn't."

"That was when I heard about Luminos. According to their website, they were training people to change the world for the better, to break the mold and disrupt the institutions that hold people back. I thought if I could learn how to do that, perhaps I could transform our educational system into a place where teachers and administrators adopted more innovative teaching methods and where students wanted to learn not only their core curricula but every course they took."

"A nice dream," Toni said.

"Unfortunately, like a lot of things in life, it was too good to be true. Don't get me wrong. The vast majority of people at Luminos were kind, generous, and wonderful individuals with a genuine desire to help others. That's who the organization attracts—idealists, dreamers, and givers. But the leaders of Luminos? They're nothing but sociopathic grifters who manipulate people for their own gain."

"Who are these so-called leaders?" Shea asked.

"The head of Luminos is Nathan Curtis Bennett, though everyone calls him NCB. He fancies himself a guru. According to him, humankind started in the Sedona-Oak Creek area rather than East Africa, and *Homo sapiens* are the result of crossbreeding between early hominids and the Emanu, extraterrestrials from the planet Annu on the other side of the Milky Way. He claims to be channeling Inagua, an ascended master of the Emanu."

Shea roared with laughter. "Oh my God! And people believe that shit? Sounds like this creep's watched too many episodes of *Ancient Aliens*."

When Robyn didn't laugh with her, Shea added, "Sorry. I'm sure he makes it sound convincing."

"NCB asserts that humanity was originally a peaceful species capable of remarkable wonders, like the Great Pyramid of Giza, Machu Picchu, and Montezuma's Castle. But somehow, we've lost our way and become embroiled with violence, drugs, greed, cruelty, and power. We've poisoned the air, land, and sea, leading to climate change and sea level rise."

"Well, he got that last part right, at least."

"NCB's vision for Luminos was to create a new tribe of humanity that would transform our species back into a peaceful, compassionate, and prosperous society that protects the earth."

"Sounds like a noble goal," Toni replied.

Shea repressed a chortle. "More like wishful thinking."

"As I said, it seemed like a wonderful concept to me at the time. But now I see the whole thing as nothing but a con. The training seminars don't deliver on their promises. They keep telling you, 'Oh, you'll learn that in the next seminar.' Each one gets progressively more expensive. They bleed people dry, shaming and coercing them into surrendering all assets to Luminos. And when members have nothing left financially, NCB robs them of their dignity."

All mirth in the conversation vanished for Shea. "How's he do that?"

"NCB likes to use Luminos members as his personal harem. The overwhelming majority of the members are women."

A fire erupted in Shea's gut. "This guy's a rapist?"

Robyn's eyes grew dull. Her arms tightened around her purse. "More of a sexual predator or harasser."

"Potayto, potahto."

"He uses coercion and persistence rather than physical force. In the training seminars, he and the other leaders talk a lot about being open and vulnerable as the key to becoming effective agents of change. They get members to open up about their darkest secrets. They also stress questioning preconceived assumptions, stating that these unexamined beliefs hold us back. And really, all of that is true. But they weaponized it. Especially NCB."

"How?"

"He pressures us into thinking that by sleeping with him, we are liberating and empowering ourselves. When we say no, he mocks us as puritanical prudes who will never change the world until we abandon our old beliefs. And any secrets he's learned about us—he uses those as leverage as well."

"What an asshole." Shea's leg prickled and burned. "If it were me, I'd tell him to fuck off."

"Easy enough to say when you're not there. I would've said the same thing before I joined. But he has this godlike status among the members. As if every word that comes out of his mouth is pure enlightenment. They fawn over him. NCB likes to regurgitate philosophies from history's influential thinkers, twisting their words to his own ends. He's this weird combination of creepy and charismatic, brilliant and sociopathically cruel."

"I think the words you're looking for are that he's a sick fuck who likes to shovel a lot of bullshit."

"I'm an intelligent, strong, educated woman who had decent self-esteem when I went in. And yet I fell for it just like the rest of them."

"You slept with this douche canoe?" Shea asked incredulously.

Tears streamed down Robyn's face, and she nodded.

Toni shot Shea a scolding look, sat on Robyn's other side, and put an arm around her shoulders. "I'm sorry you went through that. I can't imagine what that must have been like for you."

"Thank you," Robyn mumbled. "It's why I worried about Nita's daughter when she mentioned Luminos at the meeting. I didn't want Megan to suffer what I went through. I was involved for several years before I questioned what I was being told."

"What triggered your questioning?" Toni asked.

"It wasn't a single incident, but a lot of little things started nagging me. I was a red bar at the time."

"Red bar?" Toni inquired.

"It's Luminos's ranking system. Everyone in the program wears a bolo tie with a color-coded bar slide. New members are white bars. The next level up is green, then yellow, orange, red, and so forth. Luminos's inner circle wear a blue bar. NCB doesn't wear a bolo at all, supposedly because he has transcended and become a master."

"A master, right," Shea scoffed. "Master of douchebaggery."

"I was overseeing several outreach programs and building projects when this little voice inside me started noticing inconsistencies. Unfulfilled promises. The enormous amounts of money getting funneled up the chain. I wondered where it was all going.

"The tipping point was when a member named Amber Grant got sick. They discourage members from going to an outside doctor. Instead, they see Linda Steele, one of the blue bars. She claims she's an MD, but she's not. She's a nurse practitioner specializing in holistic medicine. She can write prescriptions and such. But most of what she calls treatment is baloney."

"Because what's a cult without a little medical quackery?"

"When Amber started coughing and running a fever, she went to Dr. Linda, who gave her some special tea to drink. Her cough and fever only grew worse. She begged to be taken to a hospital. But Linda said no. Not until it was too late. By the time they took her to the ER at Red Rocks Medical Center, she was barely conscious. She died a day later. I never heard any official diagnosis. And as far as I know, there was never any investigation or autopsy."

"How old was she?" Toni asked.

"I think she said she was 27."

"And no postmortem?"

"As far as I know, they wrote it off as a fatal case of the flu, even though none of the rest of us got sick. After Amber died, I paid more attention to these nagging doubts that had been building. I recognized the coercion and manipulation being used and the endless excuses for unfulfilled promises. And I found ways to avoid sleeping with NCB."

"Good for you," Shea said.

"Eventually, I walked away. Literally. I had no car. I'd exhausted my savings and maxed out my credit cards to pay for seminars, so I didn't have any money. But I walked down the mountain in the freezing cold and eventually hitched a ride back to Ironwood. I was homeless for a while. Got hooked on meth because I couldn't cope with all the stuff I'd been through or the things I'd done. Eventually found Narcotics Anonymous. People like Nita helped me get my life back on track. Been clean now for two months."

"You've talked a lot about the women," Shea said. "What about the men in the program? Is NCB sleeping with them too?"

"I don't know, honestly. I never asked. Most of the members are women. I don't know if that's because their marketing just naturally attracts more women, or if they don't accept most of the men who apply."

"Anyone else I need to watch out for besides NCB and his fake doctor?"

"Connie Brady and George Ramirez. Along with Dr. Linda, they form NCB's inner circle. The blue bars. Brady is their legal counsel and the most vicious and litigious woman I've met. She sues anyone who dares speak out publicly against Luminos. And she's good. On the rare occasion she loses, she appeals, dragging it out with motion after motion until they force defendants to surrender under a mountain of legal fees."

"Rich people justice," Toni said, sneering.

"George Ramirez is NCB's head of security. He's stalked former members, followed their children home from school, even poisoned one woman's dog. It's why I'm keeping a low profile. I don't need either Connie or George coming after me. I just want to live my life."

"Have you gone to the FBI with this?" Toni asked.

Robyn chuckled darkly. "I spoke with a deputy at the

Coconino sheriff's office. He said that what I'd experienced and witnessed—the sexual harassment, the blackmail, Amber dying from a lack of medical treatment—might be grounds for a civil lawsuit but wasn't a crime. I don't have the resources for a drawn-out civil case."

"Okay, so we've established that this cult is fucked up," Shea said. "How do I get Megan out of there? What do I gotta tell her to get her to leave with me?"

"I'm not sure, to be honest. They make you suspicious of anyone who isn't part of Luminos. If someone had come up to me and told me what was going on, I would've told them they simply don't understand. That anything bad they'd heard about the organization or NCB was fake news or mainstream media propaganda. They taught us to have an answer for everything. Circular reasoning, gaslighting, strawman arguments, appeals to ignorance. Every logical fallacy in the book, they use it."

"Damn, this is so fucked up." Shea's leg prickled and throbbed. "Why did I even agree to do this if it's hopeless?"

"It's not hopeless. I got out. Others have too. I strongly suggest getting her to reconnect to her moms. Encourage her to come home for a visit. Let her know that they still love and accept her for who she is and support her on the journey she's on to build a better world. It's all true, even if they don't want her doing it with Luminos."

"I think I can do that."

"Whatever you do, don't talk bad about Luminos. Don't mention cults or brainwashing or sexual assault or any of the other horrible things that NCB and his team do. It will only turn her off from listening to you. She'll have to change her own mind about Luminos. No one can do it for her."

"Sounds like it'd be easier to just grab her and take her somewhere for deprogramming. Even if cops consider it kidnapping."

"Honestly, Shea," Robyn replied, "it wouldn't work if

you did. Ironically, she would view you as the one trying to brainwash her. She wouldn't listen to a thing you said. And when you finally let her go, she'd run right back to Luminos. People like NCB and his inner circle are master manipulators. They figure out your buttons and play them like Thelonious Monk played the piano. Just get her to trust you and encourage her to reconnect to Nita and her other mom."

Shea wondered for the hundredth time if there wasn't someone more qualified to do this—a therapist, a preacher, a social worker, or anyone else who was good at getting people to trust them. At least Indigo was going with her. "Are there guards or anyone else packing heat? Like this George Ramirez guy?"

"I never saw any guns or heard about anyone using them. They keep people there by convincing them that the outside world is a hostile threat, or at the least that they wouldn't have anywhere to go if they left. But no guns so far as I know."

"What's the layout of the compound?"

"Members are separated by their bar rank at a half dozen smaller camps that make up the campground. Everyone stays in cabins. Some nicer than others. As a white bar, you'll be down in the Seedling camp. Crude cabins with bunk beds and no central heating or AC. The Summit camp is at the top of the hill where NCB and the blue bars live. Fancier digs. Indoor plumbing, nice accommodations."

"Where will I find Megan?"

"Probably at the Blossom or Garden camp, depending on her current bar rank. A dirt road connects the Summit camp to 89A with a fork leading to a parking area near the Seedling camp. Trails connect the rest of the camps."

"If Megan's at a different camp, what's the best way to get to her without being noticed?"

"The Seedling camp has a large dining hall. While they

take breakfast and lunch at the individual camps, everyone, regardless of rank, gathers in the Seedling dining hall for dinner. That's the best place to make an initial contact at least."

"Anything else I should know about this place?"

"Not that I can think of. I hope you can get her out before something bad happens to her." Robyn's eyes darted about, never meeting Shea's. She was holding something back.

"You sure there's nothing else?"

"What? No. I...I should be going. Have to get to work."

Shea resisted the urge to press her on whatever it was she wasn't saying.

"Well, thanks for coming by." Shea grabbed the coffee table to pull herself to her feet, wobbling slightly as she did so.

Robyn stood and shook Shea's hand. "Good luck. I hope you can get Megan out of there. I know Nita's counting on you."

CHAPTER 9
VICTIMS AND PERPS

AFTER ROBYN LEFT, Shea lay on the couch with her legs up, resting on Toni's lap.

"I don't get it, babe. Why aren't the cops doing anything about this Nathan Bennett psycho and his cult?"

Toni paused for a moment, remaining silent at first.

"It's a tough situation. It pisses me off this pendejo is hurting people. If it were up to me, he and his enablers would spend the rest of their lives rotting in a supermax prison. But even if he's coercing women into sleeping with him, prosecuting him for sexual assault would be a tough fight."

"Just give me a machete. I'll fix this guy in no time."

"I know you would. But I don't think chopping off Bennett's polla will resolve the situation. You need to get Megan out of there willingly. And without violence or anything else that would risk your own freedom. Don't need you spending the next ten years in prison."

"What about all the other women he's raping? Not to mention this nurse bitch pretending to be a doctor while refusing to let people go to the hospital?"

"No se, mi amor. I really don't. When I was with the

sheriff's office, I was part of a task force that raided a compound being used for human trafficking. Should've been clear-cut, sí? Arrest the perps and rescue the victims.

"Pero no, many of the women who'd been victimized early on had become perpetrators, making sure the newer ones did what they were told and didn't escape. Failure to do so would result in severe punishment. The culpability gets muddy when survival requires maintaining the status quo."

Shea grew dizzy thinking about the matter. She liked things simple. Protect the innocent. Fuck up the bad guys.

"I'm feeling a strong sense of déjà vu with this situation. You sending me undercover into a fucked-up situation where I don't know the good guys from the bad guys."

"The irony hasn't escaped my notice. Honestly, if you'd rather not, perhaps I can find someone else."

"No. I'd never be able to face Nita or Cat again if I walked away."

"By the way, I heard from Detective Reynolds about Paul Hudson, the driver of the pickup truck that nearly hit you. He's alive, though the surgeons weren't able to reattach his arm."

To her surprise, Shea felt sorry for the bastard, despite all the pain and trouble he'd caused her. She'd had her own arm in a sling a few times. The thought of losing an arm permanently sent shivers down her spine. "They charging him for causing the accident?"

"She's cited Hudson for failure to yield the right of way and reckless driving. She'll send you a copy of the incident report with his insurance information. Hopefully, they will compensate you for the damage to your motorcycle and reimburse your medical bills."

"Hope so."

Shea picked up her laptop from the coffee table and did

an internet search for Luminos. Most of the hits that came up were PR articles from the organization itself, promoting all the so-called benevolent projects they were doing. Organizing civil rights protests. Lobbying Congress to shore up voting rights. Facilitating research projects on climate change and alternative energy sources.

She found a few articles expressing concerns about the organization but not making any outright allegations. A few search results led to articles that had been since removed. Had Luminos's attorney forced retractions under the threat of a lawsuit?

She checked social media, which she normally avoided. Her accounts had no posts except those where others tagged her. Group photos from Athena Sisterhood events and rides. But she didn't find any relevant posts about Luminos.

She narrowed her search to the leaders of the cult. A listing on Webopedia detailed Nathan Curtis Bennett's bio and so-called accomplishments. He was a former Navy SEAL and a seventh-degree black belt in Shotokan karate and had graduated magna cum laude from Yale's business school. He held several patents and had published three international bestselling nonfiction books. All that was missing was a claim that he was a direct descendent of Jesus Christ Almighty.

On Amazon, Shea found he'd book written titled *Reshaping the Universe*, no doubt a manifesto of his twisted beliefs. She was mildly curious whether it might offer some insight into showing Megan what a fraud he was. But even if she ordered it now, it wouldn't arrive for a few days, and she wasn't interested in the e-book version.

Shea moved on to researching the other leadership members that Robyn had mentioned, starting with Linda Steele, the nurse practitioner who had refused to take the dying woman to the hospital until it was too late. She got plenty of hits for the name Linda Steele, including several in the medical field, but no one local. Shea had no idea what this woman looked like or where she was originally from. None of the hits she clicked on gave her anything conclusive.

She had the same luck with George Ramirez. Hundreds of men named George Ramirez or Jorge Ramirez all over the state. She found a news article about a Jorge Ramirez who'd been arrested for stalking an NAU student in Flagstaff seven years earlier, but the charges were later dropped. And again, Shea did not know if this guy was a blue bar in Luminos or just another man with the same common name.

A search for Connie Brady, the bulldog attorney working for Luminos, turned up quite a few results. Dozens of business defamation lawsuits filed by Luminos popped up with Brady as lead counsel, along with libel cases with Nathan Bennett listed as plaintiff. The majority were still ongoing, but the ones that had been decided resulted in large judgments against the defendants, who were former members who dared speak out against Luminos.

Shea navigated to the cult's website and signed up for the introductory seminar, "Change Yourself, Change the World." She felt wary about entering her personal information, especially her home address. Would Bennett send his goons to harass her and Toni once she'd rescued Megan? Would they stalk Annie at school? She entered the address for Iron Goddess Custom Cycles instead.

She reached a series of questions asking about education, profession, finances, and other personal history. Shea had earned her GED while in Florence State Prison. Going to college was never an option. But since this was an undercover assignment, she put down that she'd graduated with a degree in mechanical engineering from CAU, with no mention of her time in the can. She'd picked up enough from working with Lakota over the years to bluff her way through.

She wrote truthfully that she was the co-owner of Iron Goddess. If some Luminos goon ever showed up threatening her, they'd have more than Shea to worry about. Both Terrance and Lakota could hold their own in a fight. Even Kyle, despite being only four feet tall, knew how to swing a wrench or a hammer if need be.

Then came a series of essay questions. Why did she want to attend the seminar? What did she hope to get out of it? What personal qualities made her a good fit for the program? What things did she want to change in the world?

She stared at the on-screen form, trying to formulate answers that sounded educated and inspiring. Her eyelids were getting as heavy as a Harley Davidson. She imagined herself channeling Terrance, who was all about self-improvement and personal growth, and wrote a bullshit answer full of woo-woo buzzwords like "inclusivity," "own voices," "holding space," and "mindset."

Finally, she entered the payment information using a temporary debit card number generated by a privacy website. Didn't want the grifters at Luminos to get access to her actual bank information. Then she hit Send. An automated email confirmed her application had been received and would be reviewed.

She caught herself blinking out and jolting awake as she resumed her quest for anything else about Luminos and its leadership.

"Tired, querida?" Toni asked, while watching the evening news next to her.

"Yeah. My leg's aching. Should probably go to bed. You coming?"

"I'd like to finish watching the news. ¿Está bien?"

Shea nodded. "It's cool. Night, babe."

"Goodnight, amor."

She took another couple of pain pills, unsure when she'd taken the last ones. The gnawing pain assured her that at least four hours must have passed.

She could have used a swig or two of vodka to wash it down, but she didn't want Toni to see her drinking. Maybe if she woke during the night and still needed a boost, she could get up and have a small drink.

CHAPTER 10
UNRECOGNIZABLE

SHEA WOKE Friday morning feeling a little stronger. The road rash didn't burn nearly as much, and the swelling in her knee had subsided.

And then she rolled over. The pain hit her like a baseball bat wrapped in barbed wire. "Fuck."

She swallowed the last of the Vicodin and forced herself out of bed. She would not let this setback sideline her.

While changing the dressing, she saw that the scab forming over the road rash was cracked and oozy. The slightest pressure still hurt like hellfire, especially when she wrapped a roll of gauze around the nonstick pads covering the wound.

"How is it?" Toni leaned against the bathroom's doorframe.

"Hurts. No infection at least."

"Ay, pobrecita. Take it easy today and get some rest."

"I was thinking of driving up to the shop. Gotta come up with a design for a new custom motorcycle for a client. I've been trying for a week to brainstorm ideas, but every time I open up MotoCAD on my laptop, my mind goes blank."

Toni touched Shea's cheek. "How many motorcycles have you designed over the years?"

"No idea. Dozens, I suppose. Possibly close to a hundred by now."

"And why are you stuck suddenly?"

"Beats the hell outta me. Everything I come up with is shit. Same tired old ideas. Meanwhile, Terrance is also pressuring me to come up with another award-winner for Tucson Bike Week. And this"—Shea indicated her bandaged leg—"doesn't exactly help."

"Mi amor, I wish I had an answer for you. Unfortunately, I'm not a creative like you. But you're brilliant and resourceful. Not a doubt in my mind, you'll come up with something spectacular that will wow those judges in Tucson."

"I really love you, ya know that?" Shea kissed her. "And you are creative. Your shrimp tacos are worthy of the gods. Annie ate nearly a dozen of them last Saturday."

"That's not creativity, querida. Just mi abuelita's recipe. As for Annie, she's a growing teenager. She'd eat anything I put in front of her. Speaking of which, I better make breakfast."

"Hold up. C'mere, you." Shea wrapped her arms around her, and they kissed passionately. Every cell in Shea's body came alive with arousal, temporarily blocking out the pain. Maybe this was what she needed. A little sex therapy.

"Tía Toni! What's for breakfast?" Annie called from the kitchen.

Shea sighed in exasperation. "You've spoiled that kid. She used to fix her own breakfast before you moved in."

"What can I say? I enjoy having people to cook for."

During breakfast, Toni shared that Gottlieb & Sossamon, the law firm that often hired her as an investigator, had called her for a case. Annie was spending the day with her grandmother, Gramma Julia. Something about going to see a romantic comedy at the movie theater.

Shea was determined to finish the design for the Jenkins bike before she left for Sedona. In the garage, next to the washing machine, the blood-smeared, sliced-up jacket with her club colors still sat in the plastic bag from the hospital. She pulled the jacket out and crinkled her nose at the smells of dried blood and mildew.

She emptied the jacket pockets onto the dryer. Her leather pouch containing her set of lockpicks. A tube of lip balm. A pair of Bluetooth earbuds that connected to a helmet comm. Glove liners for riding in winter. A SOG spring-assisted pocketknife. A subcompact Smith & Wesson .380 pistol.

With the knife, she sliced off each patch from the ruined jacket, rinsed it off in the mop sink, and set it out to dry. She had nearly a dozen patches in all, from the large club emblem patch of a soaring owl to the small rectangular patches identifying her as the chapter vice president.

She wasn't looking forward to sewing them onto a new jacket. She'd done it when she'd been patched in a few years earlier and then again when the national charter changed the club colors from Pepto-pink and white to silver and black. Shea had hated the pink, so the chore of sewing the new patches came as a welcome relief. Putting them on a new jacket would have to wait until after they'd dried.

From her closet, she grabbed a dusty textile jacket and a pair of matching motorcycle pants. She hated the added bulk and the way they rustled as she walked. But the real problem was how they rubbed against her road rash.

After a few steps, she tore the motorcycle pants off in favor of a pair of chaps. The leather was worn and cracked but would do the job. From the top shelf, she selected a modular helmet bearing the Iron Goddess company logo.

Rather than take the pickup truck, Shea chose the Yamaha FJR from the stable of bikes filling her garage. The

FJR's paddle shifter would save her from having to shift gears with her left leg.

She took it easy driving the switchbacks up Sycamore Mountain. The trip, short though it was, refreshed her. She could smell the distant approach of autumn as she climbed the fifteen hundred feet in elevation, the ambient temperature dropping with each turn up the mountainside.

"Nice limp," Terrance teased when she hobbled over to her desk.

"Thanks," Shea retorted. "I'm thinking of showing it off down at Tucson Bike Week."

"Eh, still needs work, I think. Maybe put in more of a wobble. Maybe swing your arms more and add some props like a crutch or a knee brace."

Shea nodded. "Yeah, that might work."

"Seriously, girlfriend. How you holding up?"

"I'm vertical."

"You come up with anything for the Jenkins bike?"

She pulled the sketchbook out of her messenger bag. Most of the ideas she'd scribbled down in her alcohol- and drug-induced haze were still a jumble of nonsense sketches and indecipherable notes. But she had compiled a few ideas for where to take the bike.

"I've got enough to get started with Lakota. We should be good." Shea paused, trying to find the right words. "You know Nita over at LezBeans Coffee, right?"

"Yeah, I know her. Why?"

"She and her wife asked me to help her out with something."

"Okay, could you be a little more vague? You planning on taking time off?"

"Possibly. Their daughter's involved in a cult."

"Megan? She's such a smart girl. How would she get herself messed up in a cult?"

"I don't know. Thing is, they've lost communication with her. And they asked me to help get her back."

"Why you? Why wouldn't they go to the cops?"

"They did. Cops won't do shit. Nita asked Toni for help, since she's a PI. But Megan knows Toni used to be a cop. Might complicate things. That's when my name came up."

"Shea, no offense, but you can barely walk."

"I know. But, T, this organization Megan's involved with is seriously fucked up. People have died. Others have been sexually assaulted. You know I can't just sit on the sidelines when someone's in danger, especially the daughter of my friends."

"No, you were never one to walk away." Terrance scratched his beard. "When would you be doing this? And how long before you get back?"

"Not leaving till Sunday. Maybe I can talk to her soon after I get there, persuade her to come home, and I'll be back on Monday."

"But you're not sure."

"No."

"Your timing sucks."

"Tell me about it."

"You doing this thing alone?"

Shea shook her head. "Indigo's coming with me."

"Good. Someone who understands the meaning of tact."

"I understand tact. I simply choose not to use it."

"Ain't that the truth," Terrance replied with a snicker.

She walked over to the plate glass window that looked out onto the service bay. "That what's left of my motorcycle next to the blue V Star?"

"They dropped it off yesterday afternoon. Lakota inspected it. Thinks it's salvageable."

Shea wandered back through the service bay, saying hi to Kyle, who was replacing the clutch on a Harley Fat Boy. She stopped at her bike, which was strapped to a lift. The vehicle looked naked without the fairings. Raw. Like the chewed-up flesh on the side of her leg.

Flashes of memory of the crash stabbed at her mind like jolts of electricity. The white truck barreling into her path. Her attempts to avoid the crash. The split-second decision to lay the bike down rather than T-bone the sideways truck. The pain. The blood. So much blood.

"She's banged up good." Lakota appeared next to her. "Windshield's cracked. Left mirror's gone. Clutch lever's all twisted to hell. Chrome looks like someone took a belt sander to it. Gonna need new forks and new fairings. But the frame still looks solid. Engine's probably okay, though we won't know for sure till we start her up. That guy's insurance going to pay for the repairs?"

"Supposed to. Almost don't recognize her without the fairings."

"Amazing how a few pieces of carbon fiber can change the look of it."

"I've put together some ideas for the Jenkins bike," Shea replied, keeping her eyes on her motorcycle. "Let me put it into MotoCAD, and then we can go over it together."

"Sounds good. You feeling better?"

Her road rash was burning again. And with every step she took, it felt like someone was jabbing needles under her kneecap. She wanted to take another couple of pain pills, but she was out. She needed a new prescription. "I'm managing."

Back in the office, Shea called and left a message for the Hudsons' insurance adjuster. Then she called her doctor.

"Doctor Clooney's office. How may I help you?" asked a familiar male voice.

"Chase, it's Shea Stevens. I messed up my leg a couple of days ago and am still in a lot of pain. I've run out of the pain meds they gave me in the ER. Was hoping the doc could write me a prescription to last me a few more days. Maybe a week."

"Oh dear. What happened to your leg?"

"Road rash. Laid down the motorcycle to avoid a truck. Also have pain in my knee. Hospital said nothing was broken, but it's swollen like a melon and hurts like someone's jabbing a knife under my kneecap."

"That sounds awful. I can fit you into Dr. Clooney's schedule for an appointment two weeks from today. Say, eight o'clock?"

A growl of frustration crept into her voice. "Can't wait two weeks, man. The pain is fucking killing me."

"I understand. My suggestion would then be to return to the ER and see if they'll run some more tests. A CAT scan might reveal what's going on. Could be some soft tissue damage."

She'd just dropped a grand for her copay on her recent trip to the ER. Her insurance probably didn't even cover the cost of the ambulance ride.

"How about a compromise?" Shea replied. "I'll schedule an appointment. Meanwhile, Clooney goes ahead and writes me a prescription to help with the pain in the interim."

"I wish she could. But with the recent restrictions on opioids, she can only write a prescription after she's seen a patient. Did you want me to schedule the appointment?"

Instead of answering, Shea ended the call. "Goddamn motherfucker. Ain't like I'm some dope fiend looking for a fix."

For the second time that morning, she thought of her sister Wendy. Shea hadn't heard from her in more than a decade when she'd shown up at the shop trying to hide from Hunter, her abusive old man who had been president of the Confederate Thunder.

Turned out that Wendy had become a junkie while growing up around the Thunder. Addicted to oxy and God knew what else. Between the Thunder's drug running and their brutal misogyny, it was almost inevitable. One of the many reasons Shea had run away at sixteen after their mother was murdered and their father sent to prison.

"Problems?"

"Fucking doctor won't write me a prescription for pain unless I go in and see her. But I can't even get in to see her for two weeks. I ain't no junkie. I am a woman in legitimate pain. What the fuck am I supposed to do?"

"You could go back to the emergency—"

"Don't start, T."

Terrance looked at her with an expression of smug patience, like he was dealing with a fussy toddler. Maybe he was, Shea conceded.

"Sorry."

"You're in pain. I get it."

"You wouldn't happen to have…"

"You really gonna ask me that? I spent three years in prison for dealing Adderall in grad school. You know I don't."

"Fair enough."

"Go home and get some more rest. Take an over-the-counter pain reliever. Keep your knee elevated, if it's swelling, maybe put an ice pack on it. I'll see you when you get back from helping Nita's daughter."

Shea sighed. This guy was her brother from another mother and she his sister from another mister. "Let me get this thing done for the Jenkins bike, and I will."

She took some ibuprofen and spent the next three hours creating a digital 3D rendering of the bike she imagined from the sketches in her pad. It had a classic cafe racer look, though Shea had added some flourishes that modernized it. When she finished the rendering, she sent a text to Lakota to review the design.

"All right, I'm outta here." She pulled on her jacket and chaps.

"Take care of yourself, girl. Especially when you go up to Sedona. Call me on Monday. Let me know how things are going."

"Will do. See you round."

She ground her teeth with each hairpin turn going down Sycamore Mountain. Even though the paddle shifter helped with gear changes, leaning hard into left turns sent jolts of pain up her leg.

A half mile past the bottom of the hill, she turned right into her neighborhood. She had an idea she hoped would help with the situation. Her pulse raced when she pulled into her driveway and hobbled inside.

She went straight to their bathroom and searched the medicine cabinet. Nope, nothing. She tore into the drawers and cabinets under the sink, tossing out hair dryers, bottles of product, and Toni's makeup. Still no luck. "It's gotta be here."

She finally tore into her dresser, digging deep in the top drawer amongst the socks and underwear. Her hand wrapped around an amber pill bottle. She checked the label. Oxycodone. Jackpot.

The prescription was left over after she was hospitalized for a gunshot wound a while back. The label said they were expired, but she didn't care. Wasn't like they would've spoiled.

She'd barely used them at the time, remembering vividly how strung out Wendy had been after they reunited. Shea would not let herself end up like that.

But now, the pain was unbearable. If she didn't do something soon, she might do something more destructive. Annie had already lost her mother and father. She didn't deserve to lose her aunt as well. The best course of action, Shea assured herself, was to treat the pain, just enough to remain functional. She wouldn't overdo it. She wouldn't become a junkie.

She popped the white plastic top and poured the bottle's contents into her hands. There must have been fifty pills or more. She dry-swallowed two pills, put the rest back into the bottle, and stuffed it in her pocket. It would take half an hour before she felt any relief, but at least it was on the way.

CHAPTER 11
BOLD WOMEN OF TOMORROW

THAT NIGHT she got some decent sleep, but troubled dreams haunted her. During one nightmare, she found herself in the home that had belonged to Wendy and Hunter. Annie was there, too, as a small child.

For reasons Shea couldn't fathom, she shot both Wendy and Hunter in the head then grabbed Annie and carried her away. She woke in a cold sweat, her heart beating as fast as a hummingbird's.

Toni slumbered next to her, snoring quietly. The morning light gleamed off her skin, as if she were made of amber and lit from within. She groaned quietly in a way that set Shea's heart on fire and opened her eyes.

"Buenos días, querida. How're you feeling?"

Shea's left leg burned. "Good, unless I walk. Or stand. Or move. Think you could take Annie to camp?"

"Actually, I can't. I'm working on a case for one of Gottlieb & Sossamon's clients. I texted Julia last night. She's agreed to take her." Toni glanced at her watch. "Ay, we should get moving. Her abuela will be here soon to pick her up."

Shea sighed. "Four whole weeks without sarcastic

remarks, gossip about boys, and dramatic eye rolls. How will I survive?"

"You're not fooling me, chica dura. You're going to miss her." Toni laughed and walked out of the bedroom.

"Maybe." But Shea knew she was right.

She sat up on the edge of the bed and gasped. It felt like someone was jamming steak knives into her wound and under her patella. She opened her nightstand drawer and took two of the oxycodone. She debated about taking a third, considering her level of pain, but she decided against it. "I'm not an addict."

Thirty minutes later, Shea, Toni, and Annie were in the kitchen eating French toast and bacon at the breakfast bar. Annie inhaled hers in record time then dashed to her bedroom and reappeared, dragging two large suitcases, a gym bag, and a tote bag filled to bursting.

"Geez, girl. You pack enough clothes?" Shea set Annie's plate in the sink. "I'm sure they allow you to wash them once a week."

"I enjoy having options," Annie replied smugly.

"I'm sure you'll be the best-dressed girl there, mija."

"Thanks, tía."

A recent growth spurt made her look coltish in her shorts and T-shirt, which was screen-printed with the words Bold Women of Tomorrow—Reach for the Stars. Still, there was something different about her. Something more feminine.

"You wearing makeup? You're only thirteen."

"Almost fourteen. And lots of girls my age wear makeup. When did you get to be such a prude?"

Toni squirmed on her bar stool. "I let her have some of mine. Didn't realize it would be an issue. I'm sorry if I crossed a line."

Shea never wore makeup, not even to cover the deep scars that crisscrossed her face. She had nothing against makeup, but it wasn't her thing. She spent most of her days building and repairing motorcycles. Any makeup would just get smeared with sweat, grease, and road grime.

It was strange to see Annie suddenly looking more like a woman than a child. A miasma of feelings welled up that Shea couldn't identify. A sense of loss of Annie's childhood, the instinct to protect Annie from sexual predators. And the realization that the girl was turning into a typical teenager, drifting away from the biker culture in which she'd been raised. It felt almost like rejection.

The front door opened, and Julia walked in, wearing a large pair of sunglasses. She was a skinny woman with weather-worn skin from decades of riding. She always reminded Shea of a piece of boot leather—deeply tanned and tough but still retaining a certain softness. "Morning, ladies."

"Gramma Julia!" Annie ran and embraced her.

"Morning, Toots. You getting taller than me now."

"Morning, Miss Julia," Toni said.

"Morning, Toni. How's the patient?"

"The patient is right here." Shea limped over and hugged the woman who had raised her sister after they became orphaned. "And I'm fine."

"You always were a tough cookie. All right, Miss Annie. You ready to roll?"

"I think so."

"Give your aunties a hug and come on, then."

Annie wrapped her arms around Shea. "Bye."

A lump formed in Shea's throat. She found herself not wanting to let go. Was this what motherhood was like? The idea of not seeing Annie for a month terrified her in a way that fighting gangbangers and outlaw bikers never did.

"Be safe, kid," was all she could say.

"Bye, tía Toni."

"Vaya con Dios, mijita. You call us every night. Okay? Let us know how it's going and what you're learning."

"I will."

When Annie and Julia left, Shea stood staring at the front door. Her heart felt empty and strange. Raw and exposed like road rash.

"She'll be fine, corazón." Toni embraced her from behind.

"Hope so." Shea took a deep breath.

"I better get going. I have a client who's been wrongly charged with her husband's murder."

"I'll just stay here and stare at the walls."

"Rest, querida. You have a big job ahead of you."

An hour after Toni left, Shea again searched the web for anything she could learn about Luminos. She'd received a confirmation email that her application for the program had been accepted and another email from Indigo saying hers had too.

Shea was getting up to go to the bathroom when the adjuster from Hudson's insurance company called, a guy named Ben Davenport.

"Good morning, Ms. Stevens. I spoke with your associate Ms. White River at the motorcycle shop," Davenport said in a monied Texas accent, referring to Lakota. "She gave us an estimated repair cost of sixty-five hundred dollars. Personally, I'd prefer to have an independent shop look at it, but at this point, we're just gonna total it for three grand. We will also reimburse for medical expenses for injuries you sustained in the accident."

"Three grand? Are you fucking kidding me? This is a one-of-a-kind custom bike. I built it myself. Your customer caused this accident. And you're gonna pay for it to be fixed."

"While we are sorry that our insured's actions were cited as the cause of the accident, we'll agree to pay three thousand and not a dollar more. That's what we calculate a motorcycle such as yours is worth. Whether you choose to repair it or replace it is up to you."

"Listen up, you little pencil-necked bean counter, Iron Goddess sells bikes like that for close to six figures. Don't tell me it's only worth a measly three grand. You're either going to pay for the full repairs or you'll wish you had."

"Are you threatening me, Ms. Stevens?"

"I'm telling you my girlfriend works for Gottlieb & Sossamon, and they will sue you not only for the sixty-five hundred to fix my bike but also for pain and suffering, lost income, and for general assholery."

"You have yourself a good day, Ms. Stevens." The call ended.

Shea's knee throbbed as if a piston were hammering inside it. It took all her willpower not to hurl the phone across the room. "Fucking goddamn insurance companies."

She stood up and nearly toppled over as vertigo hit her hard. She steadied herself and paced around the room, cursing with each agonizing stride. She felt like an animal caught in a trap. Between the pressures at work and the pain from her injuries, she was going stir-crazy. Maybe going up to Sedona would be the break she needed.

When she finally got herself marginally calmed down, she hobbled out to the garage. The patches she'd cut off her ruined jacket were now dry. A few still had rust-colored stains from Hudson's blood, but they weren't too visible.

She gathered them up, grabbed a relatively new leather jacket from the collection in her closet, and started sewing them on, while also trying to keep her leg elevated. Halfway through sewing on the top rocker, she stopped to take another couple of oxycodone, wash them down with two fingers of vodka, and eat a hastily prepared ham sandwich.

When the last patch was in place, she felt a sense of accomplishment. She proudly stepped into the bedroom she shared with Toni and tried it on in front of the full-length mirror.

The reflection felt like a kidney punch. Every patch was

cockeyed. A three-year-old could have sewn them on straighter. "Fuck fuck fucking fuck!"

She tore off the jacket and threw it across the room, knocking over the lamp on her nightstand. She didn't bother to right it. Instead, she just collapsed on the bed and stared at the ceiling.

She was starting to drift off when her phone rang in the other room.

"Damn it." Maybe that tightwad of an insurance adjuster had a change of heart. She hustled to answer it. Her leg caught the corner of her bed in the rush, causing her to see stars but not slowing her momentum.

"Yeah?" Shea said through gritted teeth.

"Hey, Havoc. It's Indigo. I've talked with my boss. She's agreed to let me take next week off."

"Yeah. Good. Hate to make you use vacation time for this."

"No problem. I've needed a break for a while, and I'm getting paid to help a friend. Only wish Savage could come with me."

"Well, hopefully we won't be up there too long so that you and Savage can do something fun with your remaining time off."

"When you want me to pick you up tomorrow? I'm guessing it'd be easier if I drive, consider your injured leg."

"No, I'll drive. My leg's much better," she lied, not wanting to look like an invalid. "We're supposed to be there around ten. I'll pick you up around seven thirty."

"Okay, if you insist."

"I insist. This is an Athena Sisterhood mission, and I outrank you."

Indigo chuckled. "Okay, VP. You're in charge."

"Thanks for doing this, Indigo. I mean it."

"Always happy to have your back."

When Shea got off the phone, she saw that Toni had sent an email.

Found this in a court document search on Luminos. Thought it might help. See you tonight.

Toni had attached several multipage PDF files. Shea opened them on her personal laptop but found the legalese difficult to decipher. One was a criminal case in which Nathan Curtis Bennet was charged with sexual assault, but he was found not guilty. Most of the case documents were judgements for libel suits. Shea understood that much. But she got lost somewhere in all the wherebys and therefores.

Her takeaway was to focus on getting Megan home and have everyone keep their mouth shut. Not something that usually sat well with Shea. Especially if other people were being hurt. But she'd learned long ago she couldn't save the whole world. And she didn't need to be Connie Brady's next legal target.

She began studying satellite images of the Luminos campground to familiarize herself with the layout. While most of Sedona was scrub desert punctuated by limestone towers, the Luminos camp was situated north of town, along picturesque Oak Creek Canyon, where trees had enough water to grow. She'd ridden up the winding road to Flagstaff numerous times over the years. An interesting place to stage a rescue.

She went back and studied the organization's website in depth. The site had a blog, which she scoured for information. In one entry, she found a photo of Megan and three other young women laughing. The caption gave only her first name, but Shea recognized her. An idea formed in her head.

Nita had provided Shea with Megan's phone number. Until now, Shea had no idea if she would use it. But seeing the picture, she decided on a strategy and sent her a text.

Hey, Megan. Been tired of the world going to crap. A friend recommended Luminos. Saw your photo on their site and will be there tomorrow for "Change the World." Would love to connect and learn more from you. Shea Stevens from Iron Goddess.

Hours later, she still hadn't gotten a reply from Megan. Was Megan just busy? Or did she suspect Shea was working for her mom? Or was something or someone preventing her from replying?

~

That evening, after dinner, Shea's phone rang. "Hey, Doodlebug! How's it going?"

"Oh my god, I'm having so much fun. Everyone is super nice."

Toni poked Shea in the rib. "Put her on speaker."

Shea did so.

"¡Hola, mija! ¿Como esta?" Toni called.

"¡Hola, tía Toni! I'm having tons of fun. Learning so much it feels like my brain's gonna explode."

"How wonderful! What have you been doing?"

"In the morning, we had classes, which sounds boring, but I'm actually loving it. Wish school was this interesting. This afternoon, we hung out by the river. The camp's not too far from the Church."

The Church had been the Confederate Thunder's clubhouse. Much of Shea's childhood, and Annie's, too, had taken place around the old renovated church building. But the murder of Shea's mother and sister had poisoned the once-fond memories.

"Oh, and we saw a bobcat with babies, just like Bobbie Jean and her kittens. They were so cute."

Bobbie Jean was a bobcat that lived in the woods surrounding their neighborhood. She'd had a litter of kittens the year before, a few of which they still spotted wandering the streets or the neighboring woods.

"Sounds like you're having a great time," Shea replied. "How's the food?"

Annie paused before responding, "Not as good as tía Toni makes."

Toni's face colored with pride. "I'm sure you'll manage."

"Just hope none of my roommates snore."

"You'll survive." Shea heard muffled voices on the other end of the line.

"Yeah, okay, Sydney. I'll be right there."

"You gotta go?" A clingy sadness tugged at Shea's heart.

"They're starting a bonfire outside. S'mores and stuff."

"Okay, guess I'll let you go. Have fun and don't get eaten by bears and pumas."

"Hilarious, Aunt Shea."

"And call again tomorrow night, mijita," Toni chimed in.

"I will. Love you both."

"Love ya, Doodlebug. Good night."

Shea ended the call. Not having Annie around for a month would be tough. At least she'd have the mission of rescuing Megan to distract her for a while.

CHAPTER 12
NORTH TO SEDONA

ON SUNDAY MORNING, Shea hauled her packed duffel bag into the living room and sat down at the table, where Toni had set down chorizo and egg breakfast burritos with slices of pineapple on the side.

"This looks amazing," Shea said. "Thank you."

"Ay, corazón, I'd do anything for you. You know that." Toni kissed her gently on the lips. "How's your leg this morning?"

"It's healing up."

She had taken only one oxycodone pill instead of the usual two, trying to balance treating the pain and being able to drive.

She still hadn't told Toni about the old bottle of oxy she'd found, though she wasn't sure why. Just felt right not to bother her with the knowledge that she still needed pain medication to function.

Tears formed in the corner of Toni's eyes. "I'm sure going to miss you, chica, especially with Annie away at camp."

The sudden display of emotion hit Shea like a blow to her solar plexus. "Shit, girl. I'll be back in a day or so. Besides, you've got cases to work for the law firm. Probably be doing some stakeouts. You'll hardly know I'm gone."

"Trust me. I'll know. Do what you have to do, then hurry home. No meditating at the energy vortexes, cruising up Oak Creek Canyon to Flag, or wandering the shops in Tlaquepaque."

Shea laughed, breaking the tension. "I think you know me better than to think I'd be shopping or going all New Age woo-woo at those make-believe vortexes. And since Indigo and I are taking the truck rather than riding up on bikes, riding up Oak Creek Canyon won't have the appeal it usually does. Besides, the traffic always backs up around Slide Rock anyway, even this late in the season. Everyone wants to get a final summer swim in before it gets too cold."

After breakfast, Toni followed Shea out to her truck. Shea felt naked without a pistol holstered at the small of her back and without her old leather jacket identifying her as the VP for the Athena Sisterhood. Again, she felt exposed and vulnerable.

"See you in a few days, babe." Shea pulled on the textile jacket and kissed Toni hard. Despite her bravado, she would miss this incredible, petite woman.

She didn't deserve such an awesome girlfriend. Someone who not only accepted her for all her flaws and criminal past but had become as much a parent as Shea had for Annie. Maybe more so. All three of them had lost their own mothers at an early age.

Toni was a natural nurturer and a brilliant investigator with an indomitable spirit. The scar on her cheek from an old gunshot wound didn't diminish her beauty. It made her more beautiful. A symbol of her resilience.

"Adios, mi amor."

Shea could still feel the tenderness of Toni's soft lips as she drove north into Ironwood to the house that Indigo and Savage shared. Indigo was already waiting out front with her suitcase.

"Morning, sister. You ready for this?" Shea asked.

Indigo tossed her suitcase in the back seat of the truck's cab. "I think so. You mind if we make a quick stop in Sedona before we head to the Luminos campus?"

"Sure, no problem. Just let me know where."

Although tempted to take the scenic route through Prescott and Jerome, Shea headed due west to pick up the interstate. When she drove past where she'd crashed her bike on the outskirts of Ironwood, a chill ran through her. For just a moment, she allowed herself to ponder how much worse her injuries could have been if not for her quick reflexes.

"What's wrong, girl?" Indigo asked. "You look like someone just walked over your grave."

"Nah, I'm good. Just enjoying the cool breeze. Be glad when this summer's over."

A few miles after turning off the interstate, the towering red rock formations that made Sedona famous appeared on the horizon. Many of them had names like Courthouse Butte, Coffee Pot Rock, and Capitol Butte. There was even one called Snoopy Rock that resembled the *Peanuts* character lying atop his doghouse, complete with his buddy Woodstock.

No matter how many times Shea had been here, she always found the views breathtaking. Photos simply didn't capture the majesty and grandeur of the geologic monuments of rust-colored sandstone and white limestone.

As they got farther into town, restaurants and an assortment of businesses appeared. Indigo pointed at a quaint shop with a yellow thatched roof. "Pull in over there. The Dancing Muse Bookstore."

"Sure." Shea turned into the parking lot. "Looking for some reading material while you're up here?"

"No, I've just always wanted to stop in. Usually when we come through here, Savage and I are riding with the club and can't stop. Everyone's always eager to keep moving. Figured we could stop in today before driving to Luminos."

"No problem. Maybe I can pick up the latest thriller from S. A. Cosby."

"Not that kind of bookstore," Indigo replied as they got out of the truck.

"What kinda lame-ass bookstore doesn't carry crime thrillers?"

Shea noticed the other vehicles in the parking lot had bumper stickers like "My Other Car is a Broom" and "The Goddess is Alive and Magic is Afoot."

"You into this New Age witchy shit?" Shea whispered to her when they stepped inside. The scent of sandalwood incense pervaded the air, as did the sounds of rushing water and wind chimes, most likely from the sound system.

"It's not shit," Indigo replied tersely. "And I'm not saying I buy into all of it. But after dealing with Christianity's transphobic bullshit for years, I became open to a new way of spirituality."

Shea gazed absently at a shelf of crystals and decorative incense burners. "Shit, I'm sorry, Ind. You just never struck me as the woo-woo type. You know?"

"Why? 'Cause I'm Black?"

"Hell, no. 'Cause you're so down-to-earth."

"Maybe I'm down-to-earth because of my spiritual practice. It's made my life more peaceful and meaningful."

Shea nodded. "Sorry. Don't mind me. I'm an idiot. Closest I come to religion is naming the bike shop Iron Goddess. If this stuff makes your life more peaceful and meaningful, I'm happy for you."

"Thanks, Havoc."

They strolled past a display of pumpkin-scented incense and small fairy statues to the bookshelves. The store had sections on addiction and recovery, UFOs, herbal medicine, and nearly every non-Christian religion Shea had heard of, as well as a few she hadn't.

"You think they carry that book that Nathan Curtis Bennett wrote?"

"We don't carry that kind of garbage here," replied a woman stocking the shelves nearby. She was tall and thin, her hair tied in a French braid, and wore a shirt that bore the bookstore's logo.

"You know about this Nathan Bennett guy?" Shea asked.

Indigo looked up from thumbing through a book she'd picked up.

"I banned him and his cult members from the store." The woman's expression suggested she had more she wanted to say. "You ladies aren't with him, are you?"

Shea chuckled and shook her head. "Us? Hell no. Guy's a real asshole from what I heard."

"Some friends of ours have a daughter who's gotten involved with them," Indigo added. "They're worried since they haven't heard from her in a while."

"They should worry. Luminos used to post their flyers on the community notice board. My assistant manager went to one of their seminars. Didn't hear from her for months. No calls to say she's quitting. No emails. Nothing. Then outta the blue, she showed up asking to borrow ten grand."

A shadow passed over the woman's face. "She looked like one of those Holocaust survivors from World War II. Gaunt, haunted. Don't know what they did to her, but it messed her up good. I offered to let her stay with me, but she only wanted the money. I refused, and she left. That was seven months ago."

"I'm sorry about your friend," Shea said. "She ever get out?"

"A month ago, this guy showed up. Latino. Muscular. Asked if I'd seen her. I told him no. Few days later, another guy showed up. Skinny white guy this time. Carried a gun on his hip. When I told him I didn't allow guns in here, he… he pointed it at my face and insisted I tell him where my friend was. Even if I had known, which I didn't, I wouldn't have told him. Must've realized I was telling the truth, because he took off."

A low flame of anger lit in Shea's gut. "You call the cops?"

"Sure. They took a report. Heard nothing back. That's when I started noticing vehicles following me home. One time, I found my front door wide open. I always lock it. Always. A week ago, she called and thanked me for not giving her the money."

"She thanked you for not giving her money? How come?"

"Didn't say, and I didn't ask. She did say she'd moved back east after that psycho Bennett kept sending his goons to harass her. Before those creeps messed her up, she was a generous, sweet person who was always laughing. I don't know if she'll ever get that back."

"That's why we're in town. To make sure nothing like that happens to our friends' daughter."

"Good luck. They're a scary bunch."

"We're really sorry for your friend," Indigo said, putting a hand on the woman's arm. "Thank you for talking with us."

The woman mouthed the words "thank you" and wiped a tear from her face. "I hope you rescue the girl. May the Goddess bless your actions threefold."

"Yeah, thanks," Shea replied.

With a book in her hand, Indigo turned to Shea. "Let me pay for this, and we'll go. I really want to get Megan out of there."

CHAPTER 13
ARRIVING AT LUMINOS

THEY DROVE the rest of the way through town then continued up 89A through the winding Oak Creek Canyon. Their surroundings were an explosion of intense colors. A deep cerulean sky, unfettered by city haze, contrasted with the rolling hills of the brick-red rock landscape punctuated with the deep green of the ponderosa pines, yucca, and prickly pear cactus.

Despite all of this, Shea felt on edge. Not only was Megan in deep trouble, she probably didn't realize it. And there lay the rub.

Shea had been in countless life-and-death situations and had killed to protect herself and others. But this wasn't a straight-up fight. She'd have to cut through all of the brainwashing nonsense in Megan's mind to get her to see the danger and persuade her to get the hell out of there.

Shea felt entirely unfit for the task. Bad enough she was nursing an injured leg. While she had street smarts, she was at heart a scrapper, not an intellectual who could poke holes in philosophies and logic arguments. Never any good at talking people into doing things.

At least she had Indigo along. She had the maturity, eloquence, and tact that Shea lacked. Those traits made

Indigo good at her job as the law enforcement liaison for the Lambda Resource Center. If she could make headway with the knuckle-draggers at the sheriff's department on the needs of LGBTQ community, maybe she and Shea could convince Megan to get the hell out of that place.

They reached a small metal sign with the word Luminos on it and turned left onto a gravel road. Shortly after that, she followed a turnoff at a sign that read Parking. The road dead-ended in a small parking area occupied by a dozen vehicles.

"Despite what Toni dug up in her research, I half expected there to be razor wire fences and guard towers." Shea put the truck in park.

"Me too, the way that woman in the bookstore talked. But there are many ways to trap people." They pulled their stuff out of the back of the cab.

"You want me to carry yours?" Indigo asked.

Shea had been grinding her teeth the past few miles, winding up Oak Creek Canyon. Her entire leg felt stiff and swollen. The road rash burned. But she didn't want to look weak. "Nah, I can carry my own. But thanks."

A sign led them up a trail to the Seedling campsite, which comprised several small cabins encircling a clearing. A much longer building stood at the far end, next to a cinder-block building painted sky blue.

In the clearing, a crowd of people had gathered around an unlit fire circle flanked by log benches. The people wore matching light-green T-shirts. None of them were Megan.

As Shea and Indigo approached, the group turned toward them and erupted in warm shouts of welcome.

"Welcome to Luminos," said a woman in her thirties with short-cropped hair and suntanned skin. She wore a bolo tie with a bright-yellow round slider. "I'm Rory."

"Shea Stevens. And this is my friend, Zia Pearson." It felt

weird referring to Indigo by her legal name, but they had agreed to leave their biker names behind.

Without warning, the group surrounded them and began giving them deep hugs, as if they were family members they hadn't seen in decades. With each embrace, the hugger whispered in Shea's ear, "You are amazing. You are home."

The outpouring of affection was matched only by the intense smiles on everyone's faces. Not exactly crazed but not something she was used to seeing directed at her from strangers.

Most people reacted with either horror or pity at the deep scars crisscrossing her face. But not these people. Shea was both intrigued and alarmed. Was this what people in cults looked and acted like?

"Here, let me take your bag," offered a petite woman with dark brown skin and a prominent jaw. Like Rory, she had a yellow slider on her bowtie.

"Nah, I got it," Shea insisted. "But thanks. Just need to know where to put it."

"I'll show you. Follow me. I'm Erykah, by the way." She led them to the cabin just to the right of the long building.

"Nice to meet you, Erykah," Indigo replied. "Beautiful place you got here."

"Amazing surroundings. Amazing people. Amazing purpose."

The cabin's rustic interior smelled of dust and mildew. Erykah turned right from the common room and opened the door to a small bedroom with four sets of bunk beds. A dirty window let sunlight into the room.

"Zia, this is where you'll be staying. Top bunk by the window. Amazing view of the mountains in the distance. That trail leads down to the Nathan's Creek, where we sometimes relax and cool off on warm summer days like today."

"Guess I'll grab the bottom bunk," Shea replied.

"Oh, no. That one's already been assigned." Erykah beamed as if she'd just won an Academy Award, though Shea couldn't understand why she was smiling so. "We want you to get to know your amazing new family members."

"Family members?" Shea asked.

"One thing you'll be learning is how to see each person you meet as family. No strangers in this world, only amazing family you haven't met yet."

Shea chuckled darkly, wondering if she could turn this woman into a drinking game, taking a shot every time someone said the word *amazing*. "Hope my new family's not homicidal assholes like my original family."

Indigo gave her a concerned look but said nothing.

"I think you will be surprised by how amazing people can be once you learn to see beneath the surface," Erykah replied. "Shall I show you to your room, Shea?"

Shea felt uneasy splitting up, but it wasn't worth putting up much resistance for now. She exchanged a final glance with Indigo and said, "Sure, why not."

Erykah led her to the other end of the cabin and switched on a fluorescent overhead light that flickered for a full minute before illuminating the room. No beautiful view from this end of the cabin. No windows, in fact.

The room was smaller than the one where Indigo was staying, containing only two sets of bunk beds. The faint whiff of chemicals and claustrophobic feeling made Shea wonder if the room used to be a supply closet.

"You're in the bottom bunk in the corner there."

"Feels like a cave," Shea muttered.

"Think of it as a womb, where you will soon be reborn," Erykah said, her voice filled with hope and promise.

"I'd prefer a womb with a view," Shea quipped.

"Trust me. I'm sure your new family will more than make up for the lack of a view. Together we will help each other transform into amazing, enlightened harbingers of change."

Harbingers of change? That sounds ominous. Shea forced a smile and reminded herself why she was here.

"A friend of mine is already part of the program. Megan Thornton. I was wondering if I could talk with her."

"Oh, you're a friend of Megan's? She's so amazing."

"Yes, she is. Is she here?"

"She's around."

"Where can I find her? I'd like to say hi."

"Oh, well, she's busy in her own program at the Blossom campground."

"Blossom campground?"

"Yes, each camp has its own name. We're in the Seedling camp, where our new family members stay."

"I see."

"Megan's an orange bar, two ranks up from me." Erykah held up her bolo tie's slider. "Most of the orange, yellow, and green bars stay at the Blossom campground just up the hill."

"Uh-huh."

"We also have the Flourish campground on the other side of the hill for the red and violet bars. At the top is the Summit campground. That's where NCB stays when he's here. And the blue bars, of course. You'll meet them soon."

"NCB?" Shea said, feigning ignorance. She wanted to hear what Erykah had to say about him.

A dreamy expression washed over Erykah's face. "He's our guru. His real name's Nathan Curtis Bennett. That's how the website refers to him, of course. But here, we call him NCB because we're all family."

"So how do I get to this Blossom camp? I'd really like to talk to Megan."

"Perhaps this evening at dinner. Everyone assembles in the dining hall next door for the evening meal. You're going to love the meals here. Every meal is vegan-friendly, gluten-free, and made from locally sourced ingredients."

Shea felt a sudden craving for a steak. "Sounds wonderful."

"Our chef, Luca, used to own The Vegan Table, a five-star restaurant in Scottsdale. He quit to work here full-time. Isn't that amazing?"

"Yeah," Shea replied without enthusiasm. "Amazing."

"Well, I'll let you unpack. Showers and toilets are in the blue building next door. There's a T-shirt on your bunk and a small messenger bag with a bottle of water in an insulated pocket on the side. Got to stay hydrated, so drink up. Once you're ready, come join us back in front of the fire pit. We'll be opening the session in about ten minutes."

When Erykah left, Shea studied her new surroundings. The bunk beds were constructed from two-by-fours with a wooden ladder to the top bunk. The pillow was flat and looked cheap. She pulled back what looked like an army surplus blanket to reveal worn cotton sheets. Shea hoped they didn't have bedbugs.

She set her duffel bag on the bed, staring at one of the zippered side pockets. Despite Toni's advice against it, she'd brought along a subcompact .380 semi-automatic. She hoped she wouldn't need them. But she wouldn't leave here without Megan. If anyone tried to get in her way, she'd do what had to be done to accomplish her mission and bring Megan home safely to her moms.

Both the canvas messenger bag and the spring-green T-shirt bore the Luminos logo. The phrase "I am a work in progress" had been screen-printed on the back in a flowery font.

She shoved her duffel underneath her bunk, changed into the camp T-shirt, slung the messenger bag over her shoulder, and returned to Indigo's room. "Hey."

Indigo was pulling down her T-shirt, looking annoyed. "Hey. I think this T-shirt is a size too small."

"Figures. Don't sweat it. We won't be here long, hopefully. Erykah told me Megan's up the hill at another campsite. They got a few of them scattered about."

"Think we can sneak over there and talk with her?"

Shea shrugged. "Supposedly, everyone comes to this building to eat dinner. We can approach her then."

"What should we say?"

"I dunno yet. I want to get her away from the rest of them to talk. Not sure how best to do that."

"We'll figure it out."

"Damn right, we will." Shea slapped her on the back, and the two walked to greet the other newcomers.

CHAPTER 14
A CIRCLE OF CHANGE

THE GROUP OUTSIDE, consisting of twelve new recruits and the two yellow bar leaders, had formed a large circle, standing arm in arm.

Shea slipped into an opening next to a skinny guy with a man bun. Before Indigo could join her on her other side, Erykah waved.

"Zia, over here."

Shea felt a thrill of resentment over being separated again from Indigo. Was this some sort of divide-and-conquer strategy? Or maybe it was because Erykah and Indigo were the only two women of color among a sea of white faces. If it was the latter, Shea could hardly fault Erykah for wanting to bond with Indigo.

Shea realized how silly her thinking had become. Like grade-school-playground politics. *No, sit with me!* She reminded herself to stay focused on the mission. Perhaps when they broke for lunch, she and Indigo could find the Blossom campsite and locate Megan.

Looking around the circle, Shea realized that everyone but her and Indigo were beaming as if they'd all just won the lottery or something. It was a little unnerving. She caught Indigo's gaze and put on a fake smile to fit in. Indigo clearly got the message because a second later, she was smiling like everyone else.

"Isn't this amazing?" Rory said.

Everyone nodded.

Shea could feel the group's positive energy poking at her emotional defenses. Shea was not one to trust easily, having been hurt too deeply too many times to allow herself to be vulnerable. The tight-knit bonds she'd formed in the Sisterhood and her close relationships with the crew at Iron Goddess had taken time to get her to develop.

And here she was, embedded in a cult that violated people in countless ways. Now was not the time to let down her guard, even as she pretended to do so.

Rory continued. "Breathe in the sweet mountain air."

Shea inhaled deeply, but all she could smell was body odor coming from Man Bun next to her. Did this guy rub his armpits with rancid garlic?

"We are in the presence of greatness. Not just the amazing blue sky or the amazing red rock forest. But each one of us. We are great. You are great. Whether or not we realize it, the universe called us here to change the world. To end poverty. To end bigotry. To end war. To end all suffering. To bring about this amazing change, we much change ourselves. This greatness within us must be unblocked, shaped, and nurtured. We must free ourselves from the burdens of guilt, shame, and fear. And that's what this seminar, 'Change Yourself, Change the World,' is all about. As our amazing guru, NCB, has famously said, 'We must be the change we wish to see in the world.'"

Shea was pretty sure Gandhi was the one who had said that, but she kept quiet.

"The first thing we must change," Erykah said, "is ourselves, from strangers to friends. And we do that by sharing our truths. We are going to go around the circle and share why we are here, what brought us to this amazing place in our life journey."

Shea's road rash itched while she tried to figure out what to say.

"I'll start," Erykah continued. "My name's Erykah, spelled with a *Y* and a *K* and an *H* on the end. My mother was a big fan of the amazing Erykah Badu.

"After I earned my business degree from the University of Phoenix, I got a job with a financial company in Scottsdale. The pay was good. But it left me empty inside. What was I doing with my life? Making more money for rich people? Every day on my commute to work, I drove through a poor part of town. You could see the desperation on the people's faces. And all around them were businesses designed to keep them poor. Check cashers, bars, strip clubs."

A tear ran down her face. Indigo and the man on the other side of Erykah squeezed her tighter.

"My meemaw grew up like that. Trying to raise my daddy to be the good man he is today. Threatening him with a fate worse than death if he got mixed up in the drugs or the gangs. And even with as little as she had cleaning houses for people, she was so generous. If a neighbor needed help with anything, she was there. Food, clothing, money if necessary. I miss her so much.

"But here I was, just making money for the Man. Helping the rich get richer and not doing nothing for those less fortunate. Six months ago, I heard about Luminos and knew this is what I had to do. Not just for me but to honor Meemaw's memory. That's why I'm here."

"Thank you, Erykah, for sharing your truth," Rory said. "After someone shares in the circle, we always thank them for sharing their truth. So join me. Thank you, Erykah, for sharing your truth."

The group echoed the statement.

Erykah turned to Indigo. "Now it's your turn."

Indigo shot Shea a nervous glance and took a deep breath. "My name's Zia. I'm not really close to my birth family. I went through a lotta shit. Oh, sorry. Guess I shouldn't curse."

"It's okay. Say what you gotta say, however you need to say it. We've all heard it before."

"Thanks. I went through some rough times a while back. Won't get into the details. I did some stuff I'm not proud of just to survive. But then I made some friends who helped me get back on track. A wonderful group of women. Changed my attitude about life, you know? Instead of focusing on what I could get, I asked, 'What can I give?' Now I have a good job where I'm helping people. Helping to educate law enforcement about the challenges and issues faced by LGBTQ people. But I want to do more. I want to effect change on a more global level. That's why I'm here."

Shea and Indigo had discussed their approach to their individual backstories. Stick as close to the truth as possible without giving out too many details that could be weaponized against them.

Shea had been concerned about Indigo wanting to mention her job specifics, but Indigo thought they might really connect with the people that Luminos attracted, progressive idealists who valued diversity and inclusion. They agreed not to mention significant others who could be targeted. References to the MC would be vague for the same reason.

Erykah gave Indigo a side hug. "And we all say, 'Thank you, Zia, for sharing your truth.'"

One by one, each person in the circle shared their story. Some were recovering from addictions, some came from abusive homes or relationships, and some came from privilege but wanted to help the less fortunate.

As others shared, Shea zoned out, rehearsing her story in

her mind. Her leg went from itching to burning. Her knee felt tight. And the cool mountain air had given way to the relentless heat of the summer sun. She wanted to put some ointment on her road rash and take a couple of oxy.

"Shea? You still with us?" Rory asked, pulling Shea back into the discussion.

"What? Oh, sorry. What Caleb shared just got my mind wandering."

"Not a problem. It happens. One of the many amazing things you will learn here is how to become more present and listen to what the other is saying rather than letting our monkey minds wander. So, tell us, Shea. Why are you here?"

"I, too, grew up in a negative environment. My father murdered my mother when I was a teenager. Right in front of me and my baby sister."

Sighs of sympathy rose from the group. Rory squeezed Shea a little tighter, which she had to admit felt good.

"Rather than end up in a foster home, I ran away. To survive, I boosted cars till I got caught. Spent a stretch in the can down in Florence. When I got out, I made a new life for myself. Got a job working in a garage, fixing vehicles. Hard work. Dirty work. But honest. Learned a lot from the shop's owner. Eventually, I met Ind—Zia through mutual friends. The women's group she mentioned. Lotta good folks there. Helping other women felt good, ya know? I realized like a lotta you, I wanna do more. To pay the universe back what I took when I was stealing cars. Make the world a better place. That's why I'm here."

For an instant, she almost believed that was why she was there. But the throbbing in her leg brought her back to her mission.

That and to rescue a friend from your brainwashing, abusive psychobabble, she thought.

"Thank you, Shea, for sharing your truth," the rest of the group intoned.

When the rest of the circle had shared their stories, Rory picked up a box that had been sitting beside her. "At Luminos, we are all equals. We are all equally amazing. At the same time, we are each at different levels of enlightenment on our life journey. To symbolize these levels, we each wear one of these amazing handcrafted bolo ties made by a renowned artist right here in Sedona. You will notice the slider bars on the bolos that Erykah and I wear are yellow. But the ones you receive today will be white. The colors simply represent your level of achievement. Not your worth. Not how smart you are."

She went around the inside of the circle, handing out bolo ties. The one Shea received looked like it had been around for a while. The braided leather cord was worn and discolored. The round white ceramic slider was scratched up. She slipped it over her neck to fit in with the rest of the group. On the back of the slider, the metal was stamped with the words "Hecho en Mexico."

Handcrafted by a renowned Sedona artist? Shea thought. *My ass.*

"Now that we've all shared our amazing heartfelt stories," Erykah said, "I think we all deserve a chance to relax down by Nathan's Creek. So go change into your bathing suits, grab your beach towels, and I'll lead you down the trail. While you're hanging out by the water, getting to know each other better, we'll be calling up each of you one by one to have a private mentoring session. We all bring unique experiences, including a lot of baggage. These one-on-ones help to individualize the learning experience so that we can better serve you and guide you into becoming, as NCB says, 'the change you wish to see in the world.'"

"Now join me in one more tradition," Rory said. "Before we break up a circle, we always end with the words, 'We are one family. We are stronger together, making a better world for all.'"

They repeated the phrase, and the circle dissolved into a flurry of hugs. Shea had never considered herself a hugger, except for with family and the Sisterhood. But she went along, trying to ignore the growing burning in her leg and the stabbing pains under her knee.

Eventually, she reached Indigo. "Whaddya think?" she whispered.

"They seem harmless enough. Though if I never hear the word 'amazing' again, it will be too soon."

Shea laughed. "I hear that."

CHAPTER 15
DOWN AT THE CREEK

WHEN SHE REACHED HER ROOM, she realized that one of her roommates was Man Bun Caleb.

"Is there a bathroom to change in?" Shea asked.

"There's the shower building next door," said a woman in her fifties who had identified herself as Gayle during the opening circle. "But no stalls or privacy, really. And I'm told the hot water is in limited supply."

"Great."

It felt odd to see the women and men changing into their bathing suits together. Some of the women looked a little nervous, and one wrapped her towel around her as she changed.

Just roll with it, she told herself. *If Man Bun tries anything, he'll get a lot more than he bargained for.*

Because her road rash was still in the early stages of healing, she hadn't bothered to pack a swimsuit. No need to risk an infection, even if the wound had mostly scabbed over. Instead, she changed into a pair of gym shorts.

From one of the zipped pockets, she pulled out her bottle of oxy, popped a couple in her mouth, and washed them down with a swig from her water bottle.

"What are those?" asked Gayle.

"Uh, antibiotics. For my leg."

"I noticed that bandage. Looks mighty painful. What happened?"

She hadn't intended to talk about being a biker, but perhaps it would be okay. "I was on my bike when some asshole pulled out in front of me. Got a bad case of road rash."

"Oh, you poor thing. Looks like it must've really hurt. I swear, some people simply don't look out for bicycles, even though they're so much better for the environment."

Shea opted not to correct her. "Yeah. Life's a bitch sometimes."

She followed the group down a well-worn trail through the forest. Now that she was away from Caleb the garlic monster, she could appreciate the sweet scents of pine and juniper. Pine straw crunched under her feet, accompanied by the *pop-pop-pop* of a dozen pairs of flip-flops.

The sloping path intensified the throbbing and stabbing sensations in her knee. She took a deep breath and let it go slowly, trying to release the pain along with it. It didn't help. Ideally, the oxy would kick in soon. In the meantime, she tried to focus on the natural beauty around her.

Along the way, they passed a wooden sign with two arrow-shaped boards. One pointed down the hill with the words Nathan's Creek painted in faded yellow. The other pointed left with the words Blossom.

Shea noted it for when she would be ready to contact Megan. She caught Indigo's eye. She'd seen it too.

The trail led to a place where a rushing stream flowed into a deep pool surrounded by large, flat boulders. The burbling sound of the water soothed her mind. If it weren't for the woo-woo psychobabble and the manipulative cult, she'd probably love to hang out here. Perfect for a picnic with Toni and Annie.

Since she and Toni started dating, they had taken Annie

on a slew of day trips all over the state. Montezuma's Castle, Arcosanti, Tonto Natural Bridge, the Grand Canyon, the Mogollon Rim.

They had plans to watch the pelicans dive for fish at Gillespie Dam southwest of Phoenix and to explore farther south to Kartchner Caverns, Organ Pipe Cactus National Monument, and the historic city of Tombstone, where actors reenacted the famous gunfight at the OK Corral.

Maybe they would even stop by the tiny town of Ajo to say hello to Goblin, the mechanic who ran the chop shop she'd worked for when she was a teen. He and his crew had been like family for a time. It was why she'd taken the full seven-year sentence rather than rat him out. Introducing him to her ex-cop girlfriend probably wasn't a good idea, though.

These trips had solidified the three of them as a family. It was weird how normal it seemed. Vastly different from the chaos that had dominated her previous adrenaline-fueled life, downright refreshing in its banality.

The sun felt warm on her skin despite the gentle breeze following the creek. Shea folded her towel in half and laid it down on a rock to sit. The others cooled themselves in the water.

"Come join us. The water's amazing." Erykah appeared to be treading water in the pool. Must've been deeper than it looked.

"I'm good here, thanks. Doc says I can't go swimming for another month yet."

"Well, at least take off your shirt. You look hot sitting up on that boulder like a lizard."

Uncomfortable being the center of attention, Shea complied and peeled off her shirt, revealing the sports bra underneath.

Caleb approached, dripping water. His man bun was now unbound, and he was drying himself off. "Damn, girlfriend. You are ripped. What do you bench?"

"I don't. I'm a mechanic. Keeps me in shape. And I'm not your girlfriend."

"Sure got a lot of scars. What happened?"

"Rough living." That was her vague answer designed to shut down discussion.

"Yeah, you mentioned stealing cars and going to jail."

"Prison, but yeah. Not all of us got to attend college and major in philosophy." She felt a stab of guilt for her passive-aggressive reply, but she wasn't in the mood to discuss her past.

He must have gotten the not-so-subtle hint because he moved to another boulder to sit.

I'm not here to socialize, she told herself. *I'm here to bring Megan back home.*

Periodically, Rory arrived and called one of the new members back up the hill for something called one-on-one sessions. Shea was wary of what they were about. Was that where the real brainwashing began? Or was it some kind of absurd therapy session?

When the people returned from their one-on-ones, they seemed more subdued. Gayle looked like she'd been crying. That bothered Shea. Of all the strangers here, she seemed like a gracious grandmother type. The kind who always had freshly baked cookies when you visited.

When Shea asked Gayle what was wrong, her face erupted in a big smile.

"Don't worry about me, hon. I'm fine."

Shea wasn't so convinced.

After a while, Indigo sat down beside her. "How you doing, Havoc?"

"Managing. Could've done without trudging down that hill. Not looking forward to the climb back."

"Leg bothering you?"

"A bit."

"I have some Tylenol in my bag up the hill."

The oxy had kicked in, and she had begun to relax. "I'm good for now, but thanks."

"You change your mind, let me know."

"Thanks."

"Shea Stevens?" Rory appeared behind her on the path.

Her pulse quickened. "Yeah?"

She struggled to her feet. Her leg had gone stiff again from sitting so long. She pulled her shirt back on and gathered up her towel.

"No need to bring your towel. Just leave it here. You'll be back in no time. The others will watch over it for you."

Shea felt a little weird about leaving it there and had no desire to trudge back down the hill to retrieve it. "It's okay. I'll just take it with me."

"Don't you trust your fellow white bars?" Rory asked. "They're your family."

Shea glanced around at the others. They each wore questioning looks, as if their reputations were on the line.

"Yeah, all right." She figured she could always ask someone to bring her stuff back up with them.

"You need help getting back up the hill?" The offer seemed genuine, but a note of something in her voice set Shea's intuition on alert.

"I can manage."

Despite the oxy, the hike back was arduous. At times, she had to grab on to trees to help pull herself up. The stabbing pain in her kneecap now felt like someone was using a jackhammer. Maybe the oxy was losing its effectiveness against the pain. Or maybe she was simply pushing her body too much, despite the doctor's orders to take it easy for a few weeks. "Light duty" she had called it.

Shea was winded by the time they reached the Seedling camp. "Just up this other trail to the Summit camp. Not too much farther."

Shea cursed under her breath and followed. The trail

grew steeper and more rugged. The trees thinned out, giving her few things to pull herself up with.

By the time the trail ended at the Summit campsite, her chest was heaving, and she was gasping for breath. Five cabins stood in the clearing, two much larger than the others. A gravel road led off down the hill.

"Just over here." Rory pointed at one of the smaller cabins. She opened the door and gestured. "After you."

"Thanks."

The interior was homier and less rustic than the cabin she and Indigo were staying in. An antler chandelier hung in the main room, with a kitchenette at one end. An expensive-looking couch and a few recliners sat around a wrought-iron-and-glass table.

"Right this way." Rory led her down a hallway to an office with windows that looked out on the valley below. A door on the room's far side led out to a wooden porch.

A woman in her forties with hair pulled back into a severe bun sat behind a modern-style desk. A bolo tie with a cobalt-blue slider hung from her narrow neck. An unfamiliar electronic device the size of a toaster oven sat at one end of the desk. Electronic leads extended from the back and lay neatly folded in front of the machine.

"Shea Stevens, this is Dr. Linda."

CHAPTER 16
NO MORE PILLS

SO, *you're the nurse practitioner pretending to be a doctor. The quack who let one of their own die rather than take her to the hospital until it was too late.* Shea wondered if the other members of the cult knew she was a hack.

The woman stood as Shea and Rory entered.

"Pleased to meet you, Shea. I'm Linda Steele, though everyone calls me Dr. Linda." She smiled broadly and extended her hand. "Please have a seat."

Shea sat in a chair on the other side of the desk. Taking the weight off her leg seemed to help, but her knee still throbbed. At least the chair was softer than the rock she'd been sitting on for the past hour.

"I'll leave you to it." Rory smiled and exited, closing the door behind her.

"So, Shea. How are you liking Luminos so far?"

Shields up. Play the part. Pretend to be the naïve idealist. "Amazing."

"Yes, yes, it is. I'm glad you think so. We're very selective about the people we bring into our program. And when we find people who are the right fit, it is our job, our duty to the universe, to help them develop their potential and become positive instruments of change."

"Of course."

"Each person brings with them a lot. Potential. Assets. Talents. All of which are great. But we all bring with us baggage. Histories. Traumas. Dark secrets."

Shea's wariness increased tenfold at the word 'secrets.' "Makes sense."

"Our beloved guru, NCB, has a saying, 'We are as sick as our secrets.'"

"I thought that was an AA saying," Shea replied, sounding snarkier than she intended.

"They probably use it there too. NCB would be pleased to know they're sharing his wisdom. My point is that in order to become effective agents of change, we must free ourselves of the burden of our secrets."

Shea suppressed a laugh. A cult leader talking about not having secrets. What a sick joke.

"Okay."

"The purpose of the one-on-one sessions is to discover the secrets that are holding you back and to free you from their toxicity."

"You a shrink?" Again, the words popped out of her mouth before she could stop herself. The oxy was making it more difficult to hold her tongue and play the part.

Linda's smile broadened. "Not a fan of therapists, I gather? Not to worry. I prefer to think of myself as being responsible for our members' physical, mental, and emotional well-being. Think of me less as a shrink and more of a friend whose goal is to help you achieve and live your best life."

"I don't really have any secrets," Shea said. "I've always been a 'what you see is what you get' kinda gal."

"You do seem forthright. I respect that. Of all of our new members, you show the most promise." Linda pulled a folder out of the drawer. "I was reading over your application. Rarely do we get someone with your background. Runaway teenagers, sure, plenty of those. But not many ex-cons. Prison must have been quite an experience."

"Yeah, I shared all that in the opening circle. Like I said, no secrets."

"Of course." Linda pulled an amber prescription bottle from a drawer. She shook it, and the pills inside rattled. "Perhaps you could educate me on why you're taking these."

Shea felt she'd been sucker punched. The calm she'd been feeling from the pain pills evaporated, replaced by a ready-for-action intense focus.

Bitch has my meds. "You went through my bag?"

"Relax, Shea. This is all to help you. You are such an amazing person with an inspiring story of redemption. I'm only here to free you from all the things that are holding you back."

"Doc prescribed them after I tore up my leg."

"Yes, I see the bandages on your leg. What was the nature of your injuries?"

"Road rash. Severe. ER doc was considering a skin graft, but my fucking insurance wouldn't pay for it. Also messed up my knee. Feels like someone's jamming an ice pick into it most of the time. He wrote me a prescription to help me with the pain while I healed."

Linda nodded as if she understood. "Sounds very painful. I'm guessing you were on a bicycle or motorcycle when this happened."

"Motorcycle. I've been a rider all my life. Unfortunately, cagers don't always see us bikers. They can look right at us coming the road and still pull out in front of us."

"I'm terribly sorry that happened to you. I'm so glad you're still with us."

Shea shrugged. "Yeah, well, I'm a survivor."

"Yes, you are. You're resilient. That is an admirable

quality." Linda's gaze returned to the bottle in her hand. "Though I notice this prescription expired two years ago. So clearly, this scrip wasn't written to treat this injury."

"Look, my primary doc couldn't fit me in for three weeks. I happened to still have those around from another injury a while back." Shea deliberately neglected to mention it was from a gunshot wound, fearing that may open a whole other discussion she'd rather avoid.

"Clearly I'm not a junkie or I woulda taken 'em all long ago. I'm just doing what I gotta do to manage my pain. Now can I have them back, please?" Shea extended her hand.

The woman had the nerve to put them back in the desk drawer. "Tell you what. I'm going to hold on to them for now. We don't allow controlled substances on Luminos grounds."

"Those are mine. You have no right to take them." Shea forced herself to her feet and lunged for the pill bottle, but the oxy had slowed her reflexes.

Linda pulled a small pistol from the drawer and aimed it at Shea. *Her* pistol. "We also found this. Care to explain?"

"Un-fucking-believable." Shea resisted the urge to reach for it. *Maybe this bitch will shoot. Maybe she won't.*

"I agree. It is unbelievable. I was surprised and more than a little disappointed to find this contraband in your belongings. Bringing drugs and firearms to a seminar on self-improvement is truly beyond the pale. With all the violence going on in the world, the same violence that we hope to counter with love, this violation of our rules is downright chilling."

The two stared at each other in silence while Shea readied herself to spring into action when the opportunity arose.

"Our policy is to expel anyone caught violating these safety rules. But I really don't want to do that with you, Shea. You have so much potential for good. I can see it in you. I don't think you're a junkie. And I don't think you intended to hurt anyone here. Am I right?"

"Guess so."

"I see a phenomenal woman haunted by the fear, trauma, and secrets of a violent past, someone who is nobly struggling to put all of that behind her. If we can work together to free you from these burdens, there is no telling what you can accomplish. The world wouldn't know what hit it. People like you give me hope for our planet's future, Shea."

Shea's urge to snatch the gun out of the woman's hand faded as a wave of fatigue rolled over her. Did she really have potential for good? Were her trauma and dark secrets holding her back?

"I'm in a lot of pain."

"I know, sweetie. I can see it. But not just physical pain, though I'm sure you're feeling that too. I can also see the deep emotional pain. You wrote that you witnessed your father murder your mother when you were just a child. I can't imagine the damage that would cause to a young mind."

Flashes of that horrible morning stabbed at her memory. The screaming. Her father accusing her mother of infidelity then slashing her with a butcher knife. Shea remembered holding her mother and trying to save her life as slick blood from a neck wound ran between Shea's narrow fingers. She remembered the guilt hammering her for not seeing what a monster her father was before that fateful morning.

"It was a long time ago. I put it in my rearview."

"Those scars on your face. Did your father do that to you?"

Shea's hand reached up to her cheek. "Guard dog. I went where I wasn't supposed to. Nobody's fault but my own."

Shea recalled the guilt when she learned her father had

ordered the dog put down. The same man who never left her bedside while she recovered in the hospital.

"I'm so sorry that happened to you. Those scars have lasted a long time, and so have the wounds to your heart." Linda put the gun in the drawer with the pill bottle and made a show of locking it.

Shea didn't move, opting to see how this played out. Her primary goal was to rescue Megan. She could see about retrieving her stolen meds and gun later.

"And while we can't do much about the scars on your face, we can help heal your soul. Whether you continue here at Luminos after this seminar or you go out into the world, freeing yourself of the burden of your past traumas and darkest secrets can only help you become more effective at whatever you do. Wouldn't you agree?"

Shea couldn't argue with Dr. Linda's logic. How many times had a past lover or friend suggested Shea get professional help to work through the shit she'd endured? "I suppose so."

"Excellent. So, let's put away this contraband and get to work."

"What about the pain in my leg? It's killing me. This hiking up and down the hills ain't exactly helping."

"As I said, you are a remarkably resilient woman. How many times have you proved this? Physical pain is nothing more than your body sending electrical impulses to your brain. Most of the time, pain alerts you when something's wrong.

"But you've already received treatment for your injuries. You're on the mend. You can ignore those electrical impulses. This will be your special challenge. But I have every confidence you can meet it." She opened a different drawer and tossed Shea a small plastic bottle. "These should help in the meantime."

Shea looked at the label. "Aspirin? You think aspirin will help with this."

"As a physician, I am confident it will be enough. We can also provide you with ice packs if you think they might help. And staying hydrated will also speed healing." She reached into a mini fridge next to her desk, pulled out a bottle of water, and offered it to Shea. "Prove to me you are up to this challenge."

"Yeah, okay." Shea still wanted to throttle the woman, grab her gun and pain meds, and get the hell out of this hippie insane asylum. But she again reminded herself of her mission. "I'll do my best."

"Good. Now, to save you the trouble of going back down to the creek again, I'll ask Rory to retrieve your towel for you. We'll be having lunch soon in the main lodge. I think you'll enjoy it."

"Thanks." But she didn't feel very grateful.

CHAPTER 17

LUNCH ESCAPE

RORY WAS WAITING JUST outside the door. As promised, Linda asked her to retrieve Shea's towel. Before Shea and Rory trudged back down to the Seedling campsite, Shea swallowed a couple of aspirin and washed them down with water from the bottle. The uncoated aspirin left a bitter aftertaste that didn't go away, even with more swigs of water.

"Doing okay?" Rory asked.

Shea grunted while trying to maneuver around a large rock on the path. "Fine."

"Sorry about your leg. Must really hurt."

"Yeah."

She just wanted to locate Megan, convince her to get the hell outta Dodge, and recover at home for a few days in peace. Part of her also wanted to sneak back up to Dr. Linda's cabin and retrieve her oxy and gun. Bad enough the bitch took her meds, but leaving her in possession of a firearm with Shea's fingerprints all over it was a serious liability. If one of these wackos used the gun to shoot someone, it could come back on her.

When they reached the Seedling camp, Rory said, "Go

relax in your cabin for a bit. We'll be gathering for lunch next door in the dining hall in about an hour."

"The members from the other campsites will be there, too, right? Blossom and Twig and Bush." Shea guessed at the names of the other camps.

"Most of the other camps have picnic sites and take their lunches there. But we all get together for dinner at six. One big extended family. How was your one-on-one with Dr. Linda?"

"Amazing," Shea said with a forced smile. "Just becoming the change I want to see in the world."

"That's so good to hear. Dr. Linda spoke so highly of you based on your application, and I'm so looking forward to getting to know you better. Your story is so amazing and inspiring."

"Amazing."

"I'm going down to the creek, but I'll be back with your towel in a bit."

Shea limped to the cabin, gritting her teeth every time she bent her knee, the pain reaching exquisite levels. At least she had a bottom bunk. If she had to climb that wooden ladder every night, she'd probably murder someone in their sleep.

For a full minute, she stared at her duffel bag lying unzipped on her bunk. She felt violated and exposed.

She finished the water and tossed the bottle in the corner, missing the wicker wastebasket by a foot and not even caring. She pulled out her phone, but it had no signal. Not surprising, considering their remote location so far from downtown Sedona. Probably not a cell tower for miles.

With nothing else to do, she lay down, using her duffel bag to prop up her leg. The mattress was lumpy with a plastic lining that crinkled like a potato chip bag every time she shifted. The blanket seemed scratchy but warm.

After a while, the worst of the pain subsided into a dull

ache. At some point, she must have fallen asleep, because she found herself being shaken awake.

"Havoc, it's Indigo."

Shea opened her eyes. The room was dimly lit by a small lamp on a rough-hewn end table. "Hey."

"Rory asked me to bring your towel and an ice pack. You okay?" Indigo laid the folded towel on Shea's.

"Bitch took my pain meds and my gun."

"Your gun? I thought you said we shouldn't be carrying."

"I know. I did. It was in my duffel along with a bottle of pain meds my doc gave me for my leg. They fucking went through my bag and stole them."

A concerned look crossed Indigo's face. "Havoc, were you on pain meds when you were driving us up here?"

"Indigo, listen to me. These freaks went through my bag and stole my shit."

"Sorry. It's just…never mind. That was wrong, them going through your stuff. They kicking you out?"

"No, surprisingly enough. This Dr. Linda chick thinks I'll be a real asset to the cult. Not that she called it that. All that hippie woo-woo speak about potential and redemption and shit. How did your session with Dr. Mengele go?"

A shadow passed over Indigo's face. "She knows I'm trans, even though I never mentioned it on my application. They must've run a background check on me."

"I'm sorry, Indie."

"It's cool. I'm obviously out in my job as Lambda Center's liaison officer. Most of the sheriff's department and Ironwood PD know my T. Just felt weird that these people were checking up on me. Like an invasion of privacy. If they know that, how much more do they know? What will they do with that info after we get Megan out of here? Go after the people we love?"

Shea considered the implications. "If they come after us,

we'll push back. Hard. With the full weight of the Sisterhood behind us. When the Confederate Thunder tried to push us out, we fought back. When that drug dealer went after Orphan, we put her and her crew in the ground."

"But not without taking major losses of our own. Orphan died. So did Labrys, Pipes, Goth, and Pix. They could also sue us. After I agreed to help rescue Megan, I discovered a case where a family rescued their daughter, only to get buried in legal fees for speaking out. Even with Dragon representing us, they could bankrupt the chapter and us as individuals."

"I won't let that happen," Shea replied. "They got nothing to sue you over. I'm sure Nita and Cat will keep their mouths shut. And we will too. Despite the temptation to tell the world what a fucked-up place this is. We're just here to bring Megan home."

"So, what's the plan?"

Shea checked her watch. "We're supposed to have lunch in the dining hall in ten minutes. Rory said the other camps eat their lunches at their own campsites. They won't be coming back here until dinner. I say we sneak out during lunch and take a stroll over to this Blossom camp. See if we can't find Megan and talk with her."

"Sounds good. How's your leg doing?"

Shea swiveled around into a sitting position then pulled herself up to her feet. "Stiff. Doesn't hurt as much as it did a while ago." She considered Indigo's earlier question. "And yes, I took one oxycodone before driving us up. Didn't affect my driving, but you're right. I should've let you drive. Sorry I didn't."

Indigo put a hand on her shoulder. "Havoc, you're my sister. I'm not here to guilt trip you. You're in pain. I just don't want you ending up in worse shape than you already are."

"I appreciate it, girl." They hugged and clapped each

other on the back. "Let's grab some lunch and then slip out to find Megan."

Shea's knee protested as they walked outside, but by the time they were halfway across the lot, it had loosened up. Her kneecap still tingled a bit, but at least it didn't feel like someone was jabbing her with an ice pick. The road rash was uncomfortable but tolerable.

Most of the others were already inside the dining hall. The room buzzed with conversation. As people lined up to grab their bag lunches from the kitchen window, a few of the others expressed their concern over Shea not returning to the creek.

She assured them she was fine, that her leg just needed some rest. Their concern was touching, and she caught herself letting her guard down. Her smile felt a little less forced.

"Zia! Come join me!" Erykah shouted when they'd grabbed their lunch bags and were scouting for a seat.

"Your girlfriend's calling you," Shea teased.

"Funny."

As Shea followed Indigo toward where Erykah was sitting, another voice called. "Shea, come sit by me."

It was Gayle, waving her over.

"Guess I'm not the only one with a date," Indigo said. "Meet you out back in a few."

Shea sat down next to Gayle. "Hey."

"Hey, yourself. I worried when you didn't come back down."

"Needed to give the leg a rest." Shea opened her paper sack and pulled out a wrapped sandwich. The bread looked odd. "What're they feeding us?"

"Looks like tomato, lettuce, and facon on gluten-free bread."

"Facon?"

"Fake bacon. Looks like it's made from tempeh."

"Tempe? Like the city?"

"No, tempeh. It's a traditional Japanese food made from fermented soybean."

"Like tofu?"

"Similar."

"Yummy," Shea replied unenthusiastically.

Gayle chuckled. "You're still a meat eater, I take it."

"Always was, always will be. Keep the tofu and bean sprouts and give me a good steak any day."

"Unfortunately, the beef industry is as much responsible for global warming as the petroleum industry."

"Ah yes, the belching cows. Perhaps I'll start eating less beef and more bacon. And salmon. That's supposed to be healthy, right?"

"Yes and no. Predator fish like salmon and tuna concentrate more heavy metals like mercury. And don't even get me started on farm-raised salmon. That's like eating raw sewage." Gayle made a face.

"So, fermented soybeans. And a hardtack bun."

Gayle laughed harder. "Hardtack. You're funny, sweetie. Don't worry. You'll get used to it."

Shea took a bite of her sandwich. The flavor was almost like bacon, if she didn't think about it so much. The bread was as dry as the low desert in June. The tomato was overripe, and the lettuce was as wilted as a wet paper towel. But she choked them down with another bottle of water.

"Water tastes weird. Like a faint chemical licorice flavor." The label claimed it was bottled from a spring in Sedona.

"It's the minerals. But they're good for you. If you're used to drinking regular bottled water, spring water sometimes tastes a little different. You'll get used to it."

"Ah. Well, so long as it's good for me." She caught Indigo's gaze. "'Scuse me, Gayle. Gotta go to the latrine."

She took the apple from her lunch bag and stashed it in

her pocket then wadded up the sandwich wrapper and paper bag.

"Okay. Rory said the afternoon session starts here at two. Don't be late."

Shea checked her watch. They had thirty minutes to find Megan.

"I'll be here." She hoped to be in her truck with Megan and Indigo getting the hell out of this place by the time two o'clock came around.

She tossed her paper bag in a large bin marked Paper and the plastic wrapper in another marked Nonrecyclable then slipped out the door in the direction of the showers. She continued until she was out of sight of the windows and sat down on a rock. Didn't need anyone inside seeing her and Indigo head down the path toward the Blossom campsite.

A few minutes later, Indigo appeared. "You ready?"

"Yeah. Let's find our girl."

CHAPTER 18
MEETING MEGAN

THEY CREPT down the trail as if heading toward the creek then turned toward the Blossom campsite at the sign. The afternoon was warm, but the trail was fairly level and well-maintained. No grueling downhill to pound her joints.

"How was your lunch?" Shea asked to pass the time.

"Okay. Apparently Erykah also knew I'm trans and just started talking as if I'd been out in the open about it all along. It felt invasive. I should be the one who decides who knows and who doesn't."

"I agree. These people don't know the meaning of the word 'boundaries.'"

"On the plus side, she didn't misgender me. How was your lunch?"

"Gayle seems nice. Really, everyone seems nice except for Fake Doctor Linda. Controlling bitch. The sooner we can put this place in our rearview, the better."

In the distance, they saw a cluster of cabins peeking through the evergreen trees.

Shea stepped off the path. "Maybe we should get off the trail and circle around until we can get a better idea where she might be."

"Agreed. Think you can make it through the underbrush with your leg?"

"I'll manage."

They crept past large patches of catclaw acacia, creosote, and prickly pear cactus, staying low and scanning the campsite as it came closer into view. There were only two cabins to Seedling's four, with a shower building between them.

"See anyone?" Indigo asked as they edged along the perimeter.

"Not so far," Shea replied.

They circled around to the far side of the camp. Shea pointed. "There. A couple of picnic tables up the hill."

"I see them. Is Megan with them?"

"Too far to tell. We'll have to get closer."

Her leg ached, and the thorns of a catclaw acacia snagged the gauze around her knee. Shea carefully unsnagged her bandage from the spiny twig and smiled despite the ache. She was enjoying this. Breaking the rules. Creeping around. Spying. It felt good. She hoped every step they took was one step closer to getting the hell outta here.

Soon they were close enough to discern faces. "There!" Shea whispered. "That's Megan, I think."

"She's skinnier than I remember."

"Probably getting a lot of exercise hiking up this goddamn hill," Shea said with a smirk.

"How do we talk to her without everyone else there listening in?"

"Beats me. Wait, look."

The woman she guessed was Megan stood up from the picnic table and strode toward a pair of outhouses.

"Looks like this may be our chance. Let's move."

As silently as they could, they rushed toward the two outhouses, trying to minimize the sound of their footsteps and stay obscured behind the undergrowth. The closer they got to the camp, the less cover they had.

They reached the small wooden structures with no sign of being spotted. Megan was presumably inside. As they waited, Shea herself felt the urge to pee. She resisted the impulse to knock. Instead, they waited until the door opened.

"Megan?" Shea whispered.

The woman turned. Her face looked gaunt, but she was Megan. "Ms. Stevens? Ms. Pearson? What are you two doing here?"

Shea's prepared speech evaporated from her mind. "I… uh, wanted to talk with you." Her hand landed on the bolo tie.

"Now's not really a good time." The expression on the young woman's face was troubled, almost haunted. "How'd you know I was…wait, did my folks send you?"

"No, well, sort of." Shea shook the cobwebs from her mind.

"They're worried about you," Indigo replied. "They haven't heard from you."

"Because they think I'm stupid and spoiled and that Luminos is a cult. You can tell them it's not. I'm fine."

"They're your moms. If Annie didn't talk to me for two months, I'd go out of my skull. Especially if she was involved with…"

"A cult? Does this look like a cult to you? This is the most amazing place I've ever been. Better than any vacation we ever went on. And the people here. So kind. So caring. So amazing. We're making a difference, Shea. Unlike you two and your biker gang, who ride around talking about helping women. We're trying to change the world for the better. End poverty and discrimination."

Indigo stepped closer to Megan. "We understand that. Your moms understand that, and they believe in you. You are a wonderful young woman. No one doubts that. But look at you, girl. You're skinny as a rail. Last time I saw you…"

"I'm on a fast, okay? Not that I would expect you to understand. I'm helping to discipline my mind. And no, my moms don't understand. Otherwise, they would've paid the money so I wouldn't have to…"

"Wouldn't have to what?" Shea studied her.

"Doesn't matter. I'm fine, okay? So go back to Ironwood on your little motorcycles and tell my stingy, greedy, materialistic mothers that their daughter is fine."

Shea's phone rang in her pocket. She'd forgotten she had it with her and was surprised it was receiving a signal. She clicked the button to send the call to voicemail.

"Megan." Shea reached for Megan's hand, but she pulled it away.

"Leave me alone. If you really want to know what Luminos is about, forget all the lies my moms and the mainstream media are saying and pay attention to what's in front of your eyes. It's amazing."

Megan turned on her heel and walked back toward the picnic tables. Another member of her group was coming down the path toward them, a Latinx man who moved like he could handle himself in a fight. He spoke a moment with Megan then continued toward Shea and Indigo.

"Time to go," Shea said.

"Amen, sister."

"Hey! You two. Stop."

"What do we do?" Indigo whispered.

Shea turned and faced the man. "Sorry, dude. We were headed back toward the creek. I left my towel down there by accident."

"This camp is strictly for yellow bars and above," the guy said. His own bolo sported a deep-blue slider. A walkie-talkie rested on his belt. George Ramirez, she guessed. Camp enforcer and head of security.

"Sorry," Indigo added. "What can I say? We're just a couple of city girls lost in the woods. Probably happens a lot to us newbies. Which way back to the Seedling camp?"

He pointed down the path, a threatening expression on his face. "I see you two down here again, I'll have to report this as an infraction."

"Infraction?" Indigo asked.

"You heard of the Stick camp?"

"Stick?" Shea replied. "Nope."

"Best you stay at your own campsite, or you'll find out."

Shea offered a conciliatory smile. "Thanks for the advice. And the directions. Have an amazing day."

They turned and ambled down the path back to Seedling. Occasionally, Shea glanced back. The guy stayed in place.

"Stick camp?" Shea asked Indigo. "That like some sort of punishment?"

"As in carrot versus stick? Sounds like it. Let's definitely not go there."

CHAPTER 19
DIZZY AND HOMESICK

WHEN SHEA and Indigo reached the dining hall, the lights were off, and shades had been pulled down over the windows. A large-screen TV played a video of a man talking in front of a dark wood bookcase.

"Where were you?" Rory hissed.

"Sorry," Shea said. "Needed a little fresh air."

She handed them both bottles of water. "Don't wander off. And pay attention to the video. This is important."

They found seats in the back. Shea propped her left leg on a second chair, wishing she had an ice pack now. She considered searching the kitchen but didn't want to attract any more attention.

The guy on the screen looked like a frumpy, middle-aged gamer. Pale and overweight, with unkempt hair. The kind of guy who lived in his mother's basement and ranted about how the latest episode of *Star Trek: Whatever* wasn't canon because the aliens should have bumps instead of wrinkles running down the sides of their heads.

But this guy wasn't talking about *Star Trek*. In a high-pitched, nasal voice, he droned about how the world wasn't what most people thought it was. Some nonsense about how the paradigm created by mainstream media and scarcity politics had devolved into a delusional something or other and how the act of observation changed reality. Shea didn't bother following the meandering logic and philosophical references.

Clearly, this guy was Nathan Curtis Bennett, their beloved guru. What she couldn't figure out was why everyone seemed so enthralled with the man. He had all the charisma of a pile of dog vomit. And he made even less sense than one. Yet everyone but her seemed rapt in attention to his every word. Even Indigo. Maybe what he was saying made more sense to her. Maybe Shea was just too stupid and too uneducated to understand.

After a while, Shea caught herself nodding off. She tried keeping herself awake by working on a Plan B for getting Megan out of there. Yes, Cat and Nita had said they'd be happy just to re-establish contact.

But after her encounter with George Ramirez and his mention of some place called Stick, she didn't feel right about leaving Megan here. And this talk of fasting when Megan looked like a POW didn't sit right with her. Somehow, they had to persuade her to come with them back to Ironwood. And if necessary, take her back by force and let the chips land where they may.

"Shea," Indigo hissed.

Shea opened her eyes. The droning mushroom on the TV screen was gone. The blinds were open, and the lights were on.

"Shit. Must've fallen asleep." She checked her watch. It was nearly four in the afternoon.

Rory stood at the front of the room next to the TV. "We're going to take fifteen minutes to give everyone a chance to visit the toilet and get another bottle of water. Remember, we have to stay hydrated. We may be in a forest, but this is still the desert. And don't go wandering off. We have part two of NCB's amazing lecture coming up."

The group rose from their seats and began chatting and milling about. Shea's leg had again gotten stiff from sitting so long. She could feel the scabs along the road rash pulling, cracking, and burning.

The pain wasn't as bad as it had been the day before, but she could still use a couple of oxy to take the edge off.

She considered asking Indigo to break into Fake Doctor Linda's cabin and stealing back her meds and her gun, but Indigo wasn't as adept at breaking and entering as Shea was. And for all she knew, Fake Doctor Linda was still in her office doing her brainwashing one-on-one sessions.

"Let's go outside," Shea said to Indigo. "I need some fresh air."

She caught Rory watching her as they stepped outside the dining hall. Shea gave her a fake smile and waved.

"What'd you think of the lecture?" Indigo asked.

"The lecture? What little I remember sounded like a lot of woo-woo nonsense."

"I get that you're a skeptic. NCB used a lot of language that may seem confusing to people who aren't familiar with New Age concepts or quantum mechanics. But honestly, a lot of what he said in the video sounds legit."

"Legit?" Shea asked incredulously.

"Just try to keep an open mind."

"An open mind?" Shea's tone became a harsh whisper. "We're not here to save the world or become puppets in this psycho Bennett's little cult. We're here to rescue Megan. Did you forget?"

Indigo held up her hands in a placating gesture. "I know, but what if this place isn't a cult after all?"

"What? Are you out of your mind? Nita's friend, Robyn, is terrified after what these people put her through. And you heard that woman at the bookstore. Not to mention Megan herself looking like a fucking stick figure."

"I got the impression this fast she's on is her idea."

"Also, they took my meds and my gun. This place is not right, Indie." A wave of dizziness hit Shea, and the room wobbled. She grabbed Indigo's arm to steady herself.

"You feeling all right, Havoc?"

"Yeah, I'm fine. Just a little dizzy is all." The vertigo passed gradually. "Mountain air's a little thin. Just taking me a bit to get used to it."

"We're at roughly the same elevation as Ironwood. The air shouldn't be any thinner. Could be a side effect of coming off the pain meds you were on. When was the last time you took one?"

Shea tried to remember, but her mind was full of cotton. "Before we went down to the creek."

"That's probably it. Or you may be dehydrated. We've been doing a lot of strenuous walking today. Keep drinking water. Hopefully, the dizziness will pass soon."

"I just want to grab Megan and get the hell outta here. Maybe you don't see it, but something rotten's going on here. I can feel it."

"Havoc, even if it's as bad as you think, I'm not sure Megan's willing to leave voluntarily with us. And we can't take her by force."

"Maybe. Maybe not. Just keep your eyes open. And take nothing at face value. Just because they use all that 'we are the world' mumbo-jumbo doesn't mean this group is legit or altruistic."

"Fair enough. Let's get back in there before anyone gets suspicious."

As they found their seats, Shea remembered the call she'd received earlier and pulled out her phone. The missed call was from Annie. Probably checking in. No voicemail message was left. And no signal again, so she couldn't call her back.

She hated herself for missing the call. That empty place in her soul ached to hear Annie's voice. Even if she was sounding more and more like a typical teenage girl and less like the baby biker she had seemed for so long.

Just thinking about Annie being at camp for a month made Shea miss her all the more. And she'd only been gone for a day or so.

Her thoughts turned back to her conversation with Indigo. Was Luminos really a cult or just a group of tree-hugging idealists? Did Robyn have some unspoken agenda or grudge? Were Cat and Nita overreacting? Yeah, Megan looked skinny. But young people did all kinds of crazy things like juice fasting, joining Greenpeace, and anything else to establish their independence and annoy or worry their parents. Or in Shea's case, steal cars and go to prison.

At the very least, she had to convince Megan to get back in touch with her moms. That would allay their fears and restore the family bonds. Then Shea and Indigo could return home and, Shea could recover from her injuries in peace.

Shea found the second half of Bennett's video lecture even more confusing than the first. Lots of talk about perception, vulnerability, manifesting, mystical fulfillment, agency, and empowerment. And yet, every once in a while, he said something that made sense. She was just too uneducated and unfamiliar with most of the concepts to make sense of the bulk of his talk. Maybe he did know what he was talking about, and she was just too stupid to figure it out.

Glancing around at the others in the darkened dining hall, they seemed rapt in attention to his every word. Another thought occurred to her. Was this how they did it? The brainwashing? Get everyone sitting around in a dark room while filling their brains with new ideas, well-intentioned or not.

A wave of dizziness hit her again, followed by fatigue. She caught herself sniffling. Maybe she was coming down with something. That would be her luck. She drove up to

Sedona in all its grandeur and came down with the flu. Was it even flu season yet? Maybe it was just a late summer cold. Either way, she felt like lying down and taking another nap. Maybe she could brainstorm a way to persuade Megan to leave with them during dinner.

"Hey," she whispered to Indigo. "I'm gonna go catch some Z's in my bunk."

"You all right?"

"Just a little fatigued from all this hiking up and down hills when I should be taking it easy."

"Okay, I'll come get you for dinner."

"Sounds good. Thanks, sister."

She crept out of the room and slipped out a door. No one seemed to notice. Not even Rory and Erykah, who seemed glued to the screen.

She fell asleep quickly in the dark room despite the throbbing and burning in her leg and the persistent runny nose.

CHAPTER 20

DISCOVERED

CONNIE BRADY KNOCKED on the heavy wooden door. Linda Steele and George Ramirez stood beside her.

"Enter," said a male voice from inside.

Connie opened the door, and the three of them stepped into the room. Bennett lay in the enormous bed, its red silk sheets ruffled. Late afternoon sun filtered through the curtains.

Next to him, a young woman scrambled to pull on her clothes. The brand above her left nipple was still red and scabbed over from where she'd received it a month earlier.

"You can go," Bennett said to her.

She sat up with her back turned to Connie and the other blue bars. The young woman's ribs and spine protruded from her frame before she slipped on her shirt. Connie recognized her as a red bar but couldn't immediately recall her name. Hayden or Jaden or something similar.

Everyone stayed silent until the young woman left the room, shutting the door behind her.

"What's up?" Bennett said brightly, as if all of this were normal.

"Nate, we've uncovered something concerning about one

of the white bars." Connie handed him a manilla folder. "She has connections to law enforcement. Could be an issue."

Nate opened the folder and withdrew a piece of paper from inside. "Zia Pearson? She's a cop?"

"No, she works for a queer nonprofit down in Ironwood. She's their liaison with the local police."

"And this is a problem why?"

Ramirez stepped forward. "We think she's possibly working as a mole."

"A mole? We're in Sedona. Those law enforcement organizations don't have any jurisdiction here."

"No, they don't," Linda agreed. "But she testified in a federal case down in Phoenix involving a human trafficker. She has contacts within the FBI."

Bennett's beatific expression faded, replaced by seething anger. "Why is this only now coming to my attention?"

"When I initially ran a check on her, I assumed she was a community liaison with no direct ties to law enforcement," Connie replied, staring at the floor. "I should have looked deeper. I'm sorry. We've been looking to increase our minority representation to better tap into that market for recruits. Figured since she's a lesbian and Black, she'd be a good fit. I screwed up."

"I caught her up in the Blossom camp talking with one of the yellow bars," Ramirez interjected. "A Black girl by the name of Megan Thornton."

"They know each other?"

"Megan said she didn't," George replied.

"You believe her?"

"Not sure. They're both Black. And Thornton has two mommies. Both are from Ironwood."

"Pearson's also a transsexual," Linda added.

Bennett did a double take. "She's a he? Does he still have a...you know?"

Linda shrugged. "Not sure. I studied her social media

posts. She doesn't mention having surgery, but she could have had it years ago."

"She or he was with another white bar when I intercepted them at Blossom," Ramirez said. "A woman named Shea Stevens."

"She tied to the cops too?"

Connie shook her head. "Not as far as I could find. She's an ex-con. Spent several years in prison for grand theft auto a while back. Not active on social media. She's the co-owner of a motorcycle garage down in Sycamore Springs. No recent arrests. Nothing to show she has any direct ties to the cops or the feds."

"How does she know this Pearson he-she?"

The slur made even Dr. Linda flinch. "They both ride motorcycles, both lesbians, and they both signed up for the recruitment seminar at the last minute. But I turned up something on Stevens that we could use as leverage if necessary." A smile crept across her face.

"What's that?"

"She is the legal guardian of her niece. Not yet sure about the story behind that. But the girl, an Annie Wittmann, is currently enrolled in our Bold Women of Tomorrow Camp."

"Why is that a good thing? Sounds like a coordinated attack," Bennett said, looking genuinely worried. "Maybe this Shea Stevens and Zia Pearson are part of some undercover sting to bring me down."

"Relax, Nate," Linda assured him. "I don't think Stevens suspects that Bold Women is one of our programs. If she is working for the feds, and we have no reason to suspect she is, then we can use the niece as leverage to keep her in line and keep her mouth shut."

"Any connections to the girl who died a few weeks ago?"

"Bethany?" Linda looked at Connie. "Not as far as we know. Megan and I took care of the body. And after a week in Stick, she understands the importance of keeping quiet about it. She's fully compliant at this point."

"See that she stays that way." Bennett straightened up in the bed. "And get rid of the tranny. She's a liability. Might as well do the same with the Stevens woman. An ex-con biker?"

"Actually, I think the Stevens woman might be an asset. Her criminal history might benefit us in some of our future endeavors. Once the chlorpralozine in the water works its magic and the programming takes effect, she'd do well working with George here."

Bennett looked at the brawny man. "Georgie?"

"There's some potential there. Once she becomes compliant."

"And if not," Linda added, "we have her niece."

"Fine. Send Pearson packing. Monitor Stevens. Update me if there are any other developments."

"Will do."

CHAPTER 21
ABDUCTED

AFTER THE VIDEO LECTURE ENDED, Indigo grabbed a fresh bottle of water and stepped out into the late afternoon sun. The cool evening breeze blew her braids into her face and gave her a chill.

Her mind buzzed with ideas, tempered with the task she and Havoc had accepted.

We're here to bring Megan home, she reminded herself. *Even if this place isn't a cult, the girl shouldn't be starving herself. Does she have an eating disorder? Does Dr. Linda realize what was going on with her?*

She wandered toward her cabin to grab a jacket she had brought with her. A couple of women wearing green slider bolo ties were stacking wood in the fire circle between the cabins.

"Y'all need a hand?" Indigo offered.

The older of the two women looked up at her and smiled. "Yes, that would be amazing. Thank you."

"Let me grab a jacket from my cabin, and I'll be right back."

She slipped into the cabin and grabbed a fleece jacket bearing the Sisterhood emblem on the back, tossing the nearly full bottle of water in her bag. It was getting too cool outside to be drinking cold water.

On her way out, she checked on Havoc, who was still snoozing in her bunk. It still bothered her that Havoc had driven them up here while on pain meds. Why hadn't she asked her to drive? And why had she brought a gun up with her?

Guess old habits die hard, she thought. She'd known the woman for only four years, but it seemed like forever too. Havoc was a paradox. Fiercely compassionate but with a penchant for terrifying violence toward those who threatened people she cared about. Hardly surprising for a woman raised around an outlaw biker club.

Indigo loved this woman as family, as she did every patched member of the Sisterhood. And yet, Havoc's proclivity for mayhem sometimes frightened Indigo.

Maybe spending time surrounded by people who were consciously choosing a more loving, less violent way to change the world would help Havoc find her way to a gentler approach to life.

"Sleep tight, sister," she whispered before joining the women stacking the wood for what promised to be an enormous bonfire.

A few minutes into Indigo's helping Carla and Denise build the wooden framework, an old panel van pulled into the clearing. George Ramirez got out.

"Zia Pearson?" Something in his expression and tone unsettled Indigo.

"Yes."

"You need to come with me."

"Why?"

"You need to come with me now. No questions."

Indigo looked to Carla and Denise for support, but they continued to stack wood as if she weren't even there.

Ramirez's meaty fist gripped her arm.

"Hey! What the hell?"

He opened the passenger door, muscled her inside, and slammed it shut again.

"What's going on?" Indigo pulled the door handle, but it wouldn't open. Fear lanced through her body.

Ramirez jumped behind the wheel and floored it out of the clearing. "We need to have a talk."

"About what?"

Ramirez stayed silent.

What the hell was this about? Every likely answer she could come up with was more terrifying than the last. As a transgender woman, she'd endured her share of violence. And now, here she was in a creeper van in a cult compound with a man who clearly meant her harm.

The van lurched up the road toward Summit but then turned down a side dirt road that was partially overgrown and permeated with rocks and potholes.

She tried to devise an escape plan as she bounced around inside the van. Did she have anything to use as a weapon? No. Her pockets were empty. Even the water bottle was back in the cabin.

Her mind struggled to remember the lessons she'd learned in a self-defense class the Sisterhood had held a couple of years prior. Lesson one, never get in a vehicle with your attacker. Well, she screwed that up.

The van skidded to a stop in front of a cabin. It was small, more like a tool shed. Another man stood in front of the door. White guy, about six foot even, with a fighter's physique. Her fear turned to terror.

The white man approached her door. The instant he unlatched it, Indigo pushed against it with all her force, hoping to throw him off-balance. Instead, she pivoted around. Indigo landed hard on the rocky ground.

She gasped as the men yanked her arms behind her.

Something cinched tight around her wrists with a ratcheting sound. Zip ties. Holy shit.

"Let me go. I did nothing wrong. I'm just here to make the world a better place."

"Shut the fuck up, tranny," Ramirez growled as he and his buddy lifted her arms and dragged her into the shed and onto a folding chair.

The only light in the room came from the only door. No windows. No lamps.

"Why are you doing this?" Indigo struggled to get ahold of her fear so she could figure a way out of this. Her only chance was to talk her way out. Persuade them to let her go. But her odds seemed infinitesimal.

The two men stood over her, glaring.

"Who the fuck sent you?" Ramirez asked, muscled arms folded.

"Sent? What do you mean? I signed up. I—"

"Don't lie to me, maricón! I know you work for the cops."

"The cops? What? No! I work for the Lambda Resource Center in Ironwood. I'm not a cop." She struggled against the zip ties, but they held fast, digging deeper into her wrists.

"And what exactly is your job title?"

"Community liaison?"

"Liaison with who?"

"You've got it all wrong. I just help law enforcement understand the needs of the LGBTQ community. That's all. I don't work for the cops."

The white guy scoffed. "Right. You don't work for the cops. You just work for the cops. Fucking snitch is what you are."

"A snitch? No! Why would I be a snitch? What's there to snitch about? This is a beautiful place with beautiful people. I really like it here. I'm looking forward to becoming a better person."

"Liar!" The white guy got in her face, his bloodshot eyes just inches from her. "You're a fucking freaky liar who thinks he can sneak in and get some dirt on us."

"Dirt? What dirt? The only dirt I've seen is what's on the ground. Why are you people doing this?"

The interrogation went on for what felt like hours. They slapped her and punched her and screamed at her, demanding answers she didn't have. The light coming through the door faded and with it all hopes of survival. She was going to end up murdered like so many trans women of color. Just another statistic.

"Get her up, Donnie," Ramirez said at last. "She ain't going to tell us anything."

Indigo barely registered the words. She was beyond exhaustion, beyond despair. *Just get it over with*, she thought.

They hauled her into the back of the creeper van. The chill of the corrugated metal floor was just enough to reignite a spark of hope.

No, she told herself. *I am not going out like this. I will not let these psycho assholes kill me. Not without a fight.*

She bounced around in the back of the van, slamming into the walls as a large rectangular object slid around. When at last the van came to a halt, she positioned herself on her back with her feet to the rear doors.

The door opened. She kicked hard and connected.

"Hijo de puta! Donnie, help me get this fucking cunt out of there."

She continued kicking, but she was no match for the two men. They dragged her out and tossed her onto pavement. The zip tie holding her wrists fell away. Something heavy hit the ground next to her.

Ramirez leaned down and growled in her face. "You say one word about Luminos, I will make your pitiful life so miserable you'll wish I'd killed you and fed you to the pumas. You understand me, maricón?"

"Yes." The word came out as a rasp.

"Don't you ever step one foot in our camp again. Come on, Donnie. Let's get out of here."

For a long time, she didn't bother to move except to sob into her hands.

"Ma'am…ma'am, are you okay? Do you need some help?"

Indigo sat up, every fiber in her body screaming in pain.

A petite woman with short blond hair stood before her, a look of concern on her face. She gasped and covered her mouth. "Oh, my dear. Let me get you inside."

The woman helped Indigo to her feet. To her surprise, her suitcase lay on the asphalt beside her. She reached for it, but the woman held up her hand.

"I'll get that. Just come inside. Do you need me to call someone? The police?"

Indigo wanted to say yes. Call the police. Call the FBI. Call the fucking marines. But doing so might interfere with Shea getting Megan safely out of that insane asylum.

"No."

CHAPTER 22

DINNER CONVERSATION

NEXT THING SHEA REMEMBERED, Rory was shaking her awake. "Time for dinner."

Shea's fatigue had only deepened. When she sat up, the room spun like a carnival ride. Her limbs felt leaden. "Where's Indigo?"

"Who?"

"Uh, I mean, Zia. She was supposed to wake me."

"I'm not sure. You feeling all right?"

Shea sniffled. "Might be coming down with something."

"Or coming off something. Dr. Linda mentioned you'd been hooked on prescription pain meds."

"I'm not hooked. I was taking them for the very real pain in my leg from my very real motorcycle accident."

"Either way, cold-like symptoms are often a sign of withdrawal."

Shea had a vague memory of her brief reunion with her sister, Wendy. She had exhibited the same symptoms when she was jonesing for a hit.

"Why is Linda telling you about my private medical condition? Isn't that a hippo violation or something?"

"You mean HIPAA? Doesn't really apply here. I'm responsible for keeping you safe. It's okay for her to share relevant information. Come on. Getting some food in your stomach will help you feel better. And keep drinking water."

She'd been drinking enough water to drown an elephant. Her bladder felt near to bursting. "Gotta hit the latrine."

Her body protested when she forced herself to her feet. Her leg burned and throbbed. She took a couple of additional aspirin and told herself to power through. She was here to rescue Megan. And who knew? Maybe along the way, she might learn something from this self-professed guru.

"Oh, I brought you a present. Something to help with walking." Rory held out a polished wooden stick about five feet in length. The top was round and bulbous. The upper half had a slight twist to it, suggesting a vine had wrapped around the tree as it grew. It was beautiful.

"Wow. Thanks."

Rory escorted her to the shower building.

"You don't have to follow me. I'll head in after I pee."

"I just want to keep an eye on you, since you're not feeling well. We look out for each other here."

Big Sister is watching, Shea thought.

A few minutes later, Shea followed Rory back into the dining hall. Dozens of people wearing bolo sliders in all the colors of the rainbow filled the main room. Everyone was smiling and laughing. Scrumptious aromas filled the air. Maybe she could finally get some meat.

Shea scanned the room for Indigo. Of the few Brown or Black faces, none belonged to her. She spotted Erykah carrying a plastic tray with what appeared to be lasagna, some wilted dark green salad, and red quinoa. She only recognized the latter because Toni made it occasionally.

"Erykah, where's Zia?"

"What? Um, not sure." She looked around the room. "Maybe she went to the toilet."

"I was just there. She wasn't."

"Perhaps she needed something from her cabin. I'm sure she'll be back shortly. Grab some food. You look like you could use some fuel for that body of yours."

"Yeah, okay." But something didn't feel right. Erykah was lying.

Shea sipped from an ice-cold bottle of water while she stood in the queue for dinner, continuously scanning the room for Indigo.

"Hey, you. I wondered where you disappeared to." Gayle appeared next to her, beaming like a maniac. Without warning, the woman wrapped her in a hug. "Good to see you, sister."

Ordinarily, Shea would have resisted or at least stiffened at the uninvited physical contact. But no red flags shot up, and she leaned into the embrace and hugged her back. It felt good. It felt safe. "Good to see you too. You seen Zia around?"

"Zia? Yeah, she's here somewhere. Tell you what, we'll save a place for her when we sit down."

"Yeah, okay."

They grabbed their trays and found a few seats in the crowded room, but Shea still saw no sign of Indigo. Shea wanted to relax and enjoy being surrounded by so many amazing people, but Indigo's absence nagged at her.

Maybe she was feeling under the weather too. Maybe Shea did have a cold and had infected Indigo. She'd check on her after dinner.

The lasagna was delicious, even though the chef made it with eggplant instead of meat. The salad was appetizing, too, but it had an odd, chewy texture.

"What kind of salad is this?" she asked Gayle. "Some kind of weird kale?"

"Wakame," Gayle said with a smile.

"Waka-what?"

"Wakame. Japanese seaweed salad. It's very nutritious.

Much more so than a normal lettuce salad. Good source of iodine and other micronutrients. What do you think?"

"Texture's a little weird, but it tastes all right. What all's in it? Besides seaweed, of course."

"Sesame seeds, rice wine vinegar, and soy sauce. Possibly some other ingredients too."

Shea glanced around again for Indigo. Still no sign of her. But she spotted Megan.

"Something wrong?"

"Be right back."

Shea walked across the room and sat down in an empty chair next to Megan. Instead of having a plate in front of her, she was reading a book.

"Not hungry?"

Megan glanced briefly at her, frowned, and turned back to her book.

"Hey, girl, I'm sorry for how we left things earlier."

"Ms. Stevens, I'm not leaving with you," Megan replied in a harsh whisper.

"Relax. I'm not here to kidnap you. I'm actually starting to like it here. It really is amazing."

Megan's terse expression softened. "Yeah?"

"Yeah. Can't say I understand everything NCB was saying in his lecture today. But so much of this is new to me, ya know? We don't talk a lot about harmonizing and freeing ourselves of delusions in biker circles."

Megan chuckled. "I suppose not."

"Promise me one thing, though."

"What?" Megan's wariness returned.

"Call your moms. They're worried. You not talking to them is only making them more paranoid. And maybe, when your schedule permits, give them a visit. I assume you can leave for a day or so to spend time with them. Labor Day's coming up in a few weeks. I know they'd love to see you."

"As long as they'll treat me like an adult and not like a child. I'm not stupid. I make my own decisions. They may not be the same choices they'd make, but that doesn't make them wrong."

"I agree. I think they're more on board with you making your own decisions than you think."

"Maybe they could show it by helping me pay for my classes."

Shea had to smile at the irony of Megan's desperate need to be independent, while also wanting someone else to pay for things. The conundrum of being young.

"I think they want to. Business at the cafe's been slow this summer. Once school starts in a few weeks, they'll be better able to help you out. But you have to talk with them first."

"And yet I'm guessing they're paying you."

"They paid for Indigo and me to attend the intro class. Because they want to better understand what fascinates you about Luminos. They would have come themselves, but they're really busy."

"Too busy for me."

"Look, I get it. Sometimes we parents get it wrong. We show our love in ways that don't always feel like love. So maybe cut them some slack. They sent us to make sure you're okay." Shea studied Megan's gaunt face.

"And I can tell them you are. But you gotta reach out. Patch things up. That's what they want more than anything. And once Cat gets working on her next sculpture and the CAU students show up at the cafe again, I'm sure they'd be happy to help pay for your classes."

"Okay. I'll get in touch with them when I can."

"Glad to hear it."

Something in Megan's gaze told Shea the situation was more complicated, but she didn't press. Instead, she glanced around the room, still not seeing Indigo. "Hey, you seen Indigo since coming down for dinner?"

Megan scanned the dining hall. "You mean Ms. Pearson? No. But I've been mostly reading."

"Whatcha reading?" Shea reached to look at the cover, but Megan pulled it away defensively.

"Just some assigned reading."

Shea held up her hands in an appeasing gesture. "Okay. No problem. Probably not something I'd understand, anyway."

"Keep paying attention to the lectures," Megan said. "You'll get what we're trying to do here."

"I'm sure I will. Take care. And maybe eat a little something." Shea couldn't help the last dig as she walked away.

CHAPTER 23
LOOKING FOR INDIGO

SHEA FINISHED her water and tossed the bottle in the plastics recycle bin. She rarely drank this much water, but considering all the hiking she'd been doing, it wasn't a bad idea. But she also felt the urge to pee again.

She'd check their cabin again, looking for Indigo, on the way back from the toilet.

"Going somewhere?" Ramirez stepped in her path with the same suspicious expression as before. Did guys have resting bitch face? He also had the makings of a shiner blossoming over his right eye.

"Just gotta hit the latrine. You wanna come with?" she teased with a broad smile.

"See that you go straight there and straight back. No wandering."

"Will do." She started to turn away then stopped. "Hey, you see my friend Zia around? The one I was with earlier today?"

"Haven't seen her," he answered sharply.

Shea couldn't tell if he was lying or not. "Okay. You see her, tell her I'm looking for her?"

"Whatever." She pushed through the door.

The light outside was hazy, the sun having dipped

behind the mountain. The sky was painted in pale shades of lavender and pink, with a handful of stars piercing the deepening blue on the eastern horizon. The forest was alive with the sounds of early evening, and a cool breeze whispered through the trees.

Despite her tense encounter with Ramirez, Shea felt a sense of calm, similar to what the oxy had given her. Her leg was sore but not enough to bother her.

While she peed, she pondered her next move. Megan still wasn't willing to leave with her, but at least she'd agreed to call Cat and Nita. It wasn't ideal but was probably the best Shea could do for now. As Robyn had pointed out, cutting through months of brainwashing took time.

And really, was it brainwashing? Yes, Megan's fasting was a little concerning, as were the stories Robyn and the bookstore woman shared. But Megan didn't appear in any immediate danger. And the lectures Shea had watched got her wondering what she was doing with her life. What was wrong with wanting to build a world based on diversity, abundance, and sharing?

No one was telling her she had to obey NCB blindly. He wasn't instructing his followers to cut off communication with the outside world. Maybe all this talk of Luminos being a cult was just misunderstanding and rumor.

She nearly jumped out of her skin when her phone rang in her hand. "Hello?"

"Havoc, it's Indigo." Her voice sounded raw and raspy. "Thank goodness I reached you. I've been calling and calling."

"Where the hell are you? I've been looking all over."

"They kicked me out."

"Kicked you out? Why? Where are you?"

"Downtown Sedona. That asshole George Ramirez and one of his toadies zip-tied me and interrogated me."

"Fuck! Did they hurt you?"

"I'm...I'm okay." Her tone suggested otherwise. "But you've got to get Megan out of there as soon as possible."

"I don't get it. I was the one who brought a gun into camp. Why'd they kick you out?"

"They thought I might be a snitch. Kept asking who sent me. When I insisted I wasn't working for anyone, they told me they knew I worked as the law enforcement liaison for Lambda. I kept saying I was just trying to help them build a better world."

"Did they buy it?"

"Doubt it. When they threw me in the back of a van, I thought they were gonna kill me. I kicked one of them in the head right before they tossed me and my bags into a motel parking lot on the outskirts of town."

"Aw, shit. Indigo, I'm sorry. Let me grab my gear and the truck. We'll both get the hell out of here."

"No, you need to stay."

"Stay? After all this?"

"You need to get Megan out of there, sister. That's why her moms hired us."

"I talked to her a bit ago. She's agreed to call her moms. That's probably the best we can hope for."

"No, you must get her out of there. You were right. There's some nefarious shit going on. Why else kick me out for being the law enforcement liaison? You've got to get her out of there."

"By myself? You're the diplomat. I'm just a high school dropout ex-con. Maybe I can persuade them to let you back."

Indigo snorted with derision. "You can try, but I'm not sure how much luck you'll have."

"I can't do this alone, sister."

"Nita and Cat are counting on you, Havoc. You have to."

Shea wanted to argue. More than anything, she wanted to go home and heal up with Toni at her side.

But Indigo was right. If Megan was in trouble, Shea had

to get her out of there. Ramirez had denied seeing Indigo while sporting that shiner that she had given him.

"Fine, but I'm gonna talk to Dr. Linda and get this shit straightened out. And if I can't persuade her to let you back in…" Shea paused, unsure of what to say. "Then I'll bring Megan home one way or another. What about you? How are you getting home?"

"Savage is on her way up. Should get here in a couple of hours. The gracious lady at La Petite Sedona Motel is letting me stay in their office until she gets here. If you convince them to let me back, great. Call me. I hate leaving you there alone. Especially with your leg all messed up and you not feeling well. But Megan…"

"I know. Don't worry about me. Get home safe."

Her phone rang again. She glanced at the screen. The caller ID showed it was Annie. "Hey, Annie's calling on the other line. I missed her earlier call. I'll keep you updated."

"Watch your back, Havoc."

"Will do." She switched over to the other call. "Annie?"

"Aunt Shea, I wanna come home. Can you come pick me up?"

Shit, she thought. *Everything happening all at once.*

"Why, sweetie? What's going on?"

"I just want to come home."

"Did something happen? I thought you were having a good time."

"I…I don't know."

"Are you feeling homesick?"

"A little."

Shea felt torn. She wanted to rush in to help Annie. But keeping Megan safe from Luminos trumped Annie's homesickness.

"Okay, I'm a little tied up at the moment. Let me get ahold of tía Toni, see if she can't come get you."

"Okay." Annie sounded so forlorn it broke Shea's heart.

"Hang in there, Doodlebug. You're a tough girl. I know it's weird being away from home for so long. But we're here for you. I'll call Toni right now."

"Thanks, Aunt Shea. I love you."

"Love you, too, kiddo." Shea ended the call and punched in Toni's number.

"Hey! How's Sedona?" Toni asked.

"Long story. Annie just called me. Sounds like she's feeling homesick. Was asking for us to come pick her up."

"Aw, pobrecita. I'm on a stakeout at the moment. But let me call her, see if I can't get a sit rep on what's going on."

"Thanks, babe. I owe you."

"You doing okay up there?"

"I contacted Megan. She seems to be okay. Doubt I can persuade her to leave, but she's agreed to get back in contact with Cat and Nita."

"That's progress, I suppose. At least she's okay. They'll be relieved to hear that. And more relieved to hear from her."

"There's something else. They kicked Indigo out."

"What? ¿Por qué?"

"They learned she works with cops for Lambda. Not fans of law enforcement."

"I had a feeling that might happen. That's why I didn't take the job myself. Does Indigo need a ride back?"

"Savage is coming for her. I've agreed to stay on, see if I can't coax Megan to come home."

"Stay safe, querida. I'll take care of Annie. You just keep Megan safe and get home soon as you can."

"Will do."

She hung up. Time to have a discussion with the powers that be.

CHAPTER 24

PUSHBACK

USING her phone once again as a flashlight, she left the latrine and trekked to the trail leading up to Summit, where she'd met with Fake Doctor Linda.

It pissed her off that Ramirez treated Indigo the way they did, tossing her out like a bag of trash. Plus, Indigo would have had an easier time convincing Megan to leave than Shea would.

Shea's leg burned as the grade up the hill steepened. Shea leaned more and more on the stick that Rory had given her.

When she reached the camp, she made a beeline for Fake Doctor Linda's cabin. Without bothering to knock, she stormed into the main room, where Linda sat holding a drink and talking with another woman, who sat with her back to Shea. A bottle of wine sat between them on the coffee table.

"Shea?" Linda asked. "What are you doing here? You should be down with your group at the bonfire."

"Why the hell'd you kick out Zia? She didn't do nothing wrong." Her fists clenched as she readied for a fight.

The other woman turned to face Shea. She looked vaguely familiar. She wore a bolo with a blue slider. Shea suspected she was Connie, the bulldog attorney who sued people who spoke out against Luminos.

"Shea Stevens," Linda said, "this is Connie Brady. One of the other blue bars here."

"I don't give a shit if she's the fucking Easter Bunny. Why'd you kick out Zia and dump her in Sedona with no way to get home? I was her ride."

"We found some concerning issues in her background," Connie replied. "We felt she wasn't a good fit in our organization."

"Not a good fit? She believed all your bullshit. I'm the one who had all the contraband. But you kick her to the curb? Why? Because she works with cops? So what? Afraid she'll find something bad about you people?"

Connie sat there, stone-faced. "I'm afraid we can't discuss our findings with a third party. As for you and the contraband, Dr. Linda felt we could overlook the minor infraction, since you seem like a better fit."

"What's that even mean? A better fit? Why? Because she's Black? Or is it because she's transgender? You people talk a lot about inclusion, but Zia told me your buddy George misgendered her and called her a tranny."

Linda actually looked embarrassed. "I am terribly sorry if George said those awful things. It wasn't right. We are welcoming of all lifestyles. It was NCB who made the ultimate decision to part ways with Ms. Pearson. Unfortunately, that's the way it has to be."

"And you just dump her in downtown Sedona? What's she supposed to do? Hitchhike back to Ironwood?"

"I'm sure she has people she can call to get a ride home."

"Oh, you are, are you? I want to talk to Bennett."

"I'm afraid he's not available at the moment."

"Make him available."

"Ms. Stevens, you need to return to your campsite," Connie interjected.

"Or what? You gonna kick me out too?"

Linda stood and approached Shea with a deep smile. Shea took a wary step back.

"No one wants to kick you out, dear. You are showing so much promise. We really believe in you. I'm sorry that Zia didn't work out. Tell you what, I'll talk with NCB in the morning and ask him to consider letting her return. All right?"

"I guess." Shea wasn't sure she if was being sincere or not.

"I see you're using the walking stick I made for you. Is it helping?"

"I thought Rory gave it to me."

"I found the tree a while back. Another member cut it to length for me, and I polished it. I thought you could use it. So this afternoon, I handed it to Rory to give to you. We try to keep the camp as accessible as we can. I'm glad it's helping."

"Yeah, thanks."

Linda grabbed a bottle of water from the fridge in the kitchenette. "Here, you need to stay hydrated."

Shea accepted the bottle and took a deep pull. "Yeah."

Linda put a hand on Shea's shoulder, looking her deep in the eye. "Shea, you are so amazing. I don't think I've ever met someone as amazing as you. Your strength and resilience are inspiring. I've been doing some more reading about you. You turned that motorcycle shop into an amazing business enterprise. Providing employment opportunities to people trying to rebuild their lives? That is truly noble."

Shea shrugged, not sure what to say.

"You are proof that one can put past mistakes behind them. That's what Luminos is about. Finding that light inside of us and shining for all the world to see. Becoming an amazing example of what is possible. This is why we want you here."

Shea shrugged. "I learned from the guy who originally owned the shop. Just paying it forward."

"Of course, you are. I know there are people who think Luminos is some type of crazy cult. But nothing could be further from the truth. Cults try to control people. Our goal is the very opposite. We offer freedom. And not the way most people talk about it. If you stick with this program, you are going to know a new kind of freedom. Freedom from fear. Freedom from secrets. Freedom from pain. Freedom from limits of any kind. Imagine what that kind of freedom would feel like. That's what we're trying to help you achieve. You get this. I know you do."

Shea took another drink of water. Her mind felt muddled. "Yeah, I suppose I do."

"Why don't you head back down to camp. They'll be doing the first bonfire tonight. Should be a lot of fun. You don't want to miss it. And then you'll get a good night's sleep. Tomorrow morning, you'll wake up refreshed and rejuvenated. No more pain in your leg. The healing has already begun."

"And you'll talk to NCB about letting Zia back."

"Absolutely." Dr. Linda led her back to the front door. "Have a wonderful evening, Shea."

Shea felt that she shouldn't be so easily placated, and yet she figured she had no choice but to go along. She was still feeling off from not having any oxy for the past several hours. She simply didn't have the energy to argue.

"Yeah, okay."

She would live to fight another day, she told herself as she trudged down the hill in the dark.

CHAPTER 25

THE BRAND

THE BONFIRE WAS visible long before Shea reached the Seedling camp. A stack of wood roughly five feet tall and about ten feet in diameter had been erected and lit. Roaring flames shot high into the sky. Her fellow white bars sat on logs surrounding the fire.

Shea arrived just as they were passing out skewers for roasting marshmallows. Shea had vague recollections of spending time as a kid around a campfire with the Confederate Thunder families. Only now, the scent of weed didn't hang in the air. No music blaring from a boom box, competing with the rumble of a Harley being revved. No drunk bikers stumbling around making lewd comments toward her or getting beaten half to death by her father for making those comments.

No, this bonfire was tame and boring. Group songs, cheers, corny jokes, and ghost stories. And Shea had to admit that she liked it. Even though she was pissed at the higher-ups for kicking out Indigo. Even though her knee again felt like a ripe melon about to burst. Even though something nefarious may have been going on, leading Megan to starve herself. Still, something about this place and this group of fellow newbies felt like home. It made no sense. But she let herself enjoy it.

A couple of hours later, when the fire had burned down to smoldering embers, the white bars gathered together for one last circle, each one telling the group something they liked about another member of the group they had met that day.

More than one person said they liked Shea for her boldness and tell-it-like-it-is attitude. Shea was surprised. She wasn't used to being liked by these save-the-world types. When it was her turn, Shea complimented Gayle for her kindness.

That night, she slept soundly despite the crinkly plastic cover on the mattress. Despite the strange surroundings. Despite the discomfort in her leg. And despite a middle-of-the-night trip to the latrine.

In the morning, she woke up feeling better than she had since before her accident. Dr. Linda's words rang in her head. She would get a good night's sleep and wake up refreshed. Sure, her leg throbbed a bit, but it didn't burn or ache the way it had. Maybe it was true. Maybe Luminos would teach her how to free herself from fear and pain and limits of any kind.

Her anger over Indigo's expulsion and her concerns over what Luminos was really doing to women faded to the back of her mind.

She sat up and looked around. Gayle was wearing a long nightshirt with a graphic from the feminist punk band the Pink Trinkets. She was drying her wet hair with a towel.

"You like the Trinks?" Shea asked, surprised. She'd figured the woman would be more likely a Kenny G fan. Maybe Sarah McLachlan. But not the Trinks.

Gayle beamed. "Oh, yeah. I first discovered them when they opened for Ani DiFranco about ten years ago. Loved their style. Perfect mix of humor and feminism, with a raging, rocking beat. Kind of like a cross between Deap Vally and the Ramones."

"Definitely. My shop built their motorcycles for their Singing Mammogram tour."

"Really? That's amazing! I remember those motorcycles. Very bold. Didn't they auction one off for charity?"

Haunting memories pricked Shea's mind. A drug gang had stolen the custom bikes soon after they were completed. The same people who'd shot one of her employees, kidnapped Annie, and murdered Wendy.

"Yeah, they did," was all Shea would say about it.

"Did you know Wicked is a member of Luminos?"

Maria Wickham, also known as Wicked, was the group's lead singer. She was a member of Luminos? Something soured in her stomach.

She was seeing Luminos with fresh eyes, free from fear and rumor. If Wicked was a part of the organization, maybe the organization was as empowering as Dr. Linda had promised.

And yet, she had seen other celebrities get involved with some messed-up organizations. Part of her feared one of her feminist heroes had been seduced into something sinister—and her as well.

"You better hit the showers," Gayle said. "I hear the hot water runs out after a while."

"Thanks." Shea dug her towel and other toiletries out of her duffel bag.

She slipped her feet into a pair of flip-flops and shuffled off to the cement block building on the other side of the clearing.

The shower building had a half dozen shower stalls with no privacy walls or curtains. Shea wasn't exactly a fan of showing off her scarred and tattooed body to strangers, but she again recalled Dr. Linda's promise of freedom from fear.

Fortunately, only one other person was in the showers,

though Shea didn't recognize her. She looked to be about late thirties with a round face and freckles.

"Hey." Shea set her belongings on a nearby bench, pulled off her clothes, and turned on the spigot. She gasped when ice-cold water hit her in the abdomen. She stepped back, keeping her hand in to monitor the temperature.

The woman at the nearby shower turned toward her. "Oh, hi. I'm Sophie." A broad, overly enthusiastic smile spread across her face.

Shea spotted an angry red scar on the woman's left breast, just above her nipple. It had a vague butterfly shape, though the upper left wing had a sharp angle to it. Shea looked away, not wanting Sophie to think she was staring at her chest.

"I'm Shea," she said, meeting Sophie's eyes. "I'm new here."

"Yeah, I figured. Normally, I shower at the Blossom camp, but half the stalls are out of order. So some of us are using the Seedling showers till they're fixed."

The water wasn't warming up. Shea was not looking forward to an ice-cold shower. But after all the hiking she'd done the previous day, she needed it desperately.

"That looks painful," Sophie said, pointing at Shea's thigh.

"Road rash. Minor motorcycle accident."

"Ouch."

"That looks like it hurt too." Shea gestured at the scar on the woman's chest.

Sophie looked down at her own breast. Embarrassment colored her pale, freckled skin a bright red. "My brand."

"That's a brand? Like a cattle brand?"

"It's a butterfly. It represents transformation," Sophie said, though the tremor in her voice suggested she was trying to convince herself as much as Shea. "I got it a few weeks ago. Kinda cool, don't you think?"

"Where do you go for something like that?"

Sophie didn't exactly strike her as the body-mod type. But then, maybe Shea wasn't as good a judge of character as she thought. She never would have pegged Gayle for a Trinks fan.

"Here."

"Here? Someone here did that to you?"

"It builds character. Not that different from getting one of the many tattoos you have, I imagine. That owl across your back looks like it must've really hurt."

She had a point.

"I suppose, though you're the first person I've met with a brand. Aside from a friend who's a member of a Black fraternity."

Sophie turned off her shower and toweled off. "You'd be surprised how many people have brands these days."

Shea had never considered it. Was a brand that much more extreme than getting inked? The owl whose wings stretched across her back had taken four separate visits of several hours each. The outlining hadn't hurt much, but the filling in and shading had been more than a tad uncomfortable, especially around her spine.

Once dressed, Sophie walked toward the exit. "Enjoy your shower. Don't turn into a Popsicle."

"Yeah, thanks."

The water hadn't warmed a single degree since Shea had turned on the spigot. She plunged the rest of her body into the chill and gasped. "Fuck."

Her anger over Indigo being thrown out blazed once again, coupled with her concerns for Megan. She shivered as much with fury as from cold.

CHAPTER 26
SECRETS REVEALED

IN THE DINING HALL, Shea picked at her breakfast of tofu eggs and leathery bagels with fake cream cheese. It took two bottles of water to wash it all down.

When she was dropping off her empty meal tray in a large bin of water by the kitchen, Erykah appeared next to her. Despite the chilly morning, Erykah wore a low-cut lacy blue top.

"Good morning, Miss Shea." Her smile was as bright and unwarming as a winter sun.

"You hear about Zia?"

"Yes. So sad. She seemed so amazing. I suppose she wasn't a good fit after all. Oh well. We just have to wish her well on her journey."

Shea wanted to ask why the blue bars had been digging into Indigo's background and dumped her down in Sedona, but she figured Erykah was either not in the loop or wouldn't tell her if she was.

"Yeah," was all Shea said.

"I came to tell you that Dr. Linda needs to speak with you."

"Again? I saw her last night."

"Daily one-on-ones. It's one way we grow and free ourselves to become amazing instruments of change."

"Yes, amazing." Shea was hoping to take it easy today. Granted, her leg was feeling better, but why push it? As her gaze wandered, a hint of pink on Erykah's dark brown chest caught Shea's eye. Was it a brand like Sophie's?

"What are you staring at?" Erykah asked with a hint of scolding.

Shea felt herself blush and met Erykah's eyes. "What? No! I wasn't staring at anything. Just thinking is all."

The cool smile reappeared. "I'm just messing with you. Best head on up to talk with Dr. Linda. And grab yourself a water. Have to stay hydrated. Sometimes the one-on-ones can really take it out of you."

"Of course, thanks."

Shea grabbed another bottle of water from a glass-front refrigerator in the dining hall. She stopped by her cabin and grabbed the walking stick Dr. Linda had given her and began the long, grueling hike up to the Summit camp.

The beauty of the forest and the breathtaking views of Oak Creek Canyon made her miss Toni and Annie once more. Only a day or so had passed since she'd seen them, but it felt like ages. They would have loved how the light filtered through the trees. The sounds of the birds singing and the crunch of pine needles underfoot. The crisp air.

Her thoughts drifted to Indigo. Shea missed her too. It still miffed her that NCB's inner circle didn't feel she was a good fit.

She took another long pull from the water bottle. The water really was good. It made her feel better. More open to new ideas. Ready to free herself from her demons and become a better version of herself.

She reached the summit camp and knocked on Dr. Linda's cabin.

"Come in."

Shea stepped inside and found Dr. Linda in her office. That same odd machine was sitting on her desk. It reminded Shea of a tool that Switch had used at Iron Goddess to measure electrical current.

"Good morning, Shea. How did you sleep?"

"Amazingly well, considering the unfamiliar surroundings and not having my girlfriend beside me."

"And your leg is feeling better?"

"Yes. My leg is feeling better." That she echoed Dr. Linda's statement almost word-for-word struck her as odd, but she didn't let it bother her.

"Looks like your water bottle's almost empty." Dr. Linda reached into the mini fridge and pulled out a fresh bottle of water. "Here, I'll swap you."

Shea downed the remaining water in the bottle she'd brought with her, handed the empty to Dr. Linda, and took the cold fresh one from the fridge.

"Our goal today is to help free you from the shame and guilt of your past."

"I already served my prison sentence. I'm done with all that shame and guilt."

"Oh, of course. I'm not necessarily talking about your history of stealing cars. We all carry dark secrets with us that we fear sharing with others, especially those who love us most. And so, we bury these secrets deep in our subconscious, hoping that will make them go away."

Shea wondered where she was going with this but didn't respond.

"But these dark secrets don't really go away, do they? No, they fester like an infection. And this poisons our minds. It poisons our relationships. It robs us of joie de vivre."

"Jwa-duh-what?"

"Our joy of living. These dark, poisonous feelings hold us back because deep down we're afraid we don't deserve good things. Do you ever feel held back or blocked?"

Shea thought for a moment. "I've been struggling with creating new motorcycles for clients. I sit and stare at the design program on my computer or even at my sketch pad. But lately, nothing's been coming. At least nothing I haven't done a thousand times over."

Dr. Linda nodded knowingly. "Creative blocks can be extremely frustrating. There was a time when I, too, struggled before I joined Luminos. But the good news is that I'm here to help unblock you. You would like that, wouldn't you?"

"Sure. That would be amazing." Shea caught herself using that word. "Amazing." Oh well. There were worse habits to pick up.

"Excellent." Dr. Linda pulled some wires out of a drawer and plugged one end into the machine on her desk. "To do that, I'm going to use this device to monitor you."

She approached Shea with the other end of the electrical leads.

Shea scooted back, fending her off with raised hands. "Hold on there, doc. You ain't putting those things on me. I'm not interested in no electroshock therapy."

Dr. Linda chuckled. "Don't worry, Shea. No electroshock therapy here. These leads only measure the electrical impulses from your brain. There's no way they can shock you."

Shea eyed her warily then said, "Yeah, okay."

The woman placed leads on her forehead, her temple, and the base of her skull. "There. That's all."

"Why you need all this? Can't I just talk?"

"The machine helps me to know when we're getting close to the secrets that are blocking you. Isn't that amazing?"

"I guess. But how can it tell?"

"Different thoughts send different electrical signals from the various parts of your brain. It's a little complicated to explain. But with the proper training, which I have, a physician or psychologist can better zero in on troublesome issues and better target the therapy."

"You're gonna read my mind?"

"Not exactly. More like gauge your feelings surrounding the topics we discuss. Similar to the way a polygraph machine can detect deception." Dr. Linda sat back down. "Okay, I think we're ready to begin."

Linda began asking Shea about her childhood. Shea shared her experiences of growing up in Bradshaw City around the Confederate Thunder Motorcycle Club, where her father was the president. Through her early years, she'd been oblivious to their criminal behavior, as well as their bigoted attitudes toward anyone who wasn't straight, white, and male.

She shared about the trauma of watching her mother bleed out in her arms, despite Shea's best efforts to save her. And then her running away from the club and everyone she knew, ending up down in southern Arizona, stealing cars for a living.

"What about your sister, Wendy?" Dr. Linda asked.

"I left her behind." Shea's chest tightened. "Didn't have no choice, really. I was a teenager, and she was a little kid. Another couple in the club took her in. Julia and Monster. All in all, they did a decent job raising her. Better than I coulda done. But then…"

"Then what?"

Tears pricked her eyes. "I didn't see her for, like, ten years. Then outta the blue, she showed up at the shop. She'd had a kid, my niece, Annie. Her old man, an abusive asshole named Hunter, was the president of the Thunder. And Wendy'd turned into a junkie."

Shea took a deep breath and released it. A wave of relief hit her. She felt glad she was no longer taking the oxy, even though she had been using it to treat physical pain and not to dull her feelings.

"What prompted her to reenter your life?"

A torrent of violent memories flooded Shea's mind. "She was trying to get away from Hunter. Guess she'd heard about me and the biker shop. Hoped I'd protect her. And I agreed to. But then Annie got kidnapped."

"Oh, dear. Who took her?"

"At the time, the Thunder was in a war with a Latino street gang, Los Jaguares. We all thought it was the Jags who took Annie. We got a ransom demand for a few million bucks."

"Did you call the police?"

Shea scoffed. "We're talking the Confederate Thunder, an outlaw biker club. Ain't no way they'd call the cops. 'Specially not for something like this. He didn't have the money for the ransom neither."

"So, what did he do? What did *you* do?"

"Hunter knew about a warehouse south of Ironwood the Jags used as a base for their drug operation. We figured that's where they were keeping Annie and broke in hoping to rescue her."

"I gather it didn't go as planned?"

"She wasn't there, so Hunter and his crew stole some of the Jags' drugs to use as leverage."

"I suppose that makes sense in a criminal sort of way."

"Problem was, the Jags weren't the ones who kidnapped Annie."

"Oh?"

"A few corrupt cops had teamed up with some criminals they'd busted to grow poppies and manufacture heroin out in the Cortes National Forest. But they needed money to fund their operation. So they grabbed Annie and held her for ransom."

"And what happened?"

"Things went sideways at the ransom drop. Wendy and I rescued Annie from the trunk of a car. But Wendy was shot in the head before we could get away." Shea realized she was crying. "Cops were on the way. Had no choice but to leave her dead in the street."

"I'm so sorry." Dr. Linda handed Shea a box of tissues.

"Wendy never should've been there. Hunter had told us to stay at the Thunder's clubhouse. But I knew they would fuck it up, and they did. I let Wendy ride bitch on the back of my bike when I rode to the ransom drop. I never shoulda let her come."

"But you rescued the girl, your niece?"

"Yeah. But Hunter blamed me for Wendy getting killed. Maybe he was right. Not that he treated her any good."

"And this thing with the other drug gang, the Jaguars?"

"Things heated up between the Thunder and the Jags. Bodies started dropping. To avoid an all-out war, the Thunder agreed to return the drugs they'd stolen. I helped broker the meet. But again, things went sideways. Instead of returning the drugs, the Thunder brought a bomb. People on both sides started shooting. Then the bomb went off. It was...it was fucked up. Lotta people died. Including Hunter."

"How did Hunter die? From the gunfight or the bomb?"

Shea didn't know why Dr. Linda cared. Neither of them said anything for the better part of twenty minutes. "I did."

"Wow. Why did you kill him?"

"He came after me. Tried to kill me."

"Self-defense. Perfectly understandable reason."

"Thing is..." Shea struggled to speak the words. "I told Annie it was the Jags that killed him."

"Why not tell her the truth if it was self-defense?"

"I...I dunno. I'd already gotten Wendy killed, letting her ride with me to the ransom drop. And then shooting Hunter, shit. She was an orphan 'cause of me." Shea's chest heaved with emotion. "Ain't never told no one that before."

"That's a heavy burden to shoulder all these years."

"Five years, two months."

"A long time."

"Yeah."

"But now you're free."

"How?"

"Now you've told someone the truth. You've admitted what happened. You've unburdened your soul."

"Yeah, but Annie can't find out. I can't tell her. She'd never speak to me again."

"I understand. But you've told me. And you've let it out of that dark place in your heart. That makes the difference. Drink some water. You'll feel better."

She finished the bottle and had to admit she felt better.

"So, what now?"

"You'll head back down. And rejoin the group. Find Gayle and ask her to come up, okay?"

"Yeah."

CHAPTER 27
SWEPT UP

AS SHEA TRUDGED BACK down the hill, she felt completely raw and exposed, like the torn flesh on her thigh after the motorcycle crash. Emotional road rash.

Wendy's brutal death haunted her most. After more than a decade of estrangement, the two of them had reconnected for only a few days. And if Shea had held her ground and refused to let her ride bitch to the ransom drop, she would've still been alive.

She carried no guilt for killing Hunter. The man had been a brutal asshole who'd gotten Wendy hooked on drugs and abused her mercilessly. The Thunder's drug dealing had made them a target that led to Annie's kidnapping. When Hunter attacked Shea in the middle of the gunfight between the Thunder and the Jaguars, he got what was coming to him.

Confessing to killing Hunter should have freed her. Maybe it did, in a way. But she still couldn't risk telling Annie or even Toni the truth. The thought of losing either of them terrified her, even if she deserved it.

Something in one of NCB's videos sprang to mind. "Imagine who you could be if you had no limits? No fears.

Nothing to hold you back from being your most amazing self and living your most amazing life."

She didn't know, but a part of her wanted to find out.

Her phone rang. Toni's smiling photo appeared on the screen.

"Hey, babe!" Shea's heart beat a rapid staccato rhythm, which she told herself was from the strenuous decent back to Seedling.

"¡Ay, cariño! I just got a call from Savage. They beat the hell out of Indigo. What's going on up there?"

"They beat her up?" Shea tripped over a hidden rock. The walking stick kept her from tumbling down the trail. "She said she was okay."

"Okay? She's black and blue. And I'm not talking about her braids."

"Shit. She called me last night shortly before I talked to you. Said they kicked her out but didn't mention they hurt her. Fuck. I don't get it. Everyone's been so nice here. They're actually helping me."

"Helping you? With what?"

"All this time, you and everyone else have been telling me I need to talk to a therapist about my past traumas and shit. Well, I'm finally doing it. Dr. Linda's really helping me to move past all of that. I think, given some time, I can learn to be a better parent for Annie and—"

"Dr. Linda? The nurse practitioner who lost her license? She claims to be a therapist now?"

"I'm just saying she's helping. I'm getting something out of the program."

"Getting something out of it? Shea, you're there to rescue Megan, not become another victim of the cult."

The tempest of thoughts and emotions left Shea struggling to explain. "I know. But sweetie, I'm not entirely convinced it is a cult. I think they're really doing some good here. And Megan says she's okay."

"Shea, no. After I spoke with Indigo, I called that Robyn Phillips again. Nita's friend who stopped by before you left. I knew there was something she wasn't saying, so I pressed her. Mi amor, they're branding women like they're cattle."

The image of Sophie's breast flared back into her memory. How had she forgotten something she'd seen just a few hours ago? Her mind swam. "I…I know."

"You know? And you don't think that's cause for alarm? Where's the Shea Stevens I fell in love with? The one who wouldn't tolerate that kind of abuse? What kind of mind games are they pulling on you?"

"No mind games. I did meet a woman with a brand this morning in the showers. A butterfly. Got the impression it was voluntary. Not that different from someone getting a tattoo or a piercing."

"It's not a butterfly, Shea. It's that pinche pendejo's initials! NCB."

"His initials?" She remembered the angry red scar on Sophie's chest. The upper left wing had a funny angle. Maybe that was an N. "Yeah, I suppose. But if it was voluntary…"

"Voluntary, my ass! Robyn believes they're doping people somehow."

"Doping people? Now that's absurd. I'll admit, the vegan food they're serving isn't exactly what I'm used to, but I think I'd know if someone was doping me with something."

"Not necessarily. Indigo brought back a bottle of water from the camp. She said they kept pushing everybody to drink more."

"Of course they're encouraging people to drink water. This is the desert. They don't want people to get dehydrated, especially with all the hiking we're doing."

"I'm going to have an associate of mine at the county crime lab run a tox screen on the water in the bottle to see if there's anything that shouldn't be in there."

"Hey, knock yourself out. It's spring water. Bound to be some minerals and shit in there."

"Minerals I don't mind. Just want to make sure there're no drugs."

"Whatever."

"Whatever? Bebé, I want you to be safe. And I want Megan home safe. These cults are master manipulators."

"No one's manipulating me, Toni. I'm getting help, and now you're tossing a grenade on the whole thing. Maybe you don't want me to get help."

"Shea, do you hear yourself? All I want is for you to be happy, okay? You're mi corazón. Mi amor. I would literally take a bullet for you. I shot my old partner to save your life. Remember? And that was when I was a cop, and you were… pushing the boundaries of the law."

Shea took a breath. Toni was right. She'd risked everything to save Shea. And she had proven her love repeatedly since they'd started dating. "I'm sorry. I'm just trying to figure shit out after all these years."

"Which I applaud. But please, talk to Megan. Tell her what they did to Indigo and get her to come home with you. And stay away from the bottled water."

"And what will I drink? There're no sodas. No coffee. Maybe some green tea. But I'm sure it's made with the same water."

"I don't know. Make the best decision you can. I trust you, cariño. Just be careful."

"I will. And Toni? Babe?"

"¿Sí?"

"Thank you for caring about me. Hey, I almost forgot. How's Annie doing?"

"I think she misses us. And honestly, I miss you both. This house is too empty and too quiet."

"I'll be home soon, and I'll bring Megan with me."

By the time Shea returned to the Seedling camp, her

mind was in turmoil, and the stabbing pains under her kneecap had returned. Every step felt like someone was using a cheese grater on the side of her leg.

She longed to put two in the back of Ramirez's head, grab Megan, and get the hell out of there. Still, a part of her wondered what life could be like without the burden of her troubled past and the secrets she carried.

All the people she'd killed, either directly or indirectly, haunted her like specters in the shadowy corners of her consciousness. Even though many of them deserved their fate, she could not shake the weight of their lingering presence.

She joined the rest of the newbies in watching another video of NCB talking about how human civilization started in Sedona, not Africa's Rift Valley. He claimed humans were the offspring of early primates and the Emanu, extraterrestrials from the planet Annu on the other side of the Milky Way.

As she listened, she drank two bottles of water. They tasted fine.

If there were drugs in here, I'd know it. Besides, what else am I supposed to drink?

Shea ignored the cheap, mismatched, and often pixilated graphics NCB used in his video as he explained that humanity had gotten off track with wars and drugs and fascism and corruption. The goal of Luminos, he explained, was to re-create an enlightened tribe to help restore humanity to a peaceful, compassionate, and prosperous people that protected the earth and one another.

"People have asked me how I know these things. I am a channel for Inagua, an emissary of the Emanu. Inagua has spoken to me through my meditations and asked me to speak to you now so that we can fulfill this new mission together. Imagine the future we can create if we work together."

It had all seemed ridiculous at first mention. But Shea's skepticism ebbed the more he got into it. What did she know? She never finished high school. And never considered herself all that smart. Sure, she could design motorcycles, but even then she had to defer to Lakota's engineering expertise to make sure they were structurally sound and could deliver the horsepower she desired.

By the time the group broke for lunch, Shea had decided she would stick with the "Change Yourself, Change the World" seminar to its conclusion on Saturday. The lessons she was learning could well be the solution to her creative blocks. She could take her career to the next level. She could be a better girlfriend to Toni and a better parent to Annie. It was a win-win all the way.

Yes, Nita and Cat were worried about Megan, but Shea would make a point of checking in with her every day at dinner to make sure she was doing okay. Toni would understand. Maybe not now but eventually when she got home and explained everything she was learning.

Over the next few days, she found her thoughts more and more in line with the amazing mission that NCB and this Inagua being had set for Luminos. More than anything, she wanted to be a part of this movement to change the world, to bring justice to the oppressed and preserve the environment for generations to come. If that meant giving up her partnership in Iron Goddess, well, the sacrifice was worth considering.

When she found voicemail and text messages from Toni asking for updates, Shea simply replied with "Still working on it."

Dr. Linda's predictions seemed to be true. She no longer felt raw and exposed, even with all the guilty secrets she shared in the one-on-ones. She felt energized, empowered, and free, buzzing with possibilities. Her leg hardly bothered her at all, and she had returned the walking stick to Linda.

CHAPTER 28
BUILDING CHARACTER

AT DINNER, Shea began sitting with Megan. The two of them had solidified a level of trust, now that Shea understood what Megan had been trying to tell her moms all this time.

"Mama Nita says you built the motorcycles for the Pink Trinkets," Megan said on Thursday evening. Her plate consisted of a small block of tofu.

Shea almost felt guilty when she looked at the vegan feast on her own tray. But she reminded herself that Megan was doing what she knew was right for her.

"Yeah, me and my crew at Iron Goddess."

"Then you'll be excited to learn that Wicked will be at your graduation in a couple of days."

"Wait, what? Graduation?"

"The intro class ends on Saturday. You will earn your yellow bar."

"Wow. I can't believe it's almost been a week." Shea savored the flavors of the food on her plate. "Seems like ages. And yet at the same time, it feels like I just got here. There's so much to learn."

The words sounded strange coming out of her own mouth. And yet she believed them deeply.

Megan laughed.

"Wow. It'll be good to see Wicked again. Been a few years."

Megan winced and pressed a hand to her chest.

"Something wrong?" Shea asked.

"What? Yeah, fine. Just a little sore."

A memory wriggled to the surface. The brand on Sophie's breast. Did Megan have one too?

"Can I ask you something?" Shea whispered tentatively.

"Sure."

"Did you get branded?"

Megan stared down at the remaining crumbs of tofu on her plate. "I don't know what you're talking about."

A chill ran down Shea's spine, radiating out in tendrils of fear and anger, spoiling the veneer of serenity she had worked so hard on the past few days. She had thought this negativity was behind her.

"A few days ago, I saw Sophie in the showers. She had a brand on her chest, right above her nipple."

"Um, well, some members do get brands."

"Why?" Shea set her fork on her tray, her appetite having evaporated.

"It…uh…it builds character. It reminds us of our strength and resilience."

"Do you have a brand? Is that why you gripped your chest just now?"

"Why do you want to know? I'm on my journey, and you're on yours."

"Megan, I just want to know." Shea's newfound belief system unraveled at the edges. "You can tell me. No secrets, right?"

"Yes. I have a brand."

"And you wanted it?"

"It's part of my journey."

"Megan…"

"It builds character. We need character if we're going to change the world."

"What is it a brand of? What does it look like?"

"It's a butterfly."

"Is it NCB's initials?"

Megan looked like a frightened rabbit, unmoving, barely breathing. Just as Robyn had been that night.

"Megan, what does the brand really mean? That you're his property now?"

"Have you been talking to my moms?"

"What? No."

"Because they asked that same question."

"We're friends, you and me. We're on this mission together. I just want to know the truth."

"You sure you could handle the truth if you heard it?" Megan met Shea's eyes with a steely gaze.

"So, what? You're Jack Nicholson now?" Shea joked to lighten the tension.

The smile returned to Megan's eyes. "It will make a lot more sense once you begin the next class. You are going to continue, right? You're not just going to walk away after one class, are you?"

Shea hadn't decided yet. The original goal had simply been to get Megan home. That clearly wasn't happening. But Megan was texting her moms again. That was something, at least. By all measures, she should be heading home on Saturday, where Toni was waiting for her.

But what if Shea stayed? Just for the next seminar. She could become a yellow bar. She could make a difference.

"Yeah, I'm staying," she said.

And yet something nagged at Shea from the back of her mind. She couldn't pinpoint what. Maybe it was just her old thinking. The fear and trauma and paranoia that had haunted her much of her life.

"I'm so glad. Can't wait to tell my moms. Maybe finally

they'll get off my back once they know you see what an amazing opportunity this is."

"I gotta hit the head. I'll see you around."

"Definitely."

Shea deposited her tray, slipped a fresh bottle of water in the carrier handing from her shoulder, and stepped outside into the early evening. The night critters were giving a command performance. Cicadas, crickets, frogs, and owls. She took a deep, relaxing breath, but that something continued to nag at her. Perhaps listening to the creek would calm her nerves.

With her phone in one hand lighting her path and her walking stick in the other keeping her from pitching down the hill, she gradually reached the gurgling creek.

Her phone beeped. A voicemail message. She was tempted to ignore it. She'd trundled down to the creek to relax. But that something in the back of her mind pestered her to play it.

"Amor, call me, por favor. ¡Inmediatamente!" Toni's voice sounded urgent. Frightened, even.

She hit the redial button. "Babe, what's up?"

"Two things. First, I got the tox screen report back on the water you've been drinking. They really are doping people, like Robyn suspected. The water's laced with chlorpralozine."

"Chlor-what?"

"Chlorpralozine. It's an antipsychotic drug."

"Antipsychotic? Why would they put that in the bottled water?"

"It can make people more compliant and suggestible. It's sometimes used as a date rape drug."

"Toni, that's ridiculous. If someone had been drugging me, I'd know it."

"If the dosage is low enough, and it's given consistently,

you might never know. My friend at the crime lab ran the tests twice. There's no mistake."

"I don't understand. How would they even get it into the bottled water?"

"I don't know. My friend talked to his superior. The chain of custody is lacking, so there's not enough probable cause to get a warrant to test bottles either at the camp or at the bottling plant. I'm trying to find out if they sell this brand of water anywhere else or if it's exclusive to Luminos. This is serious, cariño."

None of what Toni said made any sense to Shea. Luminos was helping people. Why would they drug their members?

On the other hand, they had branded Megan, Sophie, and others. Robyn and the woman at the bookstore had accused Luminos of coercing women into having sex and harassing those who had left and spoken out. They had beaten up Indigo and thrown her out just for having professional ties to the cops.

"What do you want me to do?"

"For starters, stop drinking the water. Have you made any progress building a rapport with Megan? Do you think there's any chance you could persuade her to come home now?"

Shea wasn't sure how to answer the question. She didn't want to go home yet herself.

"Not yet. We've been talking a lot, but I don't think she's ready to leave yet. Give me a couple more days." At least until the graduation ceremony so she could get her yellow bar slider.

"I never should have sent you on this loco assignment. Especially not in your condition. I know we need to get Megan out of there, but after what happened to Indigo, I'm worried. I don't want anything to happen to you."

"Nothing bad's gonna happen to me, babe. I'm perfectly

fine. But if it'll make you feel any better, I'll stop drinking the water. And I'll work harder to persuade Megan to leave."

"Be careful, amor. I don't want to lose you."

Shea laughed. "Don't worry. You won't lose me. Not unless you forget where you put me."

"Idiota! Come home soon. Oh, and call Annie. She really misses you."

"I will. I love you."

"Love you too."

Shea hung up and then called Annie. She hadn't spoken with her in days and missed hearing her voice.

"Aunt Shea?"

"Hey, kiddo. How you doing?"

"I'm…fine."

"Still feeling a little homesick?"

"I guess. Tía Toni said you're at a camp too."

"Yeah, sort of. A friend of mine was here and needed some help."

"What kind of help?"

"She was worried about some things. I just came to make sure she was safe."

"What if I need help? Will you come for me?"

That nagging feeling Shea'd felt earlier resurfaced. "Annie, sweetie, are you in trouble? Is someone hurting you?"

"No, not really. I just miss being home."

"If you need Toni to come get you, say the word." Guilt nagged Shea. She should be the one to head out and pick Annie up if needed. Annie was her niece, after all. And she was the one who had made Annie an orphan in the first place.

"I'm okay. Really. Help your friend. I'll be fine. I'll see you soon, okay?"

"Okay. Call me if you need to. Although the reception up here is spotty. If you can't get ahold of me, call Toni. Okay?"

"Okay. Love you, Aunt Shea."

"Love you, too, Doodlebug."

Shea stared out at the moonlight shimmering off the dark water. A storm was brewing inside her chest. So many feelings and conflicting desires.

Guilt hammered her for the injuries and humiliation Indigo had suffered. She never would have been here if Shea hadn't asked.

And if what Toni said was true, Megan was still at risk. If Shea was honest with herself, she knew from the girl's reaction that getting branded had not been voluntary. It was written all over her face. The humiliation. The brokenness. And if they would do that to a vulnerable nineteen-year-old, what else were they doing to the other members? And what could Shea do about it in her condition?

Shea wanted to pretend it was all speculation so that she could continue working on her own issues. To be a better person, a more creative person. A more honest person. But maybe that was all just a pipe dream fueled by the water laced by this drug Toni had found.

Maybe it was time to press Megan hard about the dangers of the organization and bring her home, willingly or unwillingly.

She poured the remaining water in her bottle into the creek. She could try refilling it with water from the sink in the shower building. Just had to do it when no one was looking.

CHAPTER 29
MEETING THE GURU

SHEA TRUDGED BACK UP to camp and slipped unnoticed into the shower building. She gathered several empty bottles from the trash can, rinsed them, and filled them from the sink. She put two in her messenger bag and stashed the rest in her cabin before returning to the dining hall.

The tap water tasted bitter, leaving her wondering about its drinkability. But if Toni said they laced the bottled water with chloro-whatever, she was probably right. She'd been an excellent detective and was meticulous with evidence. Shea needed a clear mind as she formulated a strategy for getting Megan to leave with her.

When she returned to the dining hall, she discovered that the tables and chairs had all been folded away. Six Ping-Pong tables had been erected in their place. The familiar driving beats of the Pink Trinkets played over the sound system.

Sets of four people played at each of the tables. Everyone else watched, cheering as teams scored points.

Shea spotted a vaguely familiar woman across the hall wearing a red slider bolo. Periodically, she'd glance over at the woman, trying to place her, but her name and where she knew her from escaped her.

A cheer rose from the crowd as though one of the teams had won a game, though Shea couldn't see who. All six tables were in the middle of volleys. Shea followed everyone's gaze to a squat man in his forties entering the room.

Shea recognized him instantly. He was the only one in the dining hall not wearing a bolo tie. Nathan Curtis Bennett. The guru.

Shea turned to Caleb, whose man bun was loose from playing a game of Ping-Pong. "He looks a lot shorter and frumpier in person."

"I think he's amazing." Caleb looked starstruck.

Shea scolded herself for her comments. If this was a cult, she shouldn't show her hand before she was ready to make a move.

Bennett wandered through the crowd, greeting each person with a deep kiss on the lips. Shea's stomach churned at the sight. The only man she'd ever kissed had been her father and never on the lips. She wasn't about to kiss this guy.

When Bennett reached her, Shea tried to turn her head to the side and give him a half-hearted hug instead. NCB gripped both sides of her head and pulled her in for a hard kiss. She felt his tongue try to penetrate her mouth, and she pushed him away and stared at him in shock, resisting the urge to deck him.

He smiled one of those creepy Luminos smiles everyone had pasted on their faces. "Shea Stevens, right?"

"Yeah." *Play it cool, girl. Don't blow this. You have to get Megan out.*

"So pleased to meet you. I hear great things about you. I'm looking forward to getting to know you much better."

He slapped her on the ass and moved on to the woman standing beside her.

She stood there a moment, feeling dazed and more than a little violated. The kiss and slap were a wake-up call. The conversations she'd had with Cat and Nita, as well as with Toni, Indigo, Robyn, and the woman from the bookstore replayed in her mind.

She couldn't deny it any longer. This place wasn't an incubator for progressive change. It was a festering swamp of abuse and control. And she would find a way not only to protect Megan but to bring the entire organization down.

CHAPTER 30

OVERHEARD

THAT NIGHT, Shea tossed and turned. The plastic cover over the mattress rustled and crinkled every time she shifted or rolled over, like the sound of water trapped in her ear canal after swimming.

She woke in the middle of the night with her leg burning and her knee throbbing. The aspirin she'd taken before bed hadn't helped at all.

Making matters worse, her brain wouldn't shut off. She kept replaying her conversations with Toni, Robyn, and Indigo, contrasting them with what Megan and Linda had told her. Her creepy encounter with NCB blotted everything out, filling her with rage. If nothing else, she now knew without a doubt that Bennett was a sexual predator.

How would she coax Megan to leave? Especially with her drinking the drug-laced water. Maybe she could swap out some bottles of the tap water. Get her off the chloro-whatever long enough to see reality instead of NCB's delusions of extraterrestrials and world revolution.

When the dim predawn glow lit the hallway outside her room, Shea crept out of bed, grabbed a couple of bottles filled with tap water, and stepped outside in the cool morning air. Her road rash burned again as if someone had doused the gauze bandages in alcohol and lit them on fire.

"Fuck," she hissed to the gray eastern sky. Even the salmon- and lavender-colored clouds on the horizon no longer held their usual appeal.

She took a deep breath and trod along the path toward the Blossom camp. When she was halfway there, she heard footsteps and humming above her. Shea glimpsed Megan on a path farther up the hill that led from Blossom to another camp. Possibly Summit.

She suppressed her impulse to call out to her. She didn't want to alert anyone but Megan to her presence. Instead, she stepped off the path and cut up through the brambles on the rocky slope.

Her leg protested at the strain. Shea gritted her teeth. Catclaw acacia repeatedly snagged on her cargo jeans. It felt like the thorns were scraping directly against her raw skin. Her knee wasn't doing much better. She could imagine tiny tears in the tendons around her kneecap getting deeper and longer.

When she finally reached the upper trail, Megan was nowhere in sight. She rushed along the path to catch up to the girl as quickly as her leg would allow.

By the time she reached the clearing at the Summit camp, there was still no sign of Megan. Shea studied the handful of cabins. The largest belonged to Bennett, no doubt. Had he summoned her for an early-morning sexual assault? Or was she in Fake Doctor Linda's cabin for more one-on-one brainwashing?

The door to Linda's cabin was slightly ajar. Megan had to be in there. But what to do? Burst in and take back her pistol and pain meds then grab Megan and force her to come home with her? No, not a good plan. Too many ways for that to go sideways, especially if Megan refused to go.

She could wait for Megan to leave and talk with her on

the way back to the Blossom camp. That had potential. Of course, she could also listen in on their conversation, maybe get some intel that could prove useful in convincing Megan to leave.

Shea stepped inside and heard faint voices coming from inside Linda's office.

"I've tried to let go of it, Dr. Linda." The raw emotion in Megan's voice was palpable. She sounded distraught.

"Megan, if you can't get this under control, we're going to have to send you to Stick for a few days. Do you want that?" asked Linda.

"No, please. I've been fasting. Well, except for a little tofu last night."

"Well, there you have it. You haven't really been fasting, then, have you?"

"I had to. My stomach hurt so bad. I just had to eat something. I've felt dizzy and shaky."

"You're feeling dizzy and shaky because you've been doubting."

"I...It's Bethany. I still miss her so much. She died so suddenly. And it's not even like she was sick. And then..." Her voice broke. "The way we left her in the woods like that. It just feels so wrong. All of it."

"Megan, listen to me. I'm a physician. Bethany died of an aneurysm. It was something she was born with. Like a ticking time bomb. There was nothing any of us could have done to save her."

"Couldn't we have taken her to a hospital? I'm sure her family is wondering what happened to her."

"Even if we had the best neurologists or cardiologists in the world, we couldn't have saved her. She wasn't meant to continue her journey any further. You have to let this go. You have to let her go. Her time has passed. But this is your time. You can let her hold you back, or you can become the change you wish to see in the world. Are you doubting me or NCB?"

"No, never."

"I'm giving you until this evening to sort it out and let it go. Otherwise, you will spend the night in Stick. Is that clear?"

Megan sniffled. "Yes, Dr. Linda. I will. I promise."

"Good. Now complete your assignment."

The conversation stopped for a few minutes. Shea could hear shuffling. Maybe Dr. Linda was hugging her.

Shea was so busy wondering who Bethany was and where they'd left the body to realize that Megan's one-on-one session had ended. The door opened wide. Shea jumped back, sending lightning bolts of pain shooting through her leg.

"Shea?" Megan asked, wiping her face. "What are you doing here?"

"I really need to talk with you." Shea remembered the bottles of water she had with her. "Here, gotta stay hydrated after all that crying."

"You heard that?" Panic flashed across Megan's face.

"Heard what? No, but you're obviously upset over something. Some water should help."

"You're really amazing, you know that?" Megan wrapped Shea in a hug.

"It's gonna be okay, kiddo," Shea whispered in her ear. "Come on."

"Shea?" Fake Doctor Linda appeared in her office doorway. "I didn't send for you."

"I just need to talk with Megan. I'll see you later, Dr. Linda."

"Megan has work to do. But since you've made the effort to come all the way up here, step inside my office."

"See you later, Shea." Megan walked out of the cabin and disappeared.

Shea wanted to follow her but was afraid of tipping off Fake Doctor Linda. The last thing she wanted was for Linda to send Ramirez after her, or worse, after Megan.

"Shit," Shea muttered under her breath and stepped into the office.

"Good morning, Shea. I wasn't expecting you so early."

CHAPTER 31
REVELATIONS

SHEA FORCED A SMILE, determined to play along with the charade. She wanted to know more about this Bethany person and how she really died.

"I can't believe you trekked up to Summit just to chat with Megan. What's going on?" Linda asked.

"Just wanted to jump-start the day. Also, my leg's been bothering me again." Shea wasn't sure why she volunteered the information. But she needed to make some conversation to explain her being there earlier than scheduled. She took a long drink of tap water and said, "Was hoping I could have my pain meds back. Sorry."

Dr. Linda didn't respond right away but stared at Shea, seemingly studying her as if she were some kind of medical specimen. Finally, Dr. Linda said, "Let me think about it. In the meantime, let's do our one-on-one."

Shea wasn't so sure that was a good idea. She just wanted to grab Megan and get the hell out of this place. She stood. "I can come back at my scheduled time."

"Nonsense." Dr. Linda gestured for her to sit down. "If your leg's bothering you, then don't torture yourself by making an extra trip. Be kind to yourself."

The side of her leg burned all the more. She collapsed back into the chair. "Yeah, all right."

Dr. Linda attached the leads from the machine to Shea's forehead and temple then asked probing questions about her life and work at Iron Goddess. Shea tried to keep her answers short, not wanting to reveal any more information than necessary.

"You mentioned in a previous session that you and your girlfriend are raising your niece. How did you two meet?"

The question caught Shea flatfooted. This was definitely not an area she wanted Dr. Linda poking around in. Did she know Toni was a retired cop?

"Mutual friends." The answer seemed valid, though it was far from the full story.

"Tell me more."

"Just mutual friends."

"Shea, I can tell from the meters on the machine that you're holding things back. We talked about this. Our secrets are like anchors, weighing us down and preventing us from living up to our potential. If you want to be free of your creative blocks, you have to open up. Would you like some more water?"

Shea realized the remaining bottle she'd been drinking from was empty. "No, I'm good."

"What's your girlfriend's name?"

"Toni."

"Short for Antoinette?"

"Short for Antonia."

"And Toni's last name?"

"Why?"

"Shea, I'm not interrogating you. We're having a conversation."

"Her last name's Rios."

"Wonderful. See how easy that was? You're doing great.

Now, how exactly did the two of you meet? Where was it? What was the situation? I feel this is a critical point."

Shea hesitated then decided to hell with it. She was leaving soon anyway. "When my niece was kidnapped, Toni was assigned to help get her back."

"Assigned? She's a police officer?" Dr. Linda's eyes widened in surprise, though Shea could tell she was trying to act cool.

"She worked as a detective with the Cortes sheriff's department. She retired a while back."

"Really? That's very interesting. You being an ex-con and her being a police officer. A rather odd match, don't you think?"

"We never dated while she was a cop."

Shea recalled lying in the hospital, recovering from injuries caused by Toni's lieutenant running her off the road. Toni had threatened to send her back to prison on weapons charges if Shea didn't agree to become a confidential informant. For a while, she absolutely detested Toni.

"What attracted you to her?"

Shea laughed darkly. "Well, she's sexy. And even though we were on opposite sides of the law, I admired her. Not for being a cop but because she really cared about helping people and about bringing bad guys to justice. She wasn't like most of the assholes working for the sheriff's department."

She remembered Winters, the cop who gave her the third degree after the accident with the pickup truck.

"When she asked me out about a year ago, I said yes. Honestly, I was surprised it's worked out. She's smarter than me. But we have a lot in common. Both were orphaned when we were young. Both have scarred faces, mine from a dog attack, her from a gunshot wound. And she's great with Annie. They're both girly-girls, which is something I'm not."

"You're more the tomboy."

"Tomboy, butch, whatever. Never into makeup or dresses. Gimme a T-shirt and jeans, I'm good."

"And what does she do now that she's retired?"

Shea shrugged, trying not to give too much of her mission away. "She goes for hikes, watches TV, works out at the gym."

"Shea, you're holding back again."

"Occasionally, she does investigative work for defense lawyers."

"And…"

"And what? I told you." Shea felt her walls go up. This doctor wannabe wouldn't get anything more out of her.

"Are you sure? Everything? You're not leaving anything out?"

"What is this? Some kind of interrogation?"

Linda sat up taller. "Shea, I'm surprised at you. You want to change the world, right? You want to live a life without limits?"

"Yeah, I do. And I told you all there is to tell." Shea yanked off the leads. "Now can I have my meds, please? They were prescribed to me by my doctor. And you promised to give them back if I still needed them after a few days. Well, I still need them."

Linda leaned back in her chair and crossed her arms. "I'm going to hold on to them a while longer. You've been doing so well. We don't want a relapse to sabotage the amazing progress you've made."

"Fuck you."

"Hold on. I will give them back eventually. But I need you to trust me that as a physician, I'm doing what's best for you. You know as well as I do how bad the opioid crisis has become. People, good people, are becoming addicted to these drugs. I don't want that to happen to you. And with the emotional state you're in right now, that is a strong possibility for you. As a doctor, it would be irresponsible for me to give you back these medications, which as we both acknowledge were prescribed for a previous injury and have since expired."

"They still help."

"I'll tell you what. I'll make you a deal. If you sign up for the next seminar, I will give you your pain meds back right now."

"The next seminar?"

"Yes. It's titled 'Unlocking Your Best Self.' I think it's just what you need to take the next positive step in your journey. If you sign up, that will demonstrate you're committed to your recovery."

"I suppose that means I'll have to pay now too."

"It's only three thousand dollars. A minor investment compared to the rewards you'll reap. Imagine the amazing motorcycles you could create if you unlocked your best self."

Shea stared at her. She knew Linda was using another of her manipulations. "I'll have to think about it."

"If you wait until graduation, the price will go up to five thousand. I'm trying to save you money and help you grow. I'm in your corner."

"I said I'll think about it." She turned on her heel and walked out.

"I still believe in you," Linda called to her back.

Shea stormed out of the cabin, each step a new experience in agony. Every stab of pain reinforced her resolve to retrieve the meds. She wasn't an addict. She was just treating physical pain. She'd have to break into Linda's office and get her pills and gun back before she left. But her chief priority was to get Megan out of there.

CHAPTER 32
GROWING CONCERNS

"DOWN THIRTY PERCENT?"

NCB's angry shouts made Linda flinch when she walked into the office where he, George, and Connie were talking. NCB's face was beet red.

"Yavapai's jacking up our property taxes by six percent, and you're telling me our stock prices have fallen thirty fucking percent?" NCB bellowed.

"Technically 31.5, but yes," Connie replied. "Add to that, enrollments are down."

"By how much?" George asked.

"We only have six signed up for the new class starting next week."

NCB growled and stared out the window. "That's less than half our usual class."

Linda resisted the urge to walk out again. She'd seen him lose his temper like this only a few times in the twelve years she'd known him. When he did, the fallout was usually bad.

Connie continued. "And of the white bars currently enrolled, only five have expressed an interest in continuing on to the Skills Development Course. Shea Stevens, Caleb Taggert, Gayle Oliver, Juliana Babbitt, and Karen Bauer."

"You probably should count Shea Stevens out," Linda interjected. "I'm not convinced she's still onboard."

NCB whipped around to face her. His furious expression hit her like a punch in the throat. "Why not?"

"She keeps holding back. And she's asking for her pain pills again. But that's not the biggest concern."

"What is?"

Linda took a deep breath and steeled herself against the blowback she knew was coming. "Her girlfriend is a retired cop."

"What? You're just learning this now?" His shout reverberated off the walls and sent chills down Linda's spine.

"It never turned up in the background check. They're not married. No common bank accounts. The girlfriend was a homicide detective for the Cortes County Sheriff's Office but since retiring works as a private investigator. Also, Shea has been talking with Megan Thornton, one of the yellow bars. I think they know each other. Shea's been asking probing questions. Probably nothing, but…"

"This is the same woman that came in with that tranny who was a liaison with the cops?" George asked in a tone that at least sounded calming.

"Yes." Her response was almost a whisper.

NCB took a glass he'd been drinking from and threw it across the room. The glass shattered against the log walls, leaving a wet stain. "Fix this."

"I'm trying, but something's off. This morning she wasn't responding as well as I expected."

"And she's drinking the water?" NCB asked.

"Yes. We had a one-on-one just fifteen minutes ago. I watched her drink an entire bottle in front of me."

"And the bottling company is sending us the right bottles? Not the normal ones?"

"All of the blue labels are laced. I confirmed with the plant manager."

"Then what's the problem? And how are these people with connections to law enforcement infiltrating our camp?" NCB directed this last question at George.

"I don't know. I'm sorry. You want to send this Shea woman to Stick?"

NCB stood there, his hand on his chin as he appeared to consider their next move.

Linda felt consumed with guilt. She had failed to keep Shea in line and to entice more of the current class to enroll in the next seminar. There would be repercussions.

"Send her to me in an hour. Linda, leave me all of your notes on her so I can familiarize myself with all the kompromat we have on her."

"Yes, sir."

"And I want every one of the white bars enrolled in the next seminar. No exceptions. And raise the tuition by twenty percent."

"I...I will make it happen."

"Connie, I want you to max out the cards we have for that Bethany woman. George, you double- and triple-check every single person signed up for the newbie seminar. I want to know their grandmothers' maiden names. Every car they've owned. Every person they've slept with in the past ten years. And I want you to go after those who've left our fold. Get them back in. We need revenue. I will not become a homeless beggar just because you three idiots don't know how to do your jobs anymore."

"Yes, sir," they replied in unison.

CHAPTER 33

GETTING ANSWERS

WHEN SHEA WAS out of sight of the Summit camp, she pulled out her phone and called Toni.

"¡Hola, mi amor! Are you coming home yet?"

"Soon. But I need you to look into something."

"¿Qué?"

"I overheard Megan talking with Fake Doctor Linda. They were talking about leaving the body of someone named Bethany out in the woods somewhere. Maybe one of your associates can check if there are any missing women with that name."

"¡Ay Dios mio! They murdered a woman?"

"I don't know. Linda claims she died of an aneurysm, but how would she know if she never took her to a hospital? And why leave her body in the woods?"

"Do you know where her remains might be?"

"No. They didn't say."

"I really don't like you being there on your own, cariño."

"Relax, babe. I'm okay. And I'm not drinking the water anymore. Whatever they're putting into it, it's not getting into me."

"Bueno."

"On the downside, the road rash is hurting again. I don't

know if that chemical helped me deal with pain, but right now, I'm ready to chew through logs. And Fake Doctor Linda won't give me my damn pain meds back."

"¡Pobrecita!" A long pause ensued. "Maybe you should just come home. I know your mission was to bring Megan home. And the more we learn what's going on, the more worried I am about her. But…"

"But maybe I was never the right person for the job," Shea finished.

"Maybe not. Or maybe it was an impossible task to begin with. She's communicating with her moms again, so that's progress."

"I suppose." Shea couldn't help feeling as if she had failed.

"I miss you and Annie terribly. Even with my work, it's been awful quiet around here. I'm tempted to get a new cat to keep me company."

Their cat, Ninja, had passed on last February. Shea still felt the loss, though she tried not to show it.

"You're ready to replace me already, huh? Not getting enough pussy, so you're gonna buy a cat?" Shea said, trying to use humor to prevent the gnawing grief from creeping back once again.

"¡Niña tonta! I would never replace you. You are one of a kind, Shealene Stevens. A breed apart. I think Annie would appreciate a new fur baby. It's been six months since Ninja crossed over the rainbow bridge."

"Speaking of which, have you heard from Annie?"

"I'm worried about her, Shea. She really seemed upset when I spoke with her last night. More than just homesick. Something's bothering her. But when I pressed her, she said she was fine."

"I'll call her. And I'll be home soon, I promise. Let me know if you hear anything about this Bethany woman."

"Will do. Adios, cariño."

"Adios, babe."

She called Annie, but after four rings, the call went to voicemail. "Hey, kiddo. Just wanted to check in with you. Hope you're having fun. I'll try to call you again later. Reception is spotty where I am. Love you."

When she reached her cabin in the Seedlings camp, she grabbed her towel and headed to the showers. To her surprise, Megan was there. Alone.

"Megan."

The young woman nearly jumped out of her skin. "Shea! Oh my god. I didn't see you come in."

"I overheard you talking with Linda earlier."

"Isn't she amazing?" In a flash, a mask of bliss replaced the look of fear.

"I heard you talking about a woman named Bethany."

"Bethany? No, I don't think I know her. Is she new?"

"Megan, cut the bullshit. I heard you say you helped bury her body."

Megan shook her head, a blank look on her face. "No, you must've misheard. I was just up there talking about my diet."

"I didn't mishear shit. Megan, I'm your friend. I'm here to help. If something hinky's going on—"

"What? Nothing hinky's going on."

Shea stared at her, trying to bore through the delusions and brainwashing. "Megan."

"Okay, there was a woman who died of an aneurysm a couple of weeks ago. That's what I was sad about. I miss her. But life goes on, right?"

"And you just dumped her body in the woods? That makes no sense. Was she taken to a hospital? Did they do an autopsy? Come on, kid, be honest with me. No secrets."

"I am being honest. You're the one not being honest. And we didn't bury her. We left her for Inagua to take into the next world."

The shower water ran cold.

Rory and the woman Shea thought she recognized from the night before walked in.

"I'm sorry if I upset you, Megan," Shea said.

Megan turned off her shower, got dressed without a word, and marched out.

"Good morning, Shea," Rory said with a gleaming smile. "I wondered where you were."

"Just got back from doing a one-on-one with Linda."

"So early?"

"It was such a beautiful morning." Shea forced a smile. "Thought I'd get a jump on the day."

Rory took off her T-shirt. Before looking away, Shea glimpsed a brand on her chest. Chills shot down her spine and not from the icy water. All those nagging feelings she'd had in the back of her mind were coming to the fore.

"Shea, I think you may know our guest, Maria Wickham."

Suddenly, Shea recognized her as Wicked from the Pink Trinkets. Years had gone by, and the previously buxom Wicked was thin, her face haggard. Her long blond kinky hair had been shorn. She looked like a completely different person.

"Wicked?" Shea asked.

"Oh my freakin' goddess! Shea Stevens! I haven't seen you in years. How the hell are you?"

Shea felt awkward meeting her former client while naked and shivering in the shower.

"I'm…I'm good."

"I gotta say, I never figured you for Luminos material."

Shea smirked. "You and me both."

"Shea here is one of our rising stars," Rory said. "I have great expectations for her."

"Yeah, thanks. How long you been a part of Luminos?" Shea asked nervously.

"About three years. It's really changed my life. I keep wanting to bring Vicious and Nasty on board but no luck so far." Wicked pulled off her shirt to reveal a faded but distinct scar from the NCB brand.

A wave of sadness hit Shea. She wanted to shake the woman and tell her to wake the hell up but knew it wouldn't do any good.

"Guess I'll see you around."

Shea dried off and dressed. The scab on her road rash was still soft and oozy. The skin around it was pinker than she liked. Was it getting infected? Were there microbes in the shower water? She put an extra amount of ointment on it before covering it with the nonstick pads and wrapping it with gauze.

Once the other two women were busy chatting, Shea surreptitiously filled a few bottles in the sink. She stopped at her cabin to drop off her toiletries then limped to the dining hall for breakfast.

The English muffin they served was burned. Even with the blackberry preserves, it had all the flavor and texture of particle board. The oatmeal was overcooked and slimy, and the vegan sausage links smelled of old gym socks.

Not in the mood to talk with anyone, she found a seat away from the rest of her fellow campers. She was tired and hungry. The pain in her leg didn't help.

She was three-quarters into choking down the vegan sausage when Ramirez appeared.

"Shea Stevens?"

"Who wants to know?" Shea didn't bother to look at him.

"Get up."

"I'm eating my breakfast or what passes for it around here."

"Get. Up. You need to come with me now."

"Fuck off, Ramirez. My leg hurts, and I ain't in the mood."

"NCB wants to see you." Ramirez's tone went from stern to threatening. "I suggest you come willingly."

"Nathan Curtis Bennett. The great and wonderful Oz." She stayed seated. The thought of trudging back up the fucking hill held zero appeal. Meeting with the sexual predator who passed himself off as a guru held even less.

"Get. Up." He placed a firm hand on her arm.

She bolted up with her fork in hand and met his glare. Her chair toppled over behind her. Fire erupted in her leg, but she ignored it. The echoey conversations in the dining hall went quiet as a crypt.

"Ya wanna throw down, big guy? I've kicked in the teeth of bigger assholes than you."

"Don't test me, Stevens." Ramirez looked like a bull ready to charge, nostrils flaring and cheeks coloring. "If you know what's good for you, you'll come along and not make a fuss."

Shea could feel the eyes of everyone in the dining room staring at her. What would happen if she fought back? Would they join in the fray? Or just sit gawking like a flock of birds on a wire?

She decided not to press her luck. Her pain level was already at a six out of ten. Fighting this guy with her leg aching didn't seem like her best option. "Fine."

She tossed the fork on the table. The utensil bounced, clanging onto the concrete slab floor.

"I brought you some water." George held out a bottle that glistened with condensation. His expression was almost conciliatory. "Consider it a peace offering."

Shea pulled out one of her own from her bag. "Got my own. Thanks."

She stared straight ahead as George marched her out of the building. A panel van sat idling next to the fire circle. She reached into her pocket and wrapped her hand around the knife, ready to pull it.

CHAPTER 34
THE NOTORIOUS NCB

"OVER THERE." Ramirez pointed at the largest of the cabins in the Summit camp.

When they reached the door, Ramirez opened it and shoved her inside. Even compared to Dr. Linda's cabin, the living space looked less like a rustic getaway and more like something from an interior design magazine.

The overall style had a Frank Lloyd Wright flair with lots of earth tones and elongated rectangles. It reminded her of when she, Toni, and Annie had visited Taliesin West in Scottsdale.

A mahogany bookcase lined a nearby wall, filled with such titles as Sun Tzu's *The Art of War*, Robert Greene's *48 Laws of Power*, and Hitler's *Mein Kampf*. There were also books by Jordan Peterson, Donald Trump, Napoleon Hill, and General Patton. Shea hadn't read any of them and wondered if Bennett had.

Eric Clapton's "Wonderful Tonight" played on a turntable set in an elaborate entertainment center with a flatscreen television that had to be at least eighty-four inches.

Bennett himself sat on a love seat, holding a tumbler of amber liquid. A bottle of Johnnie Walker Blue Label rested on a glass coffee table in front of him. He stood when they entered, and he approached with a big smile and an outstretched hand.

"Shea Stevens, my beautiful biker goddess. I can't tell you how good it is to see you again."

"Yeah." Her tone was cool and wary but not combative.

When Shea shook his hand, Bennett immediately leaned in for a kiss. Shea deflected it with her hand.

Bennett cleared his throat. "That will be all, Georgie Porgie. Thank you for escorting Ms. Stevens safely here."

Ramirez grunted and disappeared out the door without a word.

"Please have a seat, Shea." He gestured toward the love seat where he'd been sitting. "I understand your leg's been giving you some trouble."

Shea sat instead on the sofa, perpendicular to the love seat.

"Ever the rebel," Bennett said with a chuckle and stepped over to a nearby bar cart. "I love it. Can I offer you a drink?"

Shea's wariness intensified. "It's seven forty in the morning."

"Yes, but people like you and me, we're not bound by convention, am I right? We do what we want when we want."

"I suppose."

"So, what's your poison? Bourbon? Irish whiskey? No, you strike me as a tequila kind of gal."

She knew she should keep her mind sharp, but her leg now roared in pain. "Vodka."

Bennett raised a bemused eyebrow. "A vodka girl, eh? Da, tovarisch. Ice?"

"No thanks." She didn't plan on drinking much of it.

"Nyet on the ice. Da."

Shea watched him as he poured two fingers of Ketel One into a glass, in case he tried to slip a little something extra into her drink.

He handed her the glass and clinked it with his. "Za zdarovie!"

"Whatever."

To her annoyance, he sat down beside her on the sofa. He was too close for Shea's comfort, but she refused to move and give any ground.

"So, Shea, I'm glad we finally have a chance to talk. Dr. Linda tells me you have quite the checkered past. Murdered mother. Father in prison. Runaway at fifteen. Arrested for stealing cars before you even had a driver's license." He cackled. "So bold and adventurous."

"I did what I had to to survive," Shea replied. "I also paid my debt to society."

"Yes, you did. Six years in the slammer, was it?"

"Seven."

"Wow. Must've been tough."

"I managed."

"And now you're building custom motorcycles for celebrities like our very own Maria Wickham. Impressive. A true redemption story."

"Whatever." Shea stared down at the clear liquid in her glass. She really wanted to down it and take the edge off the pain in her leg. But she needed her wits about her.

"Dr. Linda also tells me your girlfriend is a cop." His tone was still light and conversational, but Shea detected an edge creeping into his voice.

"Retired cop."

"And she's working as a private investigator now?"

Shea shrugged. "Now and then."

He put his free arm around her shoulder, making Shea's skin crawl. It took all her willpower not to drive her elbow into his nose.

"The reason I bring it up, darling, is that some people have spread nasty rumors about me and what we're trying to accomplish here. False rumors, mind you. Personally, I don't care. People entertain all kinds of crazy conspiracies these days. But this fake news has begun to have an impact on our ability to change the world for the better. You follow what I'm saying?"

"I guess."

"And there are some law enforcement organizations who've been misinformed about our mission here. Accusations of brainwashing, fraud, torture, rape, you name it. Fortunately, when these law enforcement agencies looked into these false allegations, they came up with no evidence of wrongdoing on our part."

He squeezed Shea's shoulder.

"But the thing is, my dear, some agencies don't give up so easy. Some have an agenda to bring me down for some silly reason. They have sent in undercover agents looking to dig up dirt on me."

His tone grew less cordial. "Not just dirt but outright lies. I stand for the truth while they're trying to destroy me with lies. You understand, I cannot allow that to happen. Not simply for my sake but for all our sakes. For the sake of mankind. For the sake of our future."

Shea couldn't help taking a small sip of vodka. It burned in her throat.

"So I'm going to ask you, Shea." He leaned in and whispered in her ear, "Are you working for the cops?"

"No."

"You sure? Because if you are, by law, you are required to tell me. The truth will always set you free."

"I'm not working for the cops. I hate cops."

"And yet, you're dating one."

"She ain't a cop no more. She works for defense attorneys, defending people from the cops."

"Yes, of course. I believe you." He removed his hand from around her shoulder, as if backing off.

She took another sip, resisting the urge to gulp the vodka down in one swallow.

When his hand began rubbing her thigh, she stiffened. "What the fuck are you doing?"

"Just getting to know you better, my lovely. And freeing you from the limitations in your mind."

Shea shot to her feet, spilling her drink. Her every fiber crackled with defiance. "I'm not into guys."

Their eyes locked. She could see the smarmy predator in his gaze. Gleeful, taunting, like a cat playing with prey. But she was no mouse.

"Shea, that's the story you've told yourself your entire life. And totally understandable. You grew up emulating your father in a biker culture where men have all the power. So naturally, you developed a more masculine worldview, which includes an attraction to other women."

"What the fuck do you know?"

"I know that mindset is a limitation, my dear. By defining yourself so rigidly as a homosexual, you're cutting yourself off from attractions and experiences that could further free you. You can't yet see it, but there is a part of you yearning to be free. And because I care so much about you, I want to be your liberator."

"So being attracted to only one sex is a limitation, is it?"

"Absolutely."

"So you sleep with both men and women?"

He hesitated a moment. "I work differently with the men in our organization."

"Figures."

"My point is pushing through our arbitrary boundaries is liberating, not to mention thrilling. You know the excitement of breaking the rules. That electrifying kick you got every time you got behind the wheel of a car that wasn't yours. That same thrill occurs not only from tossing aside society's arbitrary laws but removing our own internal blocks."

His hand reached out to her, beckoning. "Come, Shea. Allow me to introduce you to a whole new worldview. You won't regret it, I promise."

"Not a chance. I ain't sleeping with you. Call it a limitation or whatever the hell you want, but I'm happy with who I am. I love my girlfriend, even if she used to be a cop. I don't fool around."

"Fool around. Ah, monogamy. Did you know the concept of monogamy was nothing more than a tool that the Christian church used to keep women in line? A man who slept with a lot of women was a stud, a Casanova, a lothario. But a woman who had multiple lovers, well, she was deemed nothing but a harlot, a slut, a whore. And society hasn't changed much, has it? Women are still demonized for embracing their sexual freedom."

"I got all the sexual freedom I need. You trying to get into my pants won't change nothing. So go fuck yourself."

Rather than get angry as she expected, he broke out into laughter. "You, Shea Stevens, are a tough filly to break. Rebellious to the core. But that's a good thing. A strong spirit is what I need from my people. If we are to change the world, we need people with gumption like you."

"Can I go now?"

"Of course." He gestured toward the door. "But we will talk again. And as you leave, remember the lesson of the carrot and the stick. It is our duty to change the world. Your duty. And I am offering you the carrot. My sweet, sweet carrot. I do hope you take it. Otherwise…"

With that veiled threat hanging in the air, Shea drained her glass, tossed it at Bennett, and stormed out.

CHAPTER 35
COMPLICATIONS

RAMIREZ'S CREEPER van was nowhere in sight when Shea stormed out of Bennett's cabin. Just as well. She didn't want to be anywhere near that asshole, even if it saved her from the grueling trek down the steep hill.

Her body trembled as she limped down the trail. Her physical pain merged with her anger into a furious energy that set her heart thundering.

How fucking dare he ply her with alcohol, accuse her of being a snitch, and then try to shame her for not wanting to sleep with his sleazy ass.

The agony in her knee intensified, as if someone were prying off her kneecap. She gasped with each step, her chest heaving as she tried to focus.

She was tumbling before she realized her toe had caught on a rock. The world spun in flashes of light and blinding pain.

When she came to, she was choking on a face full of dirt and dried leaves. Her entire body had become a fireworks extravaganza of torment. She struggled to orient herself and remember where she was. Glimpses of Bennett's dorky sneer, the elaborate cabin interior, the burn of the warm vodka.

"Get up, Shea. Get. Up." Her mouth tasted salty with blood. Her words were slurred.

Shea grabbed onto a small tree trunk and tried to pull herself up. Her left knee refused to cooperate. "Fuuuck!"

She struggled to focus, but everything felt like oozy quicksand. "Okay, just breathe. Just breathe."

Breathe in. Her ribs hurt, but she managed it. Then out. Her teeth ground like a pestle crushing spices in a mortar. Gradually the spin cycle slowed, and she tried again to stand, putting all her weight on her good leg.

Her breath came in gulps. Her heart raced. Laughter filtered up through the trees from the Seedling camp below. Caleb from the sound of it. Laughing at someone's joke. She wondered if Bennett had tried to seduce him and his little man bun. She doubted it.

"Okay, girl. Now what?" The trail down seemed to stretch for miles, though it was probably only a few hundred feet.

She tried to put some weight on her left leg and immediately swore up a storm. She'd fucked up her knee good.

A sound above her caught her attention. Fake Doctor Linda gracefully trotted her direction on the trail. "Shea? Are you hurt?"

The last person she wanted to see was this bitch, but right now, she had few options. "My knee…I can't put any weight on it."

"Oh dear. I'm so sorry. If I go get George to help carry you, do you think you'll be okay here until I get back?"

Shea wanted to tell them all to go to hell, but unless she wanted to slide down the hill on her butt and hop back to her cabin, she didn't have many options

"Yeah, I'll just hold up this tree. Keep it from falling down the hill."

Linda smiled. "Still have your sense of humor. That's a good sign. Okay, I'll hurry back with George."

The fake doctor hustled back up the hill. While Shea waited, she checked her phone. Two voicemail messages. One from Indigo and one from Toni. None from Annie. Shea played the one from Indigo first.

"Hey, Havoc. Hadn't heard from you, so was wondering if you persuaded Megan to get the hell out of there. If you need help from the Sisterhood, let us know. Call me when you can, and watch your back. Also, don't drink the water. Seriously, girl, the shit's laced with some kind of date rape drug."

Shea hit the call button to return the call. The phone rang five times before rolling over to voicemail. "Hey, Indigo. Got your message. Still here at the camp. Just buggered up my knee even worse. I'm making inroads with Megan, but I'm not sure if she'll leave with me. I'm not sure I can even drive. May have to stay here a little longer. If I need the Sisterhood, I'll let you know. Also, Toni told me about the water. I'm drinking tap water from the showers for now. That and a little vodka." She chuckled darkly. "Don't ask. I'll be in touch."

She hung up and was about to listen to Toni's message when a commotion above her got her attention. Ramirez and Fake Doctor Linda were on their way down the hill.

"Heard you got into a little trouble." A hint of a smile pulled at the corners of his mouth. Was the fucker gloating?

"Fucked up my knee. Can't walk."

"Don't worry," Linda replied. "We'll take care of you."

Her tone was warm, as always, but Shea wasn't sure what to believe. Especially after hearing about them dumping a woman's body in the woods somewhere. Was she next?

"We'll carry you back up the hill," Linda explained. "I'll examine your leg and see if we can't get you mobile again."

"I'd rather just go down to my cabin."

"I understand, but we need to know the extent of the damage. We have a CT scanner in the infirmary next to my cabin. You're bleeding on the side of your head. I'll need to check for a concussion and get a good look at the damage to your leg."

"You have a CAT scanner here?"

Linda gave another big smile. "A generous donation from one of our celebrity members. You've heard of Tonia Cruz?"

"The actress? Shit."

"Well, let's not having you standing here suffering any longer than necessary. We'll use a fireman's carry to transport you to the infirmary. George, grab her bag and take her left side. I'll get her right."

Shea felt uneasy being carried by the two of them up the steep incline. George seemed to manage okay, but Linda was clearly straining with her half of Shea's weight. Shea almost felt bad. Maybe she wasn't the Dr. Mengele type after all.

When they reached the door of the cabin next to Linda's, they eased Shea back onto her good leg. "Just wait here a moment."

"I know what you did to my friend Zia," Shea growled. "You're gonna regret it."

"Bitch, I just carried your skinny white ass up this hill, and you're threatening me?"

"You carrying me doesn't change what you did to her and God knows how many others."

"What're you gonna do about it? Tell on me to the boss?" His snicker sent chills down Shea's spine. She couldn't do much of anything at this point. She was completely at their mercy.

Linda returned a moment later with a wheelchair that had clearly seen better days. Shea eased into it, and George pushed her through the door.

The cabin was second only to Bennett's in size. A narrow hallway led to a handful of rooms. A CT scanner filled the room Ramirez wheeled her into. A window separated the main room from a smaller control room.

"Let's get you lying down. Then I'll run the scans."

Shea winced and grunted as Ramirez and Linda positioned her onto the bed of the machine then placed a pillow underneath her left knee. For the next half hour, Linda ran a series of scans of both her head and her leg.

The one consolation was that she wouldn't have to pay a huge deductible or copay for the emergency treatment. She tried to relax as the machine made an odd assortment of noises.

"Okay, Miss Shea. All done," Linda said from the control room.

When Shea sat upright on the bed of the machine, the room began spinning.

"Whoa. Shit."

"Dizzy?" asked Linda with what sounded like genuine concern.

"A little."

"Good news, no concussion. As for your knee, just a sprain. I wouldn't run a marathon any time soon. But you should be fine in a day or so."

Sure as hell didn't feel like a sprain. Did this bitch even know how to read the scans she was looking at?

"Will I be able to walk?"

"Yes. We're going to wrap a compression bandage around your knee and further stabilize it with a brace. Should allow you to walk. I'll even loan you a set of crutches."

Shea winced as she thought about a compression bandage pressing on the still-raw skin on the side of her leg. "What about my road rash?"

Linda shrugged. "I'm sure you'll manage."

"How am I going to get back down to the Seedling camp?"

"I'll drive you," George said.

"What about my pain meds? Can I at least have them back? My knee's hurting a hundred times worse than it was before."

"I'm sorry. I don't think that's the best treatment. We'll keep it iced and elevated and give you some ibuprofen."

"Wow! Ibuprofen? Not just measly little aspirins? I must've won the lottery," Shea said with dripping sarcasm.

"I need you to trust me, Shea. I am providing you with the best medical treatment. All at no additional expense."

"Like you did Bethany?" Shea realized she'd overplayed her hand the instant she said that.

A confused look appeared on Dr. Linda's face. "I don't think I know a Bethany."

George said nothing, but his stern expression spoke volumes.

Great, Shea thought. *I just pissed off my ride back to camp.*

"Sorry. I'm a little mixed up," Shea said. "Pain's gotten to my head."

Linda patted Shea's shoulder. "Don't worry, dear. After a day or so of taking it easy, you'll feel much better. All the more reason to sign up for the next session. In the meantime, I will treat your abrasions before they get infected."

"Whatever." Shea struggled to get her emotions under control. Getting Megan out of there would be trickier now that she'd further injured her leg. She'd have to talk with her at dinner, away from the others.

CHAPTER 36
MISOGYNY

THE DRIVE back to the Seedling camp was tense and silent. Ramirez reminded her a bit of Victor Ganado, the former jefe of Los Jaguares. Ganado, at one time, had forged an alliance with her father's motorcycle club.

Ganado had been like an uncle to her. She had even called him tío Victor for several years. He had treated her with kindness, offering her little presents whenever she and her father visited his home. She remembered the amazing flavors of his wife's cooking.

But like her father, Ganado was a ruthless drug kingpin. In Ganado's junkyard, she'd been mauled by the dog, her face forever scarred.

Rifts emerged between the two gangs, eventually erupting into bloodshed that cost Ganado his life and all but wiped out the Jaguars.

The resemblance between Ganado and Ramirez was remarkable. The same squared face and deep-set eyes. She wondered if they were related. Ganado had fathered several kids, though none by his wife.

Ramirez stopped the van next to the entrance to the Seedling dining hall. "We're here." He made no move to get out of the van or help her inside.

"Thanks for the ride," Shea replied coolly.

"Keep your mouth shut about Bethany, or I'll put you in Stick." He didn't even look at her.

"What the hell's Stick? You people keep threatening with it."

"By the time you find out, it'll be too late."

"Whatever."

Shea hobbled out, using the worn wooden crutches that Linda had provided. The rubber padding was dirty and cracked, and it smelled of old underarm sweat.

No sooner did she shut the van door than Ramirez peeled out and vanished in a cloud of dust.

"Motherfucker." Shea hobbled to the dining hall and struggled to stay balanced on one foot while opening the heavy metal door. Fortunately, Erykah rushed over and held it open for her.

"What happened to you?" The concern in Erykah's voice sounded genuine.

"Turns out cartwheeling down the hill from Summit isn't recommended. Zero stars."

"Oh my goodness. Are you all right?"

"I'll live. I just need to elevate my leg and get some ice on it. On second thought, maybe I should lie down in my bunk."

"Best if you stay here where we can all take care of you. After all, we're family. That's what families do. We take care of each other."

Erykah helped Shea to a seat and grabbed a second chair so she could elevate her leg. Caleb hustled to the kitchen to ask the chef for some ice packs. Another member retrieved a few pillows from her cabin.

Within thirty minutes, Shea was as comfortable as she could get under the circumstances. Her knee was so swollen it felt as if the skin would split. The ibuprofen didn't come close to taking the edge off the pain.

She reached into her bag for a bottle of tap water. Instead of the two bottles she had put in there, she found four. Someone had placed two extras when she wasn't looking. Which ones were tap water?

"Shit." She tried to check to see if any were colder than the others, which might indicate they'd just been pulled from a refrigerator. But they all felt the same. And unlike water bottles from the store, they didn't have safety caps that separated when the bottles were first opened. How was it even legal to manufacture this way?

Her mouth was parched, so she opened a bottle and took a sip. It tasted refreshing with a hint of licorice. She sipped from another, which had a slight sulfur taste. This was the tap water. The one with the licorice taste was no doubt laced with the drug.

On the TV screen, Bennett droned about all the research he'd supposedly done on society, neurology, genetics, and anthropology, throwing out names of scientists and concepts she'd never heard of.

She tried to tune the noise out, but it left her mind free to obsess about how fucked her situation was. She would never get Megan out of there. The more she knew about this place, the more danger she realized that Megan and the others were in. She had failed.

"What all of this research has shown us," Bennett prattled on, "is that men are the natural warriors and leaders. It's coded in our DNA and hardwired in our brains over countless generations of evolution. The testosterone in our system drives us to dominate and control, to fend off threats to the tribe. Women, on the other hand, are natural-born nurturers. It's an inevitable result of how estrogen wires the brain to care for the young of the tribe."

"Bullshit," Shea muttered under her breath.

Gayle, who sat on the opposite side of the table from her, glanced at her, then turned back to the video.

Shea studied the people in the room with her. Everyone stared at the screen with rapt attention, clearly soaking up every bit of pseudoscience nonsense this self-appointed guru was spewing. It made her sick.

But then she remembered how she, too, had fallen under his spell. And now she wasn't. Was this chemical they were putting in the water that powerful?

"It is only natural that historically, societies have been patriarchal," Bennett continued. "I know it's not PC or woke for me to say this, but the science is clear. Men are more intelligent and logical, thus making them better leaders. Thus, women should defer to men as the heads of state and the heads of households. It's not me saying this; it's the science. And one thing we know is that science is irrefutable."

So much for changing the world, Shea thought. *This idiot only wants to revert to when women had almost no agency. No right to vote. No right to equal employment.*

"So, you may wonder, what about homosexuals and transsexuals?" Bennett continued with a sly smile. "Because I certainly wondered that when I was conducting this research. And the conclusion was obvious.

"The sudden rise in alternative lifestyles directly resulted from the women's lib movement, when ladies pushed back against their natural societal roles. As a result, this shift in power caused mass confusion. Women wanting to take charge in places where they didn't belong. And some weaker men, cowering and wanting to become women or have sex with other men. This horrifically violated nature's design."

Shea felt ill. If she had the strength, she would have walked out, packed up her stuff, and gone home. But she could not possibly work the clutch in her truck with her leg all banged up. She'd burn it out before she made it out of Sedona.

Keeping her leg elevated helped, though the ice packs

were now little more than resealable bags of water dripping with condensation and soaking into her jeans. Her tailbone ached from sitting awkwardly in the hard chair, almost as much as her knee.

Finally, the video ended, and the lights went on.

Rory appeared next to the TV screen. "Wow, that was a lot to take in." She flashed the brilliant Luminos smile and made a big show of taking a deep breath and letting it out, as if she was processing all the so-called wisdom her leader had just spewed.

"Now we'll divide up into our breakout groups and discuss."

"Don't worry, dear," Gayle said. "We'll just gather around you so that you don't have to move."

"Thanks," Shea replied with no enthusiasm.

Erykah joined their group and spoke first.

"So, what do you all think?"

"I found it amazing and compelling," Caleb said.

"Of course you did," Shea replied. "You're a guy. Why wouldn't you want to help restore the straight white patriarchy?"

"Shea," Erykah scolded. "No ad hominem attacks. If you want to make a point, you don't need to attack anyone personally."

"Are you fucking kidding me? That entire speech was nothing but grade-A, GOP-approved misogynistic bullshit. Shortly before I took a tumble down the hill, that fucker tried to shame me into sleeping with him. Acted like me being gay is a limitation and that he was there to 'cure' me."

Gayle put a hand on Shea's across the table. "I'm sure you misunderstood him. He's an amazing teacher and such a beautiful human being."

"I didn't misunderstand anything. I know what he tried to do. I was there. And I'd bet anything he's tried to do it to the rest of you. Gayle. Erykah. Jeanette. Miriam. Everyone but good old Caleb here."

All the women but Erykah looked away, refusing to meet Shea's eyes.

Erykah glared at her. "Shea, we are not here to discuss your private meeting with Bennett. And I will not tolerate you defaming him like this. We are here to discuss the wisdom and ideas presented in the video."

"Fine. The ideas are patriarchal bullshit. Actual scientific studies have proven repeatedly that women are just as smart and just as capable as men."

The other groups had gone quiet, gaping at her like goldfish. She didn't care. The truth had to be told.

"Well, I for one disagree, as previously stated," Caleb replied smugly. "Obviously, men have bigger heads, thus bigger skulls and bigger brains. It's not just empty space. It's neurons. How can men not be smarter? It's obvious."

"And what did you think about his nonsense about gays?" Shea asked. "Are you gay because women want equality?"

"Gay? What makes you think I'm gay?" he asked with entirely too much flourish.

"Hello! I'm gay. And you set off my gaydar like an air-raid siren."

She caught another look from Erykah. Maybe it would be better to play along to get along until she could get the hell out of there.

Shea held up her hands in apology. "Sorry. No more odd hominy attacks, I promise. But let me ask you, Caleb. Are you and me gay because women refused to be submissive little sheep? Are we confused about our gender roles? Or were we born this way?"

Erykah turned to Caleb. "It's a fair question. What do you think, Caleb?"

"I'm not saying I understand everything Bennett shared

about gay people. Not saying I am gay either. But he was right about other things. Men are stronger than most women."

"Bullshit!" Shea couldn't stop herself. "I'm a helluva lot stronger than most of the men I know."

Caleb scoffed. "Right."

Shea forced herself upright, holding onto the table for balance. "Ya think you could take me, Mr. Man Bun? Even with my leg all fucked up, I could still kick your scrawny little ass."

Erykah stood, forming a *T* with her hands. "Okay, time out. Let's all take a breather and process Bennett's amazing wisdom. We'll meet back here in five."

"Suits me fine," Shea replied. "I need to piss, anyway."

Shea grabbed her crutches and hobbled to the back door. Erykah caught up to her and held the door open for her.

"Shea, I know this all is a lot to take in, and I understand you're not feeling well with your injured leg. But seriously, you need to tone it down. For your sake."

"Or what? You'll kick me out like you did Zia? Or no, you'll send me to this place called Stick, wherever the hell that is?"

"Stick is no joke. It's bad. Granted, it helps those who need it. But it's not pleasant. I don't want that for you."

"Then maybe I'll just leave."

"Just take it easy, Shea." Erykah put a hand on her arm. "Tomorrow's graduation. I want to see you come back for the next session. You have so much potential."

Shea pushed past her and tottered outside.

CHAPTER 37

FOUND AND LOST

AS SHEA APPROACHED the shower building, her phone pinged. Funny how the nearest decent cell coverage was by the shitter.

After wrestling with the spring-loaded wooden door, she sat down on a seat next to one of the other campers whose name she hadn't memorized.

The woman gave Shea a worried look, like she was afraid Shea would bite her head off. No doubt a result of her outburst earlier. Shea smiled at her, but the other camper didn't return it.

When the woman left, Shea pulled out her phone, thankful the woman wasn't in a chatty mood.

Toni had sent her a text. "Call me."

When the woman left, Shea called Toni. "Hey, just got your text."

"Your voice sounds funny. You doing okay?" Toni asked.

"I'm…I'm all right. What's up?"

"An associate of mine with the FBI called. A hiker discovered a body on a trail about ten miles from the Luminos campground. They suspect the remains belong to a Bethany Vargas. She was an NAU student who went missing a while back. Her former roommate thought she'd joined Luminos."

The nagging feeling in the back of Shea's mind intensified. "Was she murdered?"

"Autopsy report hasn't come back yet. COD not determined."

"But she probably didn't die of a brain aneurysm as Dr. Linda claimed."

"Considering they dumped her remains on a trail rather than take her body to a hospital to be autopsied, I'd say foul play is a high probability."

"Fuckers." Shea sighed, growing disoriented in the latrine's gloom. "I feel like getting the hell out of here."

"Then why don't you? Megan and her folks are talking again. Still very tense, according to Nita, but it's progress."

"I can't. I fucked up my leg. Hurts like hell. I'm only walking with a pair of crutches. No way I can drive in this condition."

"Then I'll come pick you up. We can come back for your truck later. I don't trust those people."

"I can't just walk away, Toni. I can't leave Megan here with all the fucked-up shit they're doing. If she ended up dead, I could never live with myself."

"Shea, it's too big for you to tackle on your own. You're vastly outnumbered and in no shape to be doing your vigilante thing. In fact, maybe I should call Indigo to send the Sisterhood up to get you. Safety in numbers. Plus, they could pick up your truck as well."

"I will find a way to get Megan home safe. I promised her moms I would."

"Shea, corazón! Don't put yourself in this situation. I couldn't live with myself if something happened to you."

"I'll be okay, sweetie. I've been in worse situations than this. How's Annie doing?"

Shea heard Toni sigh. "That's the other thing I wanted to

talk to you about. She left a message saying she wanted to come home now. She really sounded upset. I called her back several times, but it goes straight to voicemail. I called the contact number for the camp. No answer there either. No voicemail. I'm driving up to Bradshaw City to see what the hell's going on up there."

"Fuck." The walls of the latrine felt like they were closing in on her. Footsteps approached from outside. "Let me know what you find out. I swear if those idiots hurt her, they'll regret it."

"I'll call you as soon as I know anything. Watch your back, amor. I miss you."

"Miss you too. I'll be home soon."

She hung up. Gayle opened the door. "Getting worried about you, hon. We're ready to start again."

CHAPTER 38
INCOMMUNICADO

SHEA KEPT her mouth shut the rest of the day. No one called her out for failing to take part in the discussion, which was a relief.

By chance, she discovered an open Wi-Fi signal no one had mentioned. Rather than listen to the blathering in the breakout groups, Shea texted Indigo and other members of the Sisterhood to update them on the situation. She also did more searches to find out what she could about Bethany Vargas.

Eventually, they broke for lunch. She choked down a plate of the seaweed salad and a pile of bland red quinoa. Had these people never heard of salt or spices? She knew butter was out of the question, but it would have improved the flavor dramatically. She washed her lunch down with the rest of the bottle she trusted to be tap water.

Three bottles remained in her bag. Two were laced with the chloro-whatever. She needed to get rid of the drugged water and replace it with the nasty-tasting tap water. That or simply stop drinking.

"Hey, where ya going?" asked Rory.

"Need to splash some water on my face at the shower. You want to come along and watch me?"

Her voice held more bitterness than she intended, but she felt no shame about it. She was tired of being told what to do by these people.

"Just be back in five minutes. We'll be starting the next session soon."

"Oh, goody."

She tottered out of the building on the crutches. Crossing the gravel parking was tricky. The bag kept bumping her crutches, threatening to knock her on her ass once again.

In the shower building, she emptied the laced bottles in the sink and filled them and her other empties at the tap. That should at least sustain her until the next day.

Many of the texts she had gotten from Indigo, Savage, and the other Sisters were offers to storm the gates with guns blazing to rescue her and anyone else who wanted out of there. She assured them she was okay for the moment with no immediate need for rescue.

No texts from Toni, the one person she wanted to hear from. It hurt her soul to think Annie could be in any kind of danger while she was stuck here with no way to help her.

She tried to reassure herself that her niece was probably fine. Annie had probably forgotten to charge her phone, as she sometimes did at home. Maybe a monsoon had knocked out the camp's power and, with it, their phones. Or some other perfectly reasonable explanation.

She didn't need her imagination filling her head with worst-case scenarios. She had enough to worry about here. Toni was looking for Annie.

"How are you feeling?" The unexpected sound of Fake Doctor Linda's voice behind her nearly made her topple over from surprise.

"Holy shit!" Shea said, gripping the sink to stay balanced. "Where the hell'd you come from?"

She pivoted around to face the woman. Linda's

expression was stern, not the usual fake warmth she usually offered.

"I understand you've been disruptive in your breakout group."

"What? No, just asking questions."

"Erykah says you threatened Caleb with violence and made wild, unfounded accusations against NCB."

"I'm sorry," Shea said, though she wasn't even a little sorry. She tried to look contrite. "The pain in my leg's got me in a sour mood."

"I'm also told you were on the phone the rest of the time rather than participating in the group."

"I'm sorry, but my niece, Annie, hasn't been answering her phone the past day or so. I'm worried she may be in trouble. My girlfriend has been keeping me updated. I'll try to participate more in the group without threatening anyone or accusing NCB of anything." *Even though he's guilty as hell.*

Linda held out her hand. "I'm going to have to demand your phone."

Shea stiffened. "My phone? Aw, hell no. I have to know what's going on with my niece."

"I'm sure your niece will be fine. As you said, your girlfriend is handling it. She's a detective, after all. I have every confidence she'll keep Annie safe. Maybe the camp she's at went on a field trip."

Shea didn't recall telling Linda that Annie was at a camp. How did she know? Or had Shea shared it while she was under the influence of the drug? Their interactions were all a little hazy, especially with the incredible pain she was in.

"I'm not giving you my phone. You already stole my gun and my meds."

"Shea, I didn't steal them. I'm simply holding on to them for now. This is for your own good. Your phone is a liability for you. It's holding you back. We're here to help free you from your limitations. Or do I need to contact George?"

Shea noticed she had a walkie-talkie on her belt, similar to the one Ramirez always wore.

Shea fished her phone out of her pocket and slapped it in Linda's outstretched palm. "When will I get it back?"

"When I feel you're no longer addicted to it. People have become so attached to their phones these days they miss what's going on around them. I want you to notice all the amazing things going on, Shea. It's time to grow. I do hope you'll be signing up for the next seminar. Your future depends on it."

"Whatever." Fear and vulnerability wove into Shea's physical pain like a clinging vine. How much worse could her situation get?

She hobbled back to the dining hall while debating whether to leave now or wait to talk with Megan at dinner. Driving with her knee banged up was risky. And now she had no way to call for the Sisterhood to come get her. If she managed to coax Megan to leave, maybe she could drive Shea's truck. Maybe. Did kids these days even know how to drive a stick shift?

CHAPTER 39
DOOMSDAY

SHEA SPENT the next several hours struggling to endure the pain in her knee. Despite the elevation, the ice, and the ibuprofen, the ache dug deep into her soul. The one blessing was that it distracted her from listening to NCB blathering his nonsense on the screen.

When they separated into their breakout groups, Shea occasionally inserted a nonsense response laced heavily with the word "amazing." She tried to smile, but even forcing a fake smile felt exhausting at this point.

In the late afternoon, the rest of her camp went down to the creek for some relaxation. To her surprise, Rory allowed Shea to relax in her bunk, since there was clearly no way she'd make it down the hill.

Rory escorted Shea back to the cabin, presumably to make sure she got settled okay. But Shea suspected it was to make sure she didn't go wandering off somewhere she shouldn't. Not that she'd be doing much cross-country trekking in her condition.

When she finally sat down on her bunk, Rory handed her a thick paperback book.

"What's this?"

"Something to read while you're convalescing."

"*Reshaping the Universe*?" she asked, reading the title. "By our beloved Nathan Curtis Bennett. Of course."

"There is a lot of amazing wisdom in there. He really shows his genius."

"So, this is what? His manifesto?"

"I'd prefer to think of it as his magnum opus."

"Yeah, okay. Thanks." Shea had no intention of reading it but figured it safer to play along at this point.

"Okay, get some rest."

Rory left.

Shea tossed the doorstopper of a book onto the floor and dug out her copy of Meghan Scott Molin's *The Frame-Up*. She'd rather read a cozy mystery about a comic book creator solving crimes than a manifesto by a self-absorbed, bigoted, sociopathic narcissist.

At dinner time, Erykah walked in and asked Shea if she'd like her to bring a tray in from the dining hall or if she was up to making the trip.

Though she wasn't looking forward to the usual vegan fare, Shea trundled over for dinner. Her body needed meat, the bloodier the better. Rabbit food and tofu wouldn't repair her sprained knee. But she needed to get Megan to leave, and she had a plan that might work.

Erykah helped get Shea settled at a table and brought over a tray. Gayle and a few of the others asked how she was doing. She put on a brave front and told them she was feeling better.

Dinner was a veggie burger with all the fixin's and wedge fries. She had to admit the burger was damn close to tasting like the real thing. At least something was going right.

Megan sat next to her but said little and ate even less. She had a few cubes of tofu on her plate and only ate two. She looked like skin and bones, with a sad, drawn expression on her face.

"Megan?"

"Yes?" The young woman didn't look over.

"I need your help."

Megan didn't respond right away. But after a long pause, she met Shea's eyes. "With what?"

"I need to get home. Annie's missing. And I'm…I'm no good to anyone here. I'm in a lot of pain. I'm grumpy. I'm not even listening to the lectures, as amazing as they are."

A glimmer of concern twinkled in Megan's amber eyes. "What can I do?"

"I can't drive home with my leg like this. Do you think you could take me? I know it's a lot to ask, but…" She grimaced, and only some of it was exaggerated. "I got no other choice. No one else to help me. And I'm worried about Annie."

They held each other's gaze for a long moment. Shea was finally breaking through all the brainwashing fluff and reconnecting to the girl that really cared about people. And then the connection faded, and she turned away.

"Tomorrow's your graduation. I can't rob you of that."

"I can come back when I'm feeling better. Please, Megan. Luminos is about helping people. And right now, I really need your help. Annie needs your help."

"I'm sorry. I…" A tear streaked down Megan's cheek. "I can't." She stood and hustled away.

"Fuck."

After dinner, everyone gathered outside for another bonfire. Shea explained that she needed to keep her knee elevated and that there was no good way to do that on the logs around the campfire.

Rory agreed to let her return to her bunk provided she continue reading NCB's tome of bullshit wisdom.

Once Shea reached the cabin, she began formulating a plan to get the hell out of there. Even if, regretfully, she had to leave Megan behind. How did you save someone who didn't want to be saved?

She found that between the crutches and the knee brace, she could put some weight on her knee. It hurt like hell, but surely, she could at least work her truck's clutch.

That still left her with a few problems to tackle. She could hobble down to the parking area. But carrying her duffel bag would be impossible. She'd have to leave most of her belongings behind as well. Far from ideal.

She definitely wasn't leaving her phone, pain meds, or gun behind. That simply wasn't an option. She'd have to get up to Summit somehow and sneak into Linda's office without being seen or further injuring herself.

Maybe she could drive up to there, get her shit without anyone spotting her or her truck, and then hit the road. The odds of success were lousy. But at this point, she was fast running out of options.

She pulled on her jacket, loaded the messenger bag with as much as she could fit, and skirted the perimeter of the camp carefully. The glow of the bonfire provided just enough light that she didn't trip on a root or hidden rock.

The journey seemed like it was taking forever. At any minute, she was sure someone would spot her and force her back to camp. But eventually, she was on the gravel road down to the parking area.

Her breath came in gulps. Her heart felt like a sledgehammer thudding in her chest. Her knee ached, and the compression bandage rubbed against her road rash as if made of sandpaper.

Without the light of the campfire, the road became a dim silvery shape against the darker shadow of trees. The moon above was in its last quarter. But between it and the starlight, she had enough to avoid the major obstacles of potholes and half-buried rocks if she took it slow.

Moonlight reflecting off fenders and glass in the parking lot came into view. She was doing it. She would make it.

Echoing voices ahead made her freeze.

"Yes, sir." Ramirez spoke over the walkie-talkie, just a few vehicles over from her truck.

A distorted voice replied, but Shea couldn't make it out. Definitely a male voice. Probably Bennett's.

"What? Dammit! All due respect, sir, I should have been the one to get rid of the body. Linda may know medicine, but this shit is in my wheelhouse. If I'd done the job, no one would've found her."

Another static-filled reply.

"Don't worry, sir. Megan Thornton's locked up in Stick again. I'll make sure she's not a problem."

A chill ran down Shea's spine. Whatever hellhole this Stick place was, Megan was now locked up in it. Could Shea leave without her?

"Yes, sir. I'll make some calls. If I hear anything more, you'll be the first to know."

Fuck, Shea thought. She was so close. Maybe she should just jump in her truck, forget about sneaking into Linda's office, and get the hell out. But she couldn't leave with Megan in this place they called Stick. And why was she there in the first place? Was it because they were talking at dinner?

"Hey, baby. What are you doing tonight?" Ramirez was now talking on his cellphone. "Oh yeah? What time you get off?"

Get the hell outta there, Shea thought. Fine time to make a fucking booty call.

"Oh yeah? And what time do you want me to get you off?" He laughed at his own joke. "What are you wearing?"

How long would this bullshit go on?

"I do love a woman in uniform."

Shea turned and began trudging back up the hill. Plan B

or C or whatever she was on at this point. She would bite the bullet and climb the long gravel road from the parking lot up to Summit. She would sneak into Linda's office, get her stuff back, and force someone—at gunpoint, if necessary—to help her get Megan out of Stick, and she and Megan would get the hell outta Dodge.

Maybe by that time, Ramirez would no longer be in the parking lot. And if he was, fuck him. She was ready to shoot him dead if he got in her way again.

Hobbling up the hill was grueling. She had to take frequent breaks to keep from passing out. She allowed herself to think about Toni and Annie. Were they all right? Had Toni located her? Shea was never good with such uncertainties, but now they gave her the extra energy to push her body up and up. Step. Crutch. Step. Crutch.

After what felt like a millennium, she rounded a broad turn and spotted a glow at the top of the hill from the outside lights on the Summit cabins. She took a long break to catch her breath before she made the final push.

Voices ahead caught her attention. Shea glimpsed figures walking from Linda's cabin. She was too far to make out faces, but the voices told her everything. Fake Doctor Linda and Connie, the shark of a lawyer, were walking to Bennett's cabin. Good. Shea hoped they'd stay there long enough for her to get her stuff back.

She kept to the outside of the camp and found the back door to Linda's cabin locked.

"Fuck!" she barked in hushed tones.

Think, girl, think. Her mind felt like quicksand. *Where are my lockpicks?* She remembered she'd left them on the dryer at home.

She patted her textile jacket, hoping she'd left an old cheap set of lockpicks there, but she hadn't. Then her hand came to rest on the SOG pocketknife.

She flicked open the blade and slipped it between the

door and the strike plate. With a little finesse, she slid the latch bolt enough that the door opened.

She used the rubber feet of the crutches to feel her way through the dark interior. She didn't dare turn on any lights. The office door was unlocked. Once inside, she hobbled to the desk.

In the pitch-black room, she searched the drawers by touch, starting with the main center drawer. Most of what she found was typical office stuff. Pens, a box of what sounded like paper clips, a pair of scissors, a pad of paper.

Finally, she found a phone. She pressed the power button. The glow was almost blinding in the pitch darkness. But her name and wallpaper were on the lock screen. The phone had eight percent power left and two bars worth of signal.

She unlocked it. A voicemail from Toni. She didn't have time to listen to it now. She had to find her pills and her gun and blow this joint.

When she found nothing else of value in the main drawer, she turned to the three side drawers. In the top drawer, she found pads of scratch paper and a stack of blank manila folders. She reached deep into the back of the narrow drawer. Her fingers wrapped around a plastic pill bottle. She pulled it out. It was her bottle of pain meds. She was two for two. Now to find her pistol.

The middle drawer yielded nothing but stamps and a stack of brochures.

She was about to check the bottom drawer when she heard the front door of the cabin open and voices approaching. There wasn't enough space for her to hide under the desk without bending her knee. She limped as quickly and quietly as she could behind one of the overstuffed chairs.

"Nate, let's not overreact." Connie's muffled voice grew clearer when the office door opened, and the lights came on.

Shea scrunched as small as she could behind the chair, hoping not to be spotted. Her left knee felt like the tendons were ripping apart. It took all of her will not to scream. Stars flickered in her vision.

"The feds may have found Bethany's body, but they have no way to tie her to us," Connie continued. "Anyone asks, she attended a seminar years ago then went back home. We haven't seen her since. She was an avid hiker. For all anyone knows, she went hiking and who knows? Happens all the time."

"What about that dyke Shea Stevens?" Bennett growled. "Her girlfriend used to be a cop and now works as a PI."

"We've got Stevens's phone. She won't be talking to anyone. I honestly don't think she knows anything of substance."

"I agree," Linda replied. "Poor girl is laid up back in her cabin with a sprained knee. She's not going anywhere. She won't be talking with any outsiders. And we have Megan locked down in Stick all doped up on Zylaxa. The situation is contained. No need to panic."

"Except George says Stevens isn't in her cabin. I have him looking for her."

Fuck, Shea thought. *They know I'm missing.*

"Inagua is insisting I implement Operation Fresh Start. Now. New program. New identities. No loose ends."

Inagua? This psycho really believes he's communicating with an ancient extraterrestrial entity? And what the hell was Operation Fresh Start?

"Please, NCB. There's no need for another Fresh Start," Linda begged. "Talk to Inagua. Explain to him we have alternatives this time. We can take make Shea and Megan disappear the same way we got rid of Bethany."

"Except they found Bethany's body, didn't they? The feds are doing an autopsy as we speak. I wanted to have Georgie take care of it, but you assured me that you could handle it.

Insisted she deserved a proper burial. You failed me, Linda. Inagua is very disappointed in you."

"All an autopsy will show is that she died of an aneurysm. Even if they do a tox screen, it's unlikely they'll detect the chlorpralozine, much less the insulin used to trigger the aneurysm. I was careful."

No one spoke for what felt like hours. Finally, Bennett broke the silence. "Fine. But one more screwup—even the least indicator that we're blown—you will begin preparations for Operation Fresh Start. Are we clear?"

"Yes, sir," both women said in unison.

"And if either of you refuses, for any reason, you'll be a casualty as well. Understood?"

"Yes, sir."

"Now can someone give me something for this migraine? Every time Inagua speaks to me, it feels like my skull is splitting."

"Wait here. I'll get you some Imitrex."

A metal cabinet opened and closed.

"Oh, thank Inagua," Bennett said. "Georgie, you got eyes on Shea Stevens yet?"

His walkie-talkie squawked, followed by Ramirez's distorted reply. Shea couldn't make out the words, but it didn't matter. They were looking for her.

"Well, keep looking, dammit. No loose ends. No more screwups."

Someone stormed out of the cabin. The heavy footfalls told Shea it was Bennett.

"This is bad, Linda," Connie said. "He's really losing it. Operation Fresh Start? I still have nightmares about the last one. And we didn't have but a fraction of the people we do now."

"I know. I'm not ready to give up on our people either. We really have the potential to do good. The latest class of people is amazing. Even Shea Stevens, if we can get her mind right. But a few days in Stick with regular doses of Zylaxa should do the trick."

"I've heard about the hallucinations. Brutal."

"Brutal but effective. At least in the few months that we've been using it. I have to go to the bottling plant to make sure the water is getting the proper dosage of chlorpralozine. I suspect the plant manager's been thinning it out. We fix that, and the other problems should resolve themselves."

"Let's hope so. I don't want to see all of our hard work end like so many movements. Jonestown. Heaven's Gate. We're better than that. Poisoning the entire camp? Where does that get fun?"

Shea suppressed a gasp. What the hell? Were they planning a mass murder-suicide? Fuck.

The two women walked out of the office. The room was plunged once again into darkness. Shea debated whether to keep searching for her gun. She wasn't even sure if the gun was still in the office. Her priority now was to rescue Megan by any means necessary and get the hell out of there.

CHAPTER 40
MISSING

SHEA CREPT out the back door of Linda's cabin and pondered her next move.

The moon was now a dull glow obscured by clouds. The temperature had dropped about ten degrees, and the air smelled of coming rain. Lightning flickered in the distance, accompanied by the low rumble of thunder.

The situation was getting worse by the minute. She didn't know where Megan was. And there was a good chance these psychos would murder everyone in the camp. She considered calling Fuego and having the Athena Sisterhood ride up to help her stop the carnage. But it could take hours before they'd arrive.

"Shea, Dios mio! I've been going out of my mind trying to reach you," Toni said when Shea called her.

"Sorry, babe. I'm okay. They took—"

"I can't locate Annie anywhere."

Shea's mind clouded as panic struck her. "She's not at the camp?"

"I found the Bold Women of Tomorrow complex completely abandoned. I notified Detective Johnson." Johnson was Toni's former partner on the force. "She's got patrol canvassing the area for any sign of Annie and the rest of the girls. They're getting warrants to track phones and are following up on other leads. I'm so sorry, amor."

Shea felt like a block of stone was sitting on her chest. "Don't worry. They'll find her. I'm trying to get the hell out of here." She forced herself to take a deep breath to clear the cotton from her brain.

"Toni, it's bad. This Bennett psycho has some sort of doomsday plan. Like a mass suicide or something. You need to get the cops up here."

"I'll make some calls. Get yourself out of there, my love. And Megan, too, if you can."

"I'll try. I'll call when I can. And please, find Annie."

"I will. Watch your back."

Shea hung up. The pain in her knee was excruciating. But she couldn't just hang out here. Not with a monsoon coming. The wind was already whipping the trees back and forth, blowing dust in her eyes. She had to find a place to hole up until the cavalry arrived.

Cautiously, she snuck around the perimeter of the campsite until she once again reached the road. She could hide in her truck. But that meant a precarious and agonizing trek hobbling down the gravel road in the dark.

She soon realized going downhill on crutches was much more treacherous than climbing up. She now had to contend with gravity's tendency to throw her off-balance. Every swing into the darkness felt like it could send her tumbling into disaster.

Headlights appeared coming up the hill.

"Shit." She tried to get off the road, but the underbrush blocked her way. The vehicle's lights lit her up like a stage. "Fuck."

"Stop right there." Ramirez.

"Fuck you, asshole!" she screamed, channeling all of her pain and rage.

A gunshot nearly threw her off-balance. For a second, she

wondered if she'd been hit. She was already in so much pain, it was entirely possible. But she was still standing.

"That was a warning shot, puta."

Shea considered her options. She had none. Ramirez was only ten feet away. He wouldn't hesitate to shoot her.

Shea glared at him. The creeper van's interior dome light threw ominous shadows across his square face.

"I'm leaving," Shea said, hoping for the minuscule chance he'd let her go.

"Not. Gonna. Happen."

"Look, I don't want to be any more trouble to you folks. I just want to get out of here and go home."

"You know, you and me aren't that dissimilar," he said with a certain humor in his voice.

"I doubt that." She should be agreeing with him, throw him off his guard. But she couldn't help herself.

"We're both willing to do whatever it takes to protect the ones we love. Even if it crosses someone else's arbitrary lines."

"I don't hurt innocent people."

"There are no innocent people. Haven't you learned that by now? Everyone's got an agenda, an angle, secrets, sins. Anyone that tells you they're honest is either lying to you or a chump."

Shea let the words hang in the air, trying to figure out her own angle. She remembered the conversation earlier. They wanted to dope her with some kind of drug and throw her in Stick with Megan.

"Fine. I'll go to my cabin, read some more of NCB's brilliant book, then get some sleep. That's okay, right?"

"Boss has other ideas. We tried the carrot. Now we go with the Stick. Get in."

"George, buddy…"

"Get in the fucking van, or I'll shoot you with your own damn gun."

Shea's heart sank.

"Fine."

She ambled to the passenger side of the van. Ramirez came around, took her crutches once she was in the seat, and tossed them in the back of the vehicle.

When he got back behind the wheel, he muttered, "Don't even think of trying anything. You're going to spend a few days in Stick. It won't be pleasant, but I guarantee you, it's better than the alternative."

"Why are you doing this? Don't you realize that NCB is talking about killing everyone in this camp, including you? Is this the man you choose to follow? This is like Heaven's Gate all over again."

"I do what I'm told." He put the van in gear and drove down the hill while rain began pelting the windows.

"George, you and I are a lot alike. We protect the ones we love. I know NCB means well, but you can't possibly believe he's talking with some extraterrestrial overlord. He needs help. And unless you and I work together, he won't get that help. He'll just kill himself and everyone around him."

Ramirez didn't answer. Maybe her words were somehow sinking in.

"We have to protect NCB from doing something he and you will regret for the rest of your lives. Operation Fresh Start is not a solution, George. It's an admission of failure. You know this. Deep down you can feel it. We have to save Luminos."

Ramirez drove past the turnoff to Seedling and headed farther toward the main road. A short distance later, they came to another turnoff Shea barely remembered seeing when they drove in.

The gravel road became more rugged. Every bump sent jolts of fresh pain up her leg, which made it difficult to form any sort of plan or strategy.

The van skidded to a stop unexpectedly. The headlights

illuminated a small building smaller than the three-hole latrine at Seedling. No windows. No exterior lights. This was no doubt Stick.

Ramirez got out of the driver's seat and came around to Shea's side with her crutches in one hand and her gun in his other, pointed at her.

"Get out."

"George, man. You don't have to do this."

"This is happening. Accept it."

She took the crutches and followed him to the door, which featured a large deadbolt. The rain came down harder, making the uneven ground even more difficult to navigate on the wooden crutches.

Ramirez fumbled through a large ring of keys. Just as he inserted one into the door's deadbolt lock, Shea swung one of the crutches like a baseball bat at his head. He fell to the ground, groaning, his eyes unfocused. Blood trickled from the wound at his temple.

Shea snatched the gun out of his hand and aimed it at him. Her body shook with fury and pain as her finger wrapped around the trigger. But for some reason, she couldn't bring herself to fire.

"Fucking asshole."

He moaned and mumbled something.

She stashed the gun in her cargo pants and hurriedly searched his pockets for weapons or anything else that might be useful. In his back pocket, she discovered a syringe, no doubt containing whatever drug he was going to inject her with. She flipped off the safety cap and jabbed it in his neck.

"Let's see how you like it."

"Who's there? Are you real?" called a fragile voice from inside the tiny cabin, barely audible over the torrents of rain coming down.

"Hold on, Megan. I'm gettin' you outta there."

The deadbolt's cylinder didn't turn at first, leaving Shea wondering if Ramirez had inserted the wrong key. The ring had dozens of keys on it, and she didn't have a lot of time.

She jiggled the key, and eventually the cylinder turned. The door opened to reveal Megan laying on the bare wooden floor in her underwear, her face ashen and eyes dull in the harsh glow from the headlights.

"Megan, you're safe." She did her best to kneel on her good knee.

Megan's eyes slowly focused on Shea. "Miss Shea? That really you?"

Shea covered the girl with her jacket. "Yes. We gotta move."

"Is…is that blood?"

"It's his. Not mine. He can't hurt you anymore. You're safe."

Realization slowly dawned on Megan's face, and she sat up with an expression of horror. "You killed him?" Her gaze drifted to Ramirez, whose cries had stopped. Megan's own scream echoed off the hillside.

"Megan, listen to me. They're planning to kill everyone in the camp. I couldn't let that happen to you. Your moms sent me to protect you."

"No, no, George wouldn't do that. Neither would NCB. He likes me. He says I'm his brown sugar princess."

"Wake up, Megan. Ramirez was nothing more than a thug working for a psychopath. Now come on. We gotta go, and I need you to drive."

"No, I have to stay so that I can be a better person and make the world a more loving place."

Shea shivered in the freezing downpour. She didn't have the energy or tolerance to debate any longer. She pulled out her gun and pointed it at Megan. It violated every safety protocol she'd been taught, but she had to get out this girl of this insane asylum and back to civilization.

"I don't want to hurt you, Megan. But I'll do what I gotta to get us out of here. Now get the hell up. You're driving."

Megan stared at the gun then got to her feet, sobbing like a child whose mother had died. Shea wanted to comfort her, but they had to get moving before anyone discovered them.

When they were in the van and headed back down the bumpy road, Megan said, "I have to get my stuff at the Blossom camp."

"We don't have time. I'll send the Athena Sisterhood up to get it once you're safe."

"Your biker gang?"

"Yes. They're good people. Just like me and Indigo."

"You're pointing a gun at me."

Shea put the gun away. "I know it's hard to believe, but I am truly trying to save your life. Drive down to the camp parking lot. Do you have a car here?"

"I did, but I sold it to Luminos to pay for my tuition."

Shea cursed under her breath. "Fine, we'll take my truck and head back home. You can drive a stick?" The thought just occurred to her. So many kids these days couldn't. If not, they would either have to steal the van or find some other way home.

"Cat's Subaru is a manual transmission. She used to let me drive it sometimes."

"Thank the gods for small favors. Glad to see your folks aren't neglecting your practical education."

CHAPTER 41
BUSTED

SHEA PUT the gun in her jacket pocket now that Megan was going along with the plan. When they reached the parking lot, they left the van. Shea tossed the keys out into the wet night and hobbled into the truck.

Sitting in the passenger seat of her own truck felt weird, but still she was relieved to be finally getting away from this place. She would have loved to have been able to stop NCB and his minions from executing their doomsday plan. Now that she and Megan were escaping, that became a strong possibility. But she would have to trust that Toni and her contacts in law enforcement could prevent a major catastrophe.

The truck lurched and stalled when Megan first tried to put it in gear. Lightning bolts of pain shot up Shea's leg. She ground her teeth to keep from screaming.

"Sorry! Please don't shoot me." Megan still sounded terrified.

"Megan, sweetie. I'm not gonna shoot ya." She took a deep breath, trying to get above the crushing pain. "I just want to get us both home safe. Relax and try again. You'll get it."

Megan restarted and cruised gingerly out of the parking lot.

"That's it."

They followed the gravel road back down the hill. When they reached the main road, Megan asked, "Which way?"

Shea tried to think through the pain and adrenaline coursing through her system. "Right. It'll take us into Sedona. Then we'll pick up Highway 179 back to the interstate."

"Okay."

As Megan pulled on to the road, Shea allowed herself to relax for the first time in a week. She tried thinking of what she would do once she got home to Toni and Annie. But she remembered Annie was missing. And Luminos was about to become ground zero for a major catastrophe. She couldn't relax yet.

As they drove down 89A, Shea's phone picked up a solid signal. She plugged it into her truck's power port and dialed Toni's number. "Hey! Megan and I are out of the camp and heading home. Have the cops found Annie?"

"¡Gracias a Dios! Detective Johnson still hasn't located Annie. They're conducting a full-on investigation of the organizers of the Bold Women of Tomorrow camp. Apparently, a lot of other parents reported not hearing from their kids in days. A few teens had left messages saying they were worried but no specifics."

"Fuck. What can I do?"

"Just get home. At least I won't have to worry about you."

"What about this mass suicide Luminos is planning?"

"I spoke with Special Agent Obregón at the FBI Phoenix office. They're working on it, though he couldn't give me any details."

"I can contact Fuego and the Sisterhood."

"No, leave this to the feds for now. The Sisterhood would only get in the way at this point."

"I hate feeling useless. I should have picked Annie up when she first said she wanted to come home."

"We didn't know, Shea. We still don't know what's happened. There may be a perfectly benign explanation for this, and everyone's fine. And you're not alone in feeling useless. I'm sitting here by the phone, wishing I could be out there searching for her with the rest of the sheriff's office. At least you rescued Megan."

A thought occurred to Shea. "Hey, ya think there's a link between Luminos and Bold Women of Tomorrow?"

"A link? Not that I'm aware of, but I can have both Detective Johnson and the feds look into it."

"Please do. I persuaded Megan to drive us home. We should get to Ironwood in about two hours. Maybe longer if this rain keeps up."

The truck swerved sharply onto the shoulder then lurched back onto the road.

"Megan, what the hell?"

"No! No! I promise to be good!" the girl muttered, jerking the wheel erratically. "Please, no. Please, don't. No, not the scorpions. No scorpions."

"Megan! It's okay. You're safe. There ain't no scorpions."

Shea tried to put a calming hand on Megan's arm. Megan backhanded her in the nose with remarkable speed and strength then began swatting at her own body as if scorpions were crawling over her.

"Fuck. Megan, calm down."

"Shea, what's wrong?" Toni asked over the phone.

"I don't know. She's freaking out on me." Shea realized they were in Sedona's small uptown area. "Megan, slow down."

They reached the roundabout that served as the turnoff onto Highway 179. Megan hit it straight on rather than following the curve. The truck bounced hard. Shea's head hit the window. She grabbed the wheel, trying to keep the truck from flipping.

"Megan, goddammit! Stop the truck."

Blue lights flashed behind them, accompanied by the chirp of a siren. Megan had an odd expression on her face.

"Shit. We're being pulled over. Megan, listen to me. Pull into the post office parking lot. We'll…we'll get rid of the scorpions."

To Shea's relief, Megan did as she was told.

"I know a lieutenant at Sedona PD," Toni said. "Keep me on the line. I'll talk to the officer."

"Okay."

"No, no, no, no," Megan whimpered. She whipped into a parking space and released the clutch so quickly that the truck jerked and stalled.

"Just relax, Megan. It's okay. Turn off the ignition and roll down your window," Shea said. "I got Toni on the line. She'll talk to the officer. Maybe we can get out of this without you getting a ticket. Or worse."

A white male officer in a black Sedona PD uniform appeared at Megan's open window. He looked to be in his thirties and had only stubble for hair. After a quick glance into the cab, his cool demeanor turned to wary. Shea realized her face and shirt were covered in blood from when Megan struck her.

"Ma'am, do you know why I pulled you over?" Although asking Megan, he kept his eyes pinned on Shea.

Shea held up her phone and was about to speak when Megan beat her to it.

"She's got a gun, officer," she said in a quivering voice. "She kidnapped me. Please, please help me."

"Fuck me." Shea didn't know whether to punch someone or vomit. She felt like doing both.

In a split second, the cop pointed his weapon at her chest. "Don't you move. Put your hands on the dashboard."

"Which do you want?" Shea asked calmly. "Put my hands on the dash or don't move?"

"Put your hands on the dash, slowly, smart-ass."

She dropped the phone in her lap and did as he instructed. He grabbed the handset on his radio and called for backup.

"Really, Megan? I was trying to take us home."

"No talking, either of you."

"Officer, my girlfriend is on the phone here in my lap. She's a retired Cortes County homicide detective. Will you at least speak with her?"

"I don't care if she's the goddamn pope. Don't move a muscle unless I instruct you to."

"Toni, if you're still there, I could use some help."

"Shut your mouth!"

Ten grueling minutes later, three other patrol cars arrived and surrounded the truck on all sides. Shea's best option was to let this all play out.

Six officers with weapons drawn surrounded the cab. The original patrol officer pulled open her door.

"Step out of the truck and get facedown on the ground, hands behind your head, fingers laced, feet crossed."

"Officer, my left leg is injured. I can't walk."

"Do it now!" he commanded.

"I'm sorry," Megan whispered.

Shea ignored her and forced herself up on her right leg, gripping the top of the cab for balance.

"Get on the ground now," shouted another officer behind her.

"I'm doing the best I can. My knee is busted. I have crutches in the back of the cab."

Someone grabbed the collar of her shirt and forced her onto the wet pavement. In the glare of the headlights, she could see a tiny prickly pear cactus just inches from her face, growing up through a crack in the asphalt. Jolts of pain shot from her leg throughout her body. She couldn't help but cry out, even as cuffs snapped shut on her wrists.

"What's your name, ma'am?" an unseen female officer asked.

"Shealene Eleanor Stevens."

"Do you have any weapons or anything else that could hurt me in your pockets, Ms. Stevens?"

"There's a small pistol and a pocketknife in my right front pocket."

Hands went through her pants pockets. "Gun and knife, just as she said. Pistol smells like it's been recently fired."

"Bag 'em and put in on the evidence list," the original officer said.

Shea tried to focus on her breathing to keep her mind off her pain and her legal predicament. Eventually, the officers pulled her to her feet.

"Come on," said the female officer.

"I can't walk. My left knee."

"Fine. Martinez. Gimme a hand. We'll carry her into the back of the cruiser."

A large Latinx officer who looked like a linebacker appeared. Between the two of them, they hauled Shea over to the yawning back seat of a patrol car. They bowed her head and shoved her unceremoniously onto the hard plastic seat.

"Can you bring my crutches?"

No one responded, but she watched them grab the crutches from the back seat of her truck and put them in the trunk of the patrol car. She sat there, wet and shivering, for about an hour as they scoured her truck for incriminating evidence. Not that there was anything for them to find.

Eventually, they drove her to the precinct. To her surprise, they uncuffed her and allowed her to use her crutches to go inside, with the female officer keeping a firm grip on the back of her collar.

They led her to an interview room and forced her to surrender her shirt—no doubt for evidence—and was given a rust-brown T-shirt emblazoned with the words Genuine Sedona Red Rock Dust printed on the front.

They gave her a bitter cup of coffee that helped fend off the cold. She tried to sleep, but her injuries and worries about Annie made that impossible.

After an interminable wait, the door opened.

CHAPTER 42

MISSING LINK

TWO PEOPLE, one man and one woman, walked in dressed in business attire. Plainclothes detectives, no doubt. The man carried a manila folder bearing what Shea guessed was the emblem of the Sedona PD.

They sat in the chairs opposite the small table.

"Ms. Stevens," said the woman, "I'm Detective Hawthorne. This is my partner, Detective Chapman."

"Yeah."

"Looks like you've had a helluva night."

"Guess you could say that."

"Our lieutenant spoke with your girlfriend, Toni Rios," Chapman explained. "Says she sent you to the Luminos camp to protect the young woman who was driving your truck when you got stopped. Is that true?"

"I'm not saying nothing without my lawyer."

Chapman snickered. "Rios thought you'd say that. She said to tell you that your attorney, Sydney Li, is on her way."

Li, who went by the biker name Dragon, served as the Athena Sisterhood's legal advisor, besides being a damn good criminal attorney.

"Can we get you anything?" Hawthorne asked. "Water?

More coffee? An ice pack for your swollen nose? Probably gonna be a long night."

"I'd like some water and the prescription pain meds that were in my jacket."

"I'm afraid we can't give you those just yet. We can offer you some aspirin."

"Forget it."

When they left, Shea pondered what charges they would bring against her. Much of her fate depended on what Megan told the cops and whether she was still hallucinating when she did. Kidnapping was likely.

Murder was a possibility, but that would require a body. What would Bennett or the blue bars do if Sedona PD showed up at the Summit camp with a warrant? Would they lead the cops to Ramirez's body outside the Stick cabin? Of course, doing so could corroborate Shea's plea of self-defense.

Would this incident trigger Bennett to initiate his doomsday plan and murder everyone in the camp?

After what felt like another few hours, Dragon appeared, dressed as if ready to walk into court.

"Damn, girl. You look like hell," Dragon said with a sympathetic laugh.

"I've had better days."

Shea gave her the condensed version of events.

"So far, no one has brought up any murder charges. If they do, we'll obviously claim self-defense. But the kidnapping and aggravated assault charges are a little trickier with Ms. Thornton claiming you forced her into your truck at gunpoint."

"But, Dragon, they were torturing her in that fucking hotbox of a cabin, all doped up on some drug. Not to mention there's a plan in place to murder everyone in the camp. I saved her, Dragon."

"Do you know what drug they gave her?"

"I don't remember. The water that everyone's drinking is laced with an antipsychotic drug called chlor…chlor…chlorpralozine. Toni's got the details on it. She had someone run a tox screen. But this other drug they gave Megan—Zy-something or other—it's supposed to cause hallucinations. Seriously fucked-up hallucinations."

"I'll request they run a drug screen on her, if they're not already. Your claims that Nathan Bennett and his associates are planning a mass murder staged to look like a suicide is concerning. Has anyone talked to the feds about this?"

"Toni said she was, but I don't know what's going on with it."

"I will do my best to keep you out of jail, but honestly, it's a crapshoot. Right now, all we have is your word against Megan's. Do you need medical attention for your nose?"

"My nose is fine. It's my leg that's the problem. I need to go home and keep it elevated and iced. And if they can give me back my prescription pain meds, that would help."

"I'll see what I can do."

Dragon opened the door and signaled to the detectives they were ready to talk. Hawthorne and Chapman sat opposite Shea and Dragon.

Chapman set the case folder on the table but kept it closed. "Why don't you start with explaining why Ms. Thornton is claiming you kidnapped her at gunpoint?"

"It is my understanding that Ms. Thornton has been given some sort of hallucinogenic drug," Dragon replied. "I'd like to request a drug screening."

"Why?" Hawthorne asked. "What drug? Who gave it to her?"

"A guy named George Ramirez at the camp. I don't know what the drug name is, but I overhead them saying it causes bad hallucinations. When she was driving, she thought scorpions were crawling all over her. That's what caused her to drive erratically. She's out of her mind. You can't believe a word she says."

The two detectives exchanged a glance. Shea wondered if Megan was still acting crazy. Though she hated to think Megan might be suffering, knowing that she was drugged might get the cops to dismiss the charges as bogus.

"Why would this Ramirez give her the drug?"

"To make her more compliant. They were going to do the same to me, but I fought back, grabbed Megan, and got the hell outta there."

"As you can see, my client has acted entirely in defense of self and in defense of Ms. Thornton. But detectives, there is a more serious matter at hand. The people in charge of Luminos are planning to poison everyone in the camp. Something they call Project Fresh Start. Think Jonestown, Heaven's Gate. Mass murder staged to look like a mass suicide."

Those words seemed to get their attention. "You're sure about this?"

"Absolutely. Ms. Stevens informed her girlfriend, former Detective Antonia Rios, about her discovery. Ms. Rios has been in touch with the FBI. I strongly suggest you reach out to them as well."

"Fine. Stay put. We'll be back."

They walked out of the room, and Shea buried her head in her arms. "Fuck."

Dragon put an arm on her back. "Hang in there, Havoc. We'll get you out of this."

"I should be out there trying to find Annie."

"Toni mentioned she was missing. You want me to call her, see if Annie's been located?"

A glimmer of hope sparked to life in Shea's midnight-dark mind. "Would you?"

"Absolutely." Dragon made the call. "Toni? Hey! It's

Dragon. I'm with Shea. She's okay. We're just trying to get them to drop the charges. Let me put her on."

Shea took the phone from her. "Any word on Annie?"

"Not yet, but Detective Johnson discovered a connection between Luminos and Bold Women of Tomorrow. It's a labyrinth of shell companies, but they are connected. Also, Special Agent Obregón at the FBI confirmed they were already looking into Connie Brady for credit card fraud."

"That explains this whole doomsday scenario. Shit. I swear, if they hurt Annie…"

"We'll find her, amor. I promise."

"You shouldn't make promises like that," Shea muttered.

"I will find her. I've never broken a promise to you. You know that."

"I just hope she's still alive when you do." Shea released a long breath. "Thanks, babe, for everything you're doing."

"You hang in there. We'll get you both home soon."

An hour later, the two detectives returned. Detective Hawthorne was pushing a battered wheelchair. From their grim expressions, Shea knew she was in for the worst.

"Shealene Stevens," Chapman said, "we are charging you with kidnapping and aggravated assault."

"What?" Shea tensed. "That's fucking bullshit! Megan's doped up outta her mind."

"Come on, detectives," Dragon protested. "She saved this girl from being tortured and killed. Don't do this."

"So far, we don't have any proof of that. And the girl is still pressing charges."

"She's fucking brainwashed. Dragon, call Nita and Cat. Toni has their numbers." Shea stopped short of asking Dragon to convince Nita and Cat to get Megan to drop the charges. Didn't need to be charged with witness tampering and obstruction as well.

"I will. And I'll see about getting you bailed out."

At the detectives' direction, Shea sat in the wheelchair.

They cuffed her left hand to the arm. "You people are fucking idiots. They're about to murder God knows how many people at that camp, and you're charging me with kidnapping a family friend."

"We are working with the feds, looking into your claims of a mass suicide and torture. Until we have some definite answers, though, you're going to be a guest of the city."

"Whatever."

"If it's any comfort, Ms. Stevens," Hawthorne said as she pushed the wheelchair down the corridor, "my sister got tangled up with Luminos a while back. I sympathize with you. But that doesn't give you the right to forcibly remove Ms. Thornton from the camp at gunpoint."

"Idiots," Shea muttered.

Hawthorne pushed the wheelchair out the back door of the police station into a red paved courtyard lit by a few lampposts. On the other side of the courtyard stood the city jail.

She was put in a cell with a woman who was snoring like a bulldozer. Not even the sound of the cell door opening and closing woke her. Shea lay on her own bunk and tried to sleep. But between the ache in her leg and her worries about Annie, she ended up staring at the dark wall.

Connie Brady's phone rang at two in the morning. Not that she was asleep with everything going on. One glance at the caller ID, and she cursed. Roberta Potter. Her world was collapsing around her, but if she didn't answer, it would do so faster, and the consequences would be more dire.

"Connie Brady," she said, pretending not to know who was on the other end.

"Con, it's ASAC Potter. Sorry for the hour. But what the hell's going on up there? My contact at Sedona PD's saying they've got a woman from your camp who's making all kinds of accusations, including rumors that NCB is planning to implement Operation Fresh Start. I've already got agents investigating your organization for credit card fraud. Something about a Bethany Vargas whose body turned up. Is this true? Is Fresh Start a go?"

"We've had some issues with one of our new recruits, but I think we have it contained. No plans for Fresh Start."

"Let me assure you, Connie, it is definitely not contained. I can't stall much longer. My agents are already working on a warrant affidavit to search the camp from top to bottom. And I sure as hell don't want to be cleaning up another massacre. Not after Pittsburgh."

"The Vargas thing was Linda's screwup. I'm trying to keep Nate from going nuclear. But, Bobbie, he's...he's on a rampage. If you can sideline the investigation for now, I will take care of things on our end."

"Take care of how? No, wait. I don't want to know. I do not want dozens of dead young people on my watch. Fix this."

"I will. And thank you."

"Anything for the cause."

SHEA HAD no idea what time it was when one of the COs opened the cell door and called her name.

"Stevens, Shea. Your bail's been posted." The CO looked like one of those brawny Russian women she'd seen in movies about the Cold War.

"Thank God." She pivoted and plopped her butt into the rickety wheelchair. This time, at least, she wasn't handcuffed.

The ache in her knee had subsided to a bearable level. The road rash still felt raw but didn't burn like it had. Maybe she was on the mend after all. Thank goodness for small blessings. But until Annie was safely home, she couldn't rest.

Dragon was waiting for her in the jail's lobby. She held a small box with Shea's personal effects, the crutches tucked under one arm. "How you doing, sister?"

"If I were doing any better, I just couldn't stand myself," Shea replied sarcastically. "Thanks for helping out. Any update on Annie?"

"The feds are still looking for her and the rest of the Bold Women camp." Dragon handed Shea the knee brace from the box. "You need this?"

"Yeah." Shea took it from her and strapped it around her

knee. Then she had a thought that knocked the wind out of her. "What if…what if they took Annie and her fellow campers to Luminos? And what if they do this Fresh Start mass suicide thing when she's there? Oh shit, Dragon. They gotta stop this. I can't lose Annie. I can't let that happen."

"Easy, Havoc. Between Toni and me, we're doing everything we can to put pressure on them to find the missing girls, including your niece. I talked with Cat Hamilton. They will try to convince Megan to drop the charges against you."

Dragon handed her the crutches. Shea grunted as she stood and followed Dragon out into the parking lot. A dim glow appeared in the eastern sky.

"Where's my truck?"

"City impound. Paperwork's in the box here. I'll drive you back to Sycamore Springs. You can come back up here Monday to get your truck."

"Thanks, Dragon. Don't know what I'd do without you."

"Hey, that's what the Sisterhood's for, right?"

"I suppose."

On the way down, Dragon offered to put on a Pink Trinkets album, but Shea told her not to bother. She kept picturing the brand on Wicked's breast. The thought of it made her sick. The adage of "don't meet your heroes" came to mind.

Dragon explained she'd persuaded the cops to return her cellphone, since Annie was still missing. Her gun, knife, and bloody shirt were all in evidence bags in Sedona.

Shea did have her expired pain meds once again. She considered taking a couple but didn't want to fall asleep while Annie was still missing. Even though the pain in her leg made her gasp with every bump in the road, she would cope with it until Annie was home safe.

The eastern sky was turning pale pink when Dragon pulled into Shea's driveway. Toni rushed out of the front door and hugged her tightly for several minutes when she slid out of Dragon's Mercedes. It felt good to be in her girlfriend's arms again. When Shea released her, they were both sobbing uncontrollably.

"I'll be in touch." Dragon put a hand on Shea's shoulder. "Let me know if you hear anything about Annie."

"Gracias, Dragon, for bringing my woman back home," Toni said, wiping her face.

"Yeah, thanks again, sister," Shea added.

"Any time. Try to get some rest."

Toni carried the box of Shea's stuff inside.

"Any news?"

"The feds got a warrant to search the camp thirty minutes ago. Been radio silence since. My associate promised she'd call me if they found Annie."

"Why the fuck did it take so long?"

Toni sighed as they lay down in bed. "These things take time."

"Right. If a bomb was going to blow up in a big city, I'm sure they'd move a lot faster."

"I wish I had a better answer, cariño. Justice sometimes moves slowly, especially in high-stakes cases."

"No matter who dies," Shea said bitterly. "So long as their paperwork's in order, that's what matters."

"If they screw up the affidavit, a judge may not sign the warrant or could kick the evidence they find if the defense proves the warrant was based on insufficient probable cause. For now, try to get some sleep."

"You think I can sleep with Annie in danger?"

"You'll be no good to her if you don't take care of yourself."

"I'm no good to her now, anyway. She'd probably be better off living with her grandmother."

"No, I don't trust Julia. That woman is a rattlesnake. Too many years with the Confederate Thunder. I don't care how reformed she claims to be. She kept the truth of Annie's biological father a secret for years. What other horrible secrets has she been holding onto?"

Shea considered her own dark secrets. The people she'd killed, even if they deserved it. The crimes she'd covered up in service to the Sisterhood.

"She's been a good grandma to Annie," Shea said. "Helped raise her after our mom was killed. And walking away from the Thunder, even as the widow of a patched member, was a ballsy move. Trust me, I grew up with them. They like to control women."

An hour later, Shea's phone rang. The caller ID came up as Thornton, M.

"Fuck me."

"Megan. What the hell you doing, calling me after the shit you put me through last night? I tried to save your life, goddammit." Shea struggled to tamp down the rage boiling inside her.

"Please, I'm sorry, Miss Shea. Don't be mad. I...I don't know what I was thinking. I was crazy, confused."

"They charged me with kidnapping you. I could go back to prison for ten years or more."

"I know. I'm so sorry. But I thought you should know. Annie's here."

"What?" Her anger evaporated. "Here where? Where the hell are you? Luminos?"

"Not exactly." A long pause ensued, followed by sobbing on the other end of the line.

"Megan, tell me where Annie is this minute."

"Luminos has another campground called Beta up on the Mogollon Rim."

"Where on the Rim?"

"Off Lake Mary Road, near Happy Jack."

"I need exact coordinates, Megan. This is important."

"Uh, okay. Let me pull up a map on my phone. Okay, the latitude is 34.739. Longitude is -111.395."

"Is Annie okay? Is she safe?"

"Yes, I think so. They've got her and a bunch of the other girls in a cabin here. Not sure what's going to happen. A Sedona police officer dropped me off at the entrance to the original Luminos camp and…" The sobbing came harder this time.

Shea gave Annie a moment to get it out of her system before saying, "What happened at the original campsite, Megan?"

"They're all dead. All my friends. It was like they were all sleeping in their bunks, but they wouldn't wake up. I called Linda. She had someone bring me to Beta. When I saw Annie, I…I knew I had to call you. Even if I get in trouble."

"Megan, you done good. This helps a lot. Are you safe?"

"I think so."

"You're not locked in some dark pit?"

"No. I guess they're happy I told them you kidnapped me. I'm truly sorry, Shea."

"If you keep Annie safe, all is forgiven. Especially if you drop the charges and I don't go back to prison. Okay?"

"I will."

SHEA EXPLAINED to Toni what Megan had told her. "Ay, gracias a Dios, she's alive."

"Yeah, but for how long? I gotta get up there now, Tone."

"It will take you two, maybe three hours to reach the Happy Jack area, Shea. Let me call Special Agent Obregón. They should be at the original Luminos campground by now. They can get there mucho más rápido."

"If they even bother."

Toni grabbed her phone. "Marc, it's Toni Rios. ¿Qué esta pasando? Sí, sí." She paused for a while. "¡Ay, Dios mio! ¿Cuantos cuerpos? Ay, ay, ay! I have some new intel. We got a call informing us that Annie Wittmann and the other children from the Bold Women of Tomorrow camp are at an alternate Luminos camp near Happy Jack. I can send you the coordinates. How soon can you send some agents there? No sé. Sí, entiendo. Okay, gracias." She sent him a text and hung up.

"What'd he say?"

"He'll let his ASAC know about the girls being at the Happy Jack camp. He's not sure how soon they can get out there. They've got nearly fifty bodies at the camp in Sedona. Right now, it's all hands on deck processing the scene."

"They're more worried about dead bodies than about keeping the girls alive? Typical fed bullshit. Fuck! That's it. I'm calling in the Sisterhood. If the feds don't want to save human lives, then we will."

She held Toni's gaze for a long moment, expecting her to say, "Let the feds handle it."

"Shea, your truck's in the Sedona impound. Your leg's busted all to hell. I'd say you're gonna need a ride. I'll grab my keys while you call Fuego."

Shea sat there stunned for a second. Toni really did have her back. "Yeah, okay," was all she could say at first.

Shea called Fuego, Indigo, and several other members, including a few prospects. All agreed to meet her at the clubhouse in thirty minutes. Shea grabbed a .45-caliber semiauto and a compact .38 revolver from the safe in her closet.

She pulled on the leather jacket with the mis-sewn patches and stuffed her lockpicks in the inside left pocket. On her belt, she hung a walkie-talkie that could connect with the comm systems that many of the Sisters wore on their motorcycle helmets.

Thirty minutes later, Toni's Honda Accord sat parked behind the Athena Sisterhood club house. The sun had risen, casting the lot in golden sunshine. Eight other patched members of the Sisterhood and two prospects soon arrived on their bikes.

"We'll drive north on the 17, and exit on Stoneman Lake Road," Toni explained. "After fifteen miles, we'll hang a right onto Lake Mary Road. The camp is about three miles past the Lowell Discovery Telescope. We'll turn left onto a forest service road for about two miles.

"Our primary objective is to protect the girls. Use deadly force only if absolutely necessary. Keep in mind that the Luminos members have been brainwashed and may act against their own interests. They are victims as well as perpetrators. Don't risk pulling the Sisterhood into a legal quagmire. Any questions?"

No one spoke.

"Let's go get these girls."

They synced their comms and raced north. Toni and Shea took the lead in Toni's Honda while the Sisters rode staggered behind them.

A part of Shea was envious that she was in a cage rather than on one of her bikes. At the same time, she was grateful to be riding next to Toni and impressed with how her girlfriend had taken charge of the situation.

On the way up, Shea filled her in on her experiences at Luminos. Toni, likewise, gave her accounts of some of the defense cases she'd been working on. At any moment, Shea expected Toni's phone to ring with Special Agent Obregón, telling her they'd reached the Happy Jack site and had rescued the girls. But no call came.

Shea's blood pressure rose the closer they got to the other campsite. They were almost to the turnoff onto the forest service road when Shea spotted a black Toyota sedan coming the other direction. Her spine turned to ice when she recognized the driver.

Shea dreaded what she'd find when they arrived at the new campground. She hadn't heard back from Megan. Were they still alive? Or had NCB and the other blue bars murdered them too?

Shea hopped on the walkie-talkie. "Fuego, this is Havoc. The black Toyota we just passed. That was Connie Brady, one of people from Luminos responsible for the massacre in Sedona. We can't let her get away."

"Copy, Havoc. We'll grab her."

Orders squawked over the coms. Four of the Sisters at the back of the pack broke off and went after Brady.

"Please be alive. Please be alive," Shea muttered.

Toni floored it until the GPS system told her to turn. The forest service road was primitive and poorly maintained. Shea bounced around in her seat like a pinball. The jostling set the nerves in her leg on fire. She grabbed hold of the "oh shit" handle above the door and held onto the center console with her other hand.

A glance in the mirror revealed the women behind her were struggling to keep up. Street bikes weren't designed for such terrain.

After she wound through a series of turns and up a hill, the road dead-ended at a cluster of ramshackle cabins, each painted a different color. A stone cabin stood in the center.

The Honda skidded to a stop with the motorcycles parked on either side. The sudden silence was jarring. No element of surprise working in their favor.

Fueled with anger and adrenaline, Shea burst out the door and hobbled as fast as she could, not even bothering with crutches. With her pistol in hand, she studied the seven cabins, looking for clues to Annie's whereabouts. The wooden cabins all looked alike, aside from the color of paint.

Toni appeared at Shea's side, a Glock nine-mil in her hand. The other bikers huddled around them.

"We should search the cabins in pairs," Shea suggested. "Anybody finds the girls, give a shout."

The door of the stone cabin opened. A muscular white guy stepped out. "This is private property. You people have to—"

"Where the hell's my niece?" Shea pointed her pistol at him.

"Your niece? I don't—"

"Don't you fucking lie to me, asshole. Where is she?"

A girl's scream pierced the air, crackling with terror. It came from the stone cabin.

Shea's eyes widened. "Annie."

CHAPTER 45
ALLIANCES

IN THE MIDDLE of the night, Annie Wittmann and her fellow campers had been rousted from their beds at Bold Women of Tomorrow and herded into panel vans. The drive took hours, and the campers had no way to see where they were going.

Holly Gordon, the camp program coordinator, explained they were taking part in a team-building exercise. No further explanation.

When the van stopped and they were let out, Annie realized they were in a clearing in the woods surrounded by several cabins. The air was cool and smelled of pines.

She didn't know where they were. Could be in the national forests near Prescott or Ironwood, but it wouldn't have taken them that long to get there. Her gut told her she was farther east. Someplace north of the Mogollon Rim, maybe even the White Mountains that bordered New Mexico.

Holly, along with a woman calling herself Dr. Linda and a gigantic creepy guy who looked like a professional wrestler, separated them into three groups of eight. Creepy Wrestler Guy led Annie's group to one of the musty run-down cabins and locked them in, four to a room. They had no phones, no belongings, and nothing to sleep on but a few frayed cots. Only a five-gallon bucket for a toilet. And no light except from an outside lamp that shone through a small, high-set window.

This may have been a team-building exercise, but so far, it felt like being held prisoner. Traumatic memories of the time she'd been kidnapped sent her pulse skyrocketing into panic mode. Every sound outside the locked room brought with it the threat of danger and excruciating pain.

Annie rallied to get control of her fear. Aunt Shea had once taught her that panic robbed you of the ability to find a way out of a dangerous situation. She could do this. She was smart. She was resilient. And best of all, she wasn't alone.

After they'd exhausted themselves by pounding on the door and screaming to be let out, Annie lay on her cot, concentrating on her breathing as her tía Toni had taught her until she drifted off to sleep.

Early the next morning, Annie woke to the sound of footsteps. The door opened. Creepy Wrestler Guy appeared.

For a moment, Annie dared hope he was letting them out. Instead, he shoved a cardboard box into the room and closed the door again. Annie rushed to the door but reached it a split second after the deadbolt clacked back in place.

"When are they gonna let us out?" Annie shouted.

"When they're good and ready," Creepy Wrestler Guy replied through the door. Until then, eat your breakfast, drink your water, and keep quiet."

His footsteps disappeared down the hall. A muffled cry of hope rose from the campers locked in the room on the other end of the cabin, only to dissolve into shouts to be let out and finally cries of despair.

Annie looked into the box he'd shoved into the room. Inside, she found plastic food trays and bottles of water. Each tray contained a half-frozen burger in one section and dried-out rice and slimy green beans in the others. No way was she eating that.

Annie opened a water bottle. The water had an odd flavor. Like licorice or anise. Maybe it was flavored with stevia, though she didn't see any mention of it on the label. Maybe it contained something else. She resealed the water and tossed it back in the box.

"That man told us to keep quiet. We should probably do as he says," Abigail said, hastily chugging a bottle of water. She had cheerleader looks and what her Aunt Shea called Jesus Tourette's syndrome.

"Screw that. They lock us in here all night and give us this goddamn crap to eat? I don't think so."

"You shouldn't take God's name in vain. It's a sin."

"Maybe if God got up off his ass and helped us get outta here, I'd reconsider it. And where the hell is Holly? What gives her the right to keep us locked up like a bunch of animals?"

"It's a team-building exercise," replied Mandy, a heavyset girl with sad eyes. "Maybe we're supposed to work together to figure a way out."

"Like you'd be smart enough to figure out how to get out of a locked room, lardo," Abigail said with a snort.

Sydney, a girl with a head full of shoulder-length braids, sneered at her. "You know, Abby, you like to bandy 'Jesus' about, but you sure don't act like him."

"Yeah, just shut the hell up, Abby," Annie added, putting a hand on Mandy's shoulder. "Don't listen to her, Mandy. She don't know nothing."

"*Doesn't know anything*, you ignorant redneck. Shows you what a public education is good for. You can't even speak proper English."

Annie punched Abigail in the face, sending her tumbling over the box and onto the floor. Delivering the blow hurt

Annie's hand much more than she expected, but it was worth it.

Sydney stepped between them. "Easy, girl. She's not worth it."

"She hit me!" whined Abigail. "She hit me. I'm telling Holly and my parents. They're gonna sue you to the poorhouse."

"Ignore her, Annie. Let's find a way out of here."

Annie nodded. "Let's blow this joint."

"How?" asked Mandy. "We have nothing to break out with. There's only a small window, and it's five feet off the ground."

Annie studied the door. "If I had something to pick this lock with..."

"You know how to pick locks?" Sydney asked.

"My aunt Shea taught me." Annie recalled tía Toni's protests when Shea showed her the basics.

"Figures a lowlife criminal would know something like that," Abigail said with a sneer.

"Will this work?" Mandy pulled a barrette out of her long hair.

The barrette's clip was made of a thick wire that might work as a tensioner.

"I think so. I'll have to break the metal part off and bend it."

Mandy shrugged. "It's okay. I got plenty more at home. If we ever get home."

The girl teared up, triggering a lump in Annie's throat. "I'll try to get us out."

Annie separated the clip from the barrette and bent the end at a ninety-degree angle. "You have another barrette?"

"Sorry. Just the one."

"How about this?" Sydney offered her a paper clip. "Found it in the box."

Annie straightened it out, leaving a slight hook at the end. "Yes, I think this should work."

Annie knelt in front of the door, trying to remember what Aunt Shea had taught her. She inserted the short end of the bent hair clip in the lock and applied a gentle pressure to it while testing the pins with the straightened paper clip.

She counted six pins in the lock. Typical for a deadbolt. She probed and raked and set at least a few, but the others refused to catch. She reset several times without success.

"I thought you knew how to pick locks," Abigail snorted. "Even as a criminal, you're inept."

"I do know how. I'm just used to using actual lockpicks. And this is a deadbolt. It's got security pins that make it harder to pick."

"You're just a liar is all you are. Trying to act cool like you know something you don't."

Annie resisted the urge to belt the snotty bitch again. The darkening bruise on the girl's face would have to suffice. She had to focus on helping them get out of there.

After several more minutes of trying, she tossed the makeshift picks aside. "I can't get it."

Sydney and Mandy tried to kick the door open, but it remained solid and shut.

"Maybe when that creep shows up again with the food and water, we jump him," said Sydney as they sat on the floor, catching their breath.

"Maybe. But who knows when him or anyone else will show up again?"

Mandy sat on her cot and cried. Annie and Sydney sat on either side of her with arms over her shoulders, but they didn't speak. Abigail sat alone in the corner cot.

"I wasn't always fat," Mandy said after a long while.

Annie wasn't sure what prompted the comment. "Yeah?"

"I used to be skinny and pretty like Abigail."

"You're still pretty."

"Not like I was. Thought I was all that, you know? In eighth grade, all the boys were asking me out. I even did a bit of modeling. I got to be a bit of a snob."

"What changed?" Sydney asked.

"My mom started dating this guy a few years ago. He seemed nice at first. Called me his little goddess. But then…"

Annie knew right away where this was going. "He turned out to be a perv."

Mandy began sobbing quietly. "I couldn't bring myself to tell anyone. I thought it was my fault for being such a…a bitch."

"Not your fault he was a perv, Mandy," Annie said.

"I started eating more. It was the only thing that made me feel good. After a while, my mom's boyfriend stopped messing with me. Guess he didn't want a fat goddess."

"Mandy, you are still a goddess, girl," replied Sydney. "Your dress size ain't got nothing to do with that."

"Something similar happened to me," Abigail whispered. "Except I stopped eating. It was like the only thing in my life I had any control over."

Annie looked up at the girl across the room, wary that she was up to something. But the sadness on her face looked genuine. "I'm sorry that happened to you."

"My mom has schizophrenia," Sydney whispered.

"You mean like multiple personalities?" Mandy asked.

"Nah, that's something different. It's like her mind disconnects from reality. When she's not on her meds, she hears and sees things that aren't there. My dad, he's like a saint. Always there for her. He knows that the disease ain't her. It's just the disease. When she's on her meds, which she is most of the time, she's a great mom. But sometimes…it's just hard, you know?"

Annie nodded. "Sounds tough."

"How about you, Annie?" Mandy asked.

Annie squirmed. Her life had been anything but

normal. Growing up around a biker gang. Getting kidnapped. Losing her parents. But that was just stuff that happened. Some of it bad stuff. But it didn't define her. She knew that. But there was one thing that did. Or that she thought did.

She had shared this secret with Holly in one of their one-on-one interviews. Holly had insisted that secrets held you hostage to your fears. Sharing your truths freed you to claim your power and change the world.

Now, confined in this cabin with the other girls, she found the courage to speak her truth.

"About a year ago, this guy shows up claiming to be my bio dad. I had to take a DNA test to see if he really was."

"Like a paternity test?" Sydney asked.

"Yeah. Only…it showed something weird."

"What?"

"It showed I'm intersex."

Sydney cocked an eyebrow. "Intersex?"

Annie took a deep breath and let it out. "I was born…I was born with XY sex chromosomes. Everybody thought it was a mistake at first. That my DNA sample got mixed up with someone else's. I mean, you've seen me in the showers at camp. I'm a girl, right? All girl parts. No boy parts. Except it turns out I was born with androgen insensitivity syndrome."

Mandy wiped her face and met Annie's eyes. "What's that?"

"It means my body makes testosterone like a boy but doesn't know what to do with it. So, I developed like any other girl. My DNA is just…confused."

Her pulse was racing. She expected the others would freak out at any moment. Or worse, call her a freak.

Mandy replied with a quiet "Wow."

"I have seen you in the showers," Sydney said. "You definitely a girl."

"Oh, you been checking me out, have you?" Annie teased, despite her nervousness.

"Nah, ain't like that. I'm just saying. DNA don't determine who you are. Just as my mom's schizophrenia doesn't define who she really is."

"You get a period?"

Annie shook her head. "No."

"Lucky," replied Sydney.

Annie looked across the room and found Abigail staring at her. "Go on, say it. I'm a freak. An abomination."

Abigail didn't respond right away. Annie felt her fists curling.

"That..." Abigail started. "I can't imagine what that must have felt like for you. To know you're a girl, and yet this stupid test says something else. Must've been hard."

"Yeah, it was at first. Fortunately, my aunts were really supportive. My grandma too. I guess I'm really lucky."

"Must be nice having a family that looks out for you." The sorrow on Abigail's face cut a gaping hole in Annie's animosity toward her.

"Come here." Annie raised her arm and beckoned the girl.

Abigail walked over, head bowed, and sat next to Annie. The four of them squeezed together on the cot. Annie expected it to rip apart and send them all sprawling.

"I'm sorry for what I said earlier," Abigail said. "To all of you."

"Sorry I hit you."

Thunder rumbled in the distance. The light coming in from the window had dimmed dramatically.

"Sounds like a monsoon coming on."

FOR THE REST of the day and throughout the night, thunder shook the cabin walls. The roof leaked over Abigail's cot, so they all shifted over to stay dry. Some of the lightning strikes sounded so close, Annie wondered what would happen if lightning struck the building itself and set the place ablaze. How would they get out?

At first light the next morning, Annie was back picking the lock. But try as she might, she could not set all the pins. It felt at times like she had, but the cylinder refused to turn. Damned security pins.

She stopped when she heard multiple footsteps approaching. Annie and Sydney exchanged a glance and crouched, ready to pounce.

The door opened. Annie lunged at Creepy Wrestler Guy with fists flying. But neither she nor Sydney were any match for him. He tossed them back into the room as if they were rag dolls. "Get back, bitches."

"Donnie! Language." Holly appeared in the doorway. "We don't talk to our girls that way."

"Holly!" Annie got back to her feet. "Please let us out. We've formed a team. We want to go home now."

"Soon. I promise. But first, I need Sydney to come with me."

Annie tried to push past, but Creepy Donnie again pushed her back inside.

"Annie, you'll have to wait your turn. Soon, I promise. But Sydney first."

She didn't want to wait. She wanted out now. But it was clear she wouldn't get past Creepy Donnie.

Sydney stared at the two adults with a wary gaze. "Why just me? Why not all of us?"

"Trust me. All will be revealed in time."

Creepy Donnie grabbed Sydney by the wrist and hustled her out of the room then once again shut the door, the lock clacking in place.

Annie tried to make sense of what was going on. Maybe Holly was telling the truth, and they would all be let out. Maybe they were interviewing them individually first to see how everyone did. But something told her it would not be that simple.

Annie looked at her fellow campers. They were exhausted and hungry. Mandy was crying. Abigail was in the corner on her knees, praying. This was hopeless.

Annie grabbed her makeshift picks and started working again on the lock until a low rumble grew outside.

"What is that?" Mandy asked, wiping her face. "Another monsoon?"

The rumble became a sustained roar, growing louder by the second.

Abigail stopped praying. "Sounds like a rockslide."

"No." A glimmer of hope blossomed inside Annie. "Motorcycles. Lots of them."

When the engines went silenced, she banged on the door and shouted. "In here! We're in here!"

They all kept shouting until a distant scream silenced them.

The room went dead silent for a moment. Then it erupted in shouts, sobs, and wailing. Annie snatched up the improvised lockpicks and furiously began working on the deadbolt.

Shea and the other women roared past the big guy and charged through the door of the stone cabin with guns raised.

The smell of burned meat hung in the air of the warm, dimly lit room. Fake Doctor Linda stood over a shirtless dark-skinned girl who sat sobbing in a chair next to a metal tray table of medical supplies. Linda appeared to be treating a wound on the girl's chest. Some women Shea didn't recognize huddled around the two of them.

"What the ever-loving fuck is going on? Where the hell's my niece?"

Linda turned and glared at her. "You should not be here. This is a private ceremony on private property."

"Bullshit! You're branding girls, you fucking monster. Get the fuck away from her."

"Shea Stevens," said an all-too-familiar voice from next to the fireplace. Bennett stood facing the fireplace, stirring the coals with a poker. Ramirez turned and glared at the Sisterhood, a dark bruise scoring the side of his face.

"It seems the fates keep pulling us together," Bennett purred.

"Jig's up, you sick motherfucker. Where the hell's my niece?"

Bennett removed the end of the poker from the coals to reveal it was a branding iron. The glyph of his initials glowed at the end. He slowly turned and met her gaze. "I must say, you have proved yourself to be remarkably resourceful. Bested old Georgie Porgie here. And with a bum leg, no less. Very impressive. Maybe I should hire you as my head of security."

"You have exactly ten seconds to put that thing down and tell me where my niece is. Or I will put every one of you sadistic fuckers in the ground. Do you hear me?"

"Shea," he crooned in an appeasing tone. "No need for violence. We are all friends here. How lovely you brought some of your biker companions."

"Eight." Shea counted down.

"Put down the branding iron, Mr. Bennett," Toni ordered. "Do it now."

"I would, ma'am, but the floor is wood. I'd hate for the cabin to catch fire and burn us all up."

"Seven."

"Set it down in the fireplace then get down on the floor. All of you," Toni continued.

"I'm treating a patient," Linda insisted.

"Six."

"Did those screams alarm you, ladies? They were screams of delight. Young Sydney here was transitioning to a new stage of her spiritual journey."

"Bullshit! You fucking branded her." Shea's finger hovered over the trigger. "Four."

"Okay, okay." Bennett held out his free hand in a calming gesture. He set the fiery end of the iron in a small metal bucket beside the fireplace. The poker sizzled and sent up a cloud of steam. "We will bring Annie here to you, all right? Holly, would you be so kind as to retrieve Miss Annie Wittman from her cabin?"

A woman wearing a Bold Women of Tomorrow polo shirt nodded obediently. "As you wish."

"Raven, Banshee, go with her," Fuego ordered. "Make sure that puta don't try nothing stupid."

"You got it, Prez," Raven replied.

"Savage, check on the girl," Shea added. "I don't trust this fake doctor."

"Gladly."

"This is my patient." Linda stepped defiantly between Savage and the girl. "I am her doctor."

Savage gripped her by the lapel. "You're going to need a doctor if you don't move out of my way."

Linda glared at her but stepped aside.

"Hi, Sydney. My name's Chelsea," Savage said in a gentle tone. "I'm an emergency medical technician. Do you know what that is?"

"Like a paramedic?" Sydney asked between choked sobs.

"You got it. You're a smart girl. I'm just going to look at that burn, okay?"

CHAPTER 47
REVELATIONS

"WHAT ARE THEY DOING TO SYDNEY?" Mandy cried.

"I don't know." Annie worked furiously on the lock.

Despite the chill in the air, sweat trickled down her face and burned her eyes. Three pins set. Four. Five. When it felt like the sixth one caught, she put more pressure on the improvised tensioner. To her surprise, the cylinder turned.

For a moment, she simply stared at the lock. "I…I did it."

She leapt to her feet and opened the door. "Come on. Let's get out of here."

No sooner did she step into the dark hallway than several silhouetted figures appeared near the cabin's front door.

"Get out of our way or we'll kill you," Annie shouted with as much ferocity as she could muster.

"Annie?" replied a familiar voice.

"Raven?" A glimmer of hope filled Annie's chest. She rushed toward the woman and embraced her with relief. "How'd you find me?"

"Long story." Raven's tan round face broke out into a smile. Holly and Banshee, one of the Sisterhood's prospects, stood next to her. "Come on, girl. I'll take you to your aunts."

"Wait." Annie glared at Holly. "There are other girls here locked in the rooms. We have to let them out."

"Okay, you head to the stone cabin. Banshee and I will see to the other girls."

"Thank you." A burst of energy and relief flowed through Annie. She raced into the sunlight and toward the stone cabin's open door.

"Aunt Shea!"

Shea's heart leapt, and she hobbled to the front door. Annie was flying past the motorcycles in the clearing. Shea met her on the cabin's front porch and wrapped her in a tight hug.

"Oh my god, sweetie. It's so good to see you. I've been so worried."

"I'm okay. I'm okay. I'm okay. Thank you for coming to get me."

Shea just stood there with her arms around the gangly teen. For a moment, gratitude and joy blotted out every scintilla of pain. It was as if she'd just woken from the worst nightmare, only to realize her greatest dreams had come true.

When at last Shea pulled away, she met Annie's eyes. "I'm so sorry I didn't come sooner." Guilt came crushing down on her positivity like a power hammer at her shop. "I…"

Annie wiped the tears from her face. "It's okay. You were trying to help Megan. Toni told me."

"I know, but you're my number-one priority. You know that, right? More than anyone else. More important than me.

More important than even Toni, and you know how much I love her."

Annie nodded. "I know. I love you too."

"Come on. Let's go say hi to Toni and the others."

Shea led her back inside the stone cabin where the bitter smell of scorched flesh still lingered. "How is she, Savage?"

Savage stooped over Sydney, whose chest was now bandaged and covered with a towel. "I used the antibiotic ointment and burn gel they have here, but she needs to see a doctor. A real doctor."

"Coconino Sheriff's office is on their way," Toni announced. "I've also contacted Cortes County and the FBI."

The cabin began filling up with girls from the Bold Women of Tomorrow camp. Megan emerged from the crowd and hugged Shea.

"Thank you, Miss Shea. You…you rescued me twice in twenty-four hours. I don't know how to thank you."

"You can start by telling the Sedona cops to drop the kidnapping charges against me."

"Yes, yes, of course. I was so stupid, so…I don't know. Crazy, I guess."

"They drugged you like they did everyone else. It's not your fault."

"But you didn't fall for it."

"I came in knowing they were up to no good. And I had some people helping me."

Megan's grateful expression dissolved into grief. "All my friends. They're dead now. I would've been too. Maybe I should've been."

"No, Megan. You shouldn't. You're alive. And the best thing you can do is testify against Bennett and his cronies. That's the best way you can honor your friends' memory."

"Yeah, okay. I can do that."

The Sisters did what they could to keep the girls calm while they all waited for the cops. The situation was chaos, but for the first time in a week, it seemed to Shea like a good chaos. Until she realized that people were missing.

"Hey!" Shea glanced around the room. "Where the hell's Bennett and Ramirez?"

"¡Mierda! Those pinches pendejos were just here," Fuego growled. "Where'd they go?"

Shea noticed a sly grin creep across Fake Doctor Linda's face. She pressed the muzzle of her gun to the woman's face. "Tell me where they went, bitch."

"What do I know? I'm just an unlicensed nurse practitioner."

"Talk, bitch or, so help me…"

"Amor, don't." Toni put her hand on Shea's arm. "Not in front of the girls. This puta isn't worth it."

"You want me to talk? I'll talk. Let's talk about you and your secrets."

"What? Tell me where Bennett and Ramirez went."

Somewhere outside, a car engine roared to life.

"We're on it," Fuego said. "We'll get them."

Raven and Indigo followed her outside.

"Tell me, Ms. Rios, did Shea here ever tell you how poor Annie came to be an orphan?"

Suddenly it dawned on Shea where this bitch was going with that. "Keep your fucking mouth shut."

Annie, who had been sitting with her friends, suddenly stood at the mention of her name.

"She murdered the poor girl's daddy and blamed it on a Mexican drug gang."

Rage once again exploded in Shea's mind. She raised her arm to coldcock the woman. Toni pulled her away and wrapped her in a bear hug.

"No, babe. Let it go."

"Shut up, bitch!" Shea shouted through tears. "Shut up, shut up. Don't listen to her, Annie."

"Aunt Shea?" Fear and confusion trembled in Annie's voice. "What's she talking about?"

"And your mommy? Oh, child, your auntie was told to stay at your daddy's clubhouse while he and his friends went to rescue you. But no, she had to be a hero and brought your mommy along for the ride. She wasn't even supposed to be there. But your aunt Shea insisted."

"It's a lie. It's a fucking lie."

"Aunt Shea? What's she saying?"

"Annie, don't listen to this woman," Toni replied in a calming tone.

"You bitch!" Shea screamed. "You fucking, lying bitch."

"Sorry, Shea," Linda said in a singsong manner. "The truth deserves to be told. I'm simply freeing you from your dark secrets."

In a burst of energy, Shea broke free of Toni's grip and pistol-whipped Linda with every ounce of strength she had. The woman fell to the floor and didn't move. Shea's chest felt like it would explode with all the emotions blazing inside her.

"Shea. Mierda." Toni knelt. "Savage, a little help."

"Let the bitch bleed," Savage replied.

Shea spat at her. "Amen, sister."

CHAPTER 48
HOME

THE COPS ARRIVED twenty minutes later, and the feds followed an hour after that. Everyone was questioned, though Shea's interview with Special Agent Obregón was not nearly as grueling as the ones she'd endured in Sedona. Just a straightforward interview without the usual jumping back and forth in the timeline to trip her up. Probably because they already knew most of what had led up to the situation.

When Shea was finally released, she met up with Toni, Annie, and the Sisterhood in the clearing.

"We tried to catch Bennett and that other puto, but they got away. Sorry, Havoc," Fuego explained.

Shea shook her head, too exhausted to feel much of anything. "It's okay. Annie, Megan, and the other girls are safe."

"On the plus side, Brillo and Dragon caught that loca lawyer a few miles north of here. Apparently, the feds had a warrant out for her. Credit card fraud or some shit."

"Good. Glad we got her at least." Shea's left knee buckled, but Toni kept her from falling to the ground.

"We need to get your leg looked at," Toni said.

The last thing she wanted was to spend another few hours in an ER, but she didn't have the strength to protest. "Yeah, okay."

Shea hugged Fuego and the others. "Thanks for helping me out."

"No worries, chica," Fuego replied. "We'll see that Megan gets home safe. Hermanas por siempre." *Sisters forever.*

"Forever sisters." Shea said in response.

On the ride back, Shea rode in the back seat of the car with her arms wrapped around Annie, never wanting to let her go. Toni played an album from the Buena Vista Social Club on the stereo. Shea didn't know why, but Cuban jazz always seemed to lift her mood, even in dark times. Something about the brightness of the horns and the energetic beat. It was the sound of joy in the face of trauma.

A few hours later, they helped Shea into the Ocotillo Urgent Care facility, where her leg received an X-ray and a CT scan. After an interminable wait for the results, she learned that she'd torn the meniscus in her left knee. The good news was that the doctor didn't recommend surgery, though she'd have to spend the next few weeks staying off it and going to physical therapy.

On the drive back to Sycamore Springs, Shea checked the news on her phone. Media outlets were reporting the deaths at Luminos as a mass suicide. A few called it what it was. Murder.

A part of her felt guilty she couldn't save the rest of them. Gayle, Erykah, Rory, and so many others. She hadn't heard whether Wicked was among the dead. But what more could she have done? How did you save someone who didn't want to be saved?

At home, they went straight to bed. At one point, Annie crawled between Shea and Toni, and the three of them slept for nine hours straight.

Shea crept out of bed at four the next morning, limped outside to the front porch, and stared out at the night. A neighborhood bobcat they'd nicknamed Bobbie Jean strolled into the glow of her porch light, leading a new litter of kittens.

"Keep 'em safe, girl."

When they vanished once again into the darkness, she pulled out her phone. Three voicemail messages had been left overnight.

The first was from Cat Hamilton, thanking her for rescuing Megan. Apparently, Megan had fully cooperated with the feds and faced no charges of her own. Cat and Nita had talked and were going to pay Shea and Indigo for their trouble, including the deposit on her bail.

The second message was from Detective Hawthorne, informing her that the Yavapai county attorney had dropped all charges against her after Megan admitted that Shea had acted to protect her.

The last message was from Wicked.

"Hey, Shea. It's Maria Wickham, a.k.a. Wicked from the Pink Trinkets. I heard through the grapevine that you went undercover to bring down Luminos. Gotta admit, at first, I was angry, thinking you betrayed us. But now...now, I'm just ashamed. I realize now what Vicious and Nasty have been telling me over the past few years. I helped recruit so many women whom NCB abused." Her voice cracked with sorrow.

"I don't know how I can live with myself. I thought I was making the world a better place. And now dozens of people are dead, and hundreds have been traumatized, in part because of my stupidity. Thank you, Shea, for doing what I couldn't. You're a genuine hero. Stay safe, my friend."

"¡Hola, mi amor," Toni whispered and sat down next to her. "¿Como estás?"

"I'm okay. Feels weird to be home. But good."

"I got an email from Special Agent Obregón. ASAC Potter has been arrested."

"Who's that?"

"Assistant Special Agent in Charge of the Flagstaff Field Office. Apparently, she's a member of Luminos and was sandbagging the investigation. She's facing some serious conspiracy charges."

"Wow. Sedona PD dropped the charges against me."

Toni's tired face brightened. "Really? ¡Gracias a Dios!"

"Any word on Nathan Bennett?"

"Still in the wind, last I heard. But he's on the FBI's most wanted list, along with George Ramirez."

"Motherfuckers."

"At least Annie and Megan and all the girls from the Bold Women camp are home safe. And you're on the mend."

"Annie's gonna need some serious therapy," Shea admitted.

Toni clasped Shea's hand. "Surprised to hear you say that. I thought you didn't believe in therapy."

"I'm willing to concede it can help sometimes. It helped her get over the death of her folks."

As soon as she said that, she recalled Linda blurting out the truth about their deaths.

"Dígame, amor. Did you kill Annie's father?"

"Am I talking to my girlfriend or the cop?"

"Your girlfriend. Tell me the truth. Just between you and me."

"I'd arranged for the Confederate Thunder to return the drugs they'd stolen from the Jags. The hope was to end the bloodshed between the two gangs. But Hunter had other plans."

"The bomb."

"Right. Suddenly, the whole thing went sideways. Everybody started shooting. I tried to get the hell outta there, but Hunter followed me. He hated me for protecting Wendy when she tried to leave him. He blamed me for Wendy getting killed at the ransom drop."

"That wasn't your fault, chica. A mother's love knows no bounds. Nothing you could have done to stop her coming with you."

"My fault or not, Hunter tried to kill me. Almost did. I just got lucky and killed him first. Just seemed easier to blame his death on the Jaguars. Especially after your lieutenant and partner tried to murder me when I was driving away."

Toni leaned her head against Shea's shoulder while the two of them sat in silence, holding hands.

Shea felt relieved that Toni knew what had really happened. Even if it felt a little awkward confessing to killing someone to a retired cop. Would she tell her buddies back in the Cortes County Sheriff's Office? Could she still be charged with something? Murder? Interfering with an investigation?

No, Shea was not getting that vibe. This woman had her back. And Shea had hers.

"Self-defense," Toni said at last. "So why not tell Annie what really happened?"

"I...I don't know. She was too young. And I was afraid if I told her the truth, she'd want to go back to living with Julia, Monster, and the Confederate Thunder. After what happened to my mother and later Wendy, I couldn't risk it. Since then, just never knew how to tell her."

Toni nodded. "Pobrecita. It's a heavy burden to bear. But now that that puta spilled the beans, you owe it to Annie to tell her the truth."

"The truth about what?"

Shea nearly jumped out of her skin. She hadn't heard Annie walk outside.

"You're up early," Shea said, pasting on a smile.

"I woke up, and you two were gone."

Shea couldn't help but laugh. "Maybe because some teenager kept kicking me in her sleep. Tomorrow night, you sleep in your own bed."

"Toni said you owe me the truth about something."

And just like that, the heavy burden of the secret fell hard on her chest.

"I'm going to make a pot of coffee while you two talk." Toni disappeared into the house.

"You remember that woman at the camp saying I was responsible for your parents' deaths?"

"She was crazy."

Shea told Annie the entire story. Both were crying by the time she was done. Shea was sure Annie would hate her. And Shea wouldn't blame her if she did.

"I miss my mom," Annie said at last, her words muffled through sobs.

"I miss her too. Shoulda never took her with me to the ransom drop."

"It's not your fault she's dead." Annie hugged her. "Those evil men who kidnapped me killed her."

"Yeah," Shea replied, not knowing what else to say.

"My dad used to hurt my mom a lot. If you say he attacked you, I believe it. I know you, Aunt Shea. You're a good person. You rescued me from the kidnappers before you'd ever met me. When we found out I was intersex, you helped me accept that about myself. I'm glad I have you. And yesterday, you rescued me again."

"I had a lotta help."

"But you were there for me when I needed it."

The three of them sat in silence for a while. The eastern sky brightened from gray to apricot.

"I saw Bobbie Jean a while ago. She had a new litter of kittens with her."

"Really? Aww, wish I'd seen them."

"I was thinking, maybe later today we could drive over to the Four Paws Animal Rescue and adopt a couple of kittens."

Annie's tear-strewn face brightened. "Really?"

"Really."

A FEW WEEKS LATER, Shea arrived at Iron Goddess, riding her FJR. She was early. No one, not even Terrance or Lakota, had arrived.

As always, the service bay smelled of rubber, oil, and steel. She'd forgotten how much she missed it. This was a place of second chances and new beginnings. Her first job out of prison had been here. The motorcycle shop of misfit toys, as someone once had dubbed it. A place where broken people with tarnished pasts could build a new life.

Standing alone in the quiet service bay, she realized that she, too, was ready for a new start. She had a lot of shit to put behind her. But for the first time in a while, her creativity juices were starting to flow again.

"Damn, am I seeing things? Is this the ghost of Shea Stevens?"

Shea turned to see Lakota striding toward her with arms outstretched. Shea embraced her.

"Feels good to be back."

"Good to have you back, girl. You seen the new bike?"

"No."

Shea followed her to where a partially assembled

motorcycle was on a stand. It looked like the sketches she had made but better.

"I had to make some modifications to the design," Lakota explained. "And we're still wiring it up. Just came back from the paint shop yesterday. Still waiting on the pipes to come back from chrome."

"Looks amazing. Guess you didn't need me here after all."

Lakota chuckled. "Oh, no. Would've been a lot easier if you were here. I've been working long days. If Terrance hadn't hired the new gal, I'd still be fabricating everything, and we would've missed the deadline."

"New gal?"

"Mystic. Got out of lockup a month ago. Good welder. Had some machining experience."

Shea's heart skipped a beat. *Couldn't be. Could it?* "What's her real name?"

"Lauren Randall, I believe. Why? You know her?"

"Yeah. A lifetime ago. Before I got locked up."

"Should we not have hired her?"

"I'm sure it'll be fine. What was she in for?"

"Manslaughter. Killed an ex-boyfriend."

"Ex-boyfriend, huh?" Shea nodded. "Should be interesting."

"Hey, I read that article in *Phoenix Living* about the Luminos cult. What a horrible tragedy. I'm glad you and Annie got out okay."

Once the story of the Luminos massacre broke, a flurry of media inquiries had flooded into the shop. Local and national news organizations, not to mention a handful of true crime podcasters. Terrance had fielded the calls, but Shea had granted an interview only to a reporter from the weekly alternative newspaper based out of Phoenix.

She wanted the truth known, but after all the fallout, she was in the mood to share it only once. The last thing she wanted was to become the media darling of the week. She hadn't even bothered reading the article when it came out.

The rest of the crew trickled in, greeting her with hugs and slaps on the back. Her reunion with Mystic was awkward but professional. They had dated so long ago, and both had been through a lot since. If things worked out, they'd eventually talk. But Shea wasn't ready just yet.

After a few hours of helping Lakota and Mystic wire up the new bike, their head sales rep, Monica Austin, walked into the service bay. "Hey, boss. Glad you're back."

"Thanks. What's up?"

"Some guy up front asking for you?"

"A guy?" Considering they primarily sold bikes designed for women, his presence seemed a little odd. "He give you a name?"

"Paul Hudson."

The name rang a faint bell, but she couldn't place it.

"Big guy. Missing part of an arm," Monica added.

Suddenly, it clicked. The asshole driver of the pickup truck that wrecked her bike. What the hell did he want? Her insurance company was suing his for the cost of repairing her custom bike. But why should he care?

"All right. I'll be right there."

"Everything okay, girl?" Lakota asked.

"Not sure."

She stood up and limped down the hall, thinking about the prescription bottle in her pocket.

When she and Monica reached the showroom, Monica pointed at a stocky guy with a shaved head and a scraggly beard. If not for the missing arm, she wouldn't have recognized him.

"I'm Shea Stevens. Whaddya want?" she muttered warily.

He glanced down at the brace on her leg. "That from the accident?"

"Yeah."

"Sorry."

Shea didn't expect an apology and wasn't sure what to say in response. "Okay."

"Cops say you saved my life. Woulda bled out otherwise."

"Cops say a lotta crazy shit."

"Yeah, well. I wanted to repay the favor."

"And how do you plan to do that?"

"I read that article about you and Luminos."

"What about it?"

"I used to be a member."

Shea's senses tingled. Where the hell was this going? "Lemme guess, you're here to tell me not to testify when Fake Doctor Linda and that fucking Connie the shark lawyer go to trial."

"Nah, nothing like that."

"Then what?"

"I used to be NCB's enforcer. I helped train George Ramirez. He and I still talk from time to time."

"Get to the fucking point."

"I think I know where they are."

In pitch darkness, Shea worked the tumblers on the cabin's back door. Her fingers were stiff from the freezing rain. Winter came earlier up here in the north Georgia mountains. Even with the heavy coat and balaclava, she felt like a human Popsicle, which didn't make picking the lock any easier.

She'd spent two months following up on the lead that Hudson had given her. In that time, she'd learned that Nathan Curtis Bennett was born Dmitriy Ivanovich Turgenev, the only son of Russian immigrants.

He had been the leader of an independent evangelical church in Pittsburgh until a fire had wiped out nearly the entire congregation during an evening prayer service.

No one could explain why the doors were locked, or why Turgenev was one of the few to escape. A hung jury had resulted in a mistrial and an acquittal of all manslaughter charges. Turgenev disappeared and reinvented himself as Nathan Curtis Bennett.

Bennett now faced multiple counts of first-degree murder charges, aggravated assault, and kidnapping, as did George Ramirez, Connie Brady, Linda Steele, and George's lackey, a guy named Donnie Likowski.

But despite facing the death penalty, none of Bennett's cronies were willing to give up his location or testify against him in court. Even if the feds found him, it seemed likely that Bennett and possibly Ramirez would slither free once again. The man was more slippery than a greased rattlesnake.

It was with this information in mind that Shea told Toni what she had learned and what she intended to do about it. She didn't want any secrets between them. And to her relief, Toni agreed that, at least in this case, justice would be best served via "extrajudicial" means.

Ramirez had called Hudson from the Gold Strike motel in Dahlonega, inviting him to join them for Bennett's latest venture. Hudson passed, citing the recent loss of his arm. Upon reading the article in *Phoenix Living*, he contacted Shea.

She'd driven nearly two thousand miles on an Iron Goddess custom sport touring bike. It had been a helluva ride, especially once she got out of the desert, midway across Texas. She'd hit rain in Louisiana and hail just north of Atlanta. She'd never seen so many trees. And to see them dressed in their autumn splendor was quite a sight for a desert rat like her.

Ramirez was long gone from the motel by the time she

reached it. With the help of the Georgia Chapter of the Sisterhood, they canvassed the area for any sign of Bennett or Ramirez. Back in Arizona, Toni followed up on electronic leads that might indicate their whereabouts.

At a New Age bookstore in Helen, she found a flyer on the community bulletin board inviting people to join a new group promising wisdom and a new dawn for mankind. It wasn't terribly dissimilar from other posts on the board. But something in the wording told her this was Bennett's latest gambit.

She was tired, sore, and freezing when she reached the campground. The weeks of physical therapy had helped repair her meniscus, but the damp cold soaked into her bones. Her knee ached, much as it had when she was at Luminos. But she had a mission to complete.

At last, the cylinder in the back door's deadbolt turned. The hinges creaked when she opened it, but the noise could barely be heard above the clatter of the sleet on the roof and the increasingly tense voices within.

"Please, no. I don't want to do this." The voice was female and young.

"Now, Sonya, what have I told you about limitations? Nothing more than self-sabotage. You are holding yourself back. You'll never change the world until you learn to let go and trust. I'm here to liberate you. Deep down, you know you want this." This voice was all too familiar. It was why she was here.

The smells of weed and patchouli hung thick in the air. A man lay on top of a struggling teenage girl. Shea emerged from the dark of the hallway into a dimly lit bedroom and raised her pistol.

"Get off her."

The girl screamed. The man whipped around and faced Shea. His fly was open, and his erect penis was sticking out.

Bennett had lost weight since she'd seen him last. He also now sported a well-groomed goatee.

"Sonya, run on outta here," Shea said. "He ain't gonna hurt you no more."

The girl grabbed her clothes and rushed out of the cabin.

"Get out of my house," Bennett roared. "George! George!"

"George Ramirez is dead. I snapped his neck about five minutes ago." Shea pulled off the balaclava.

"Well, well, Shea Stevens. The big hero. Been a while. How's the leg?"

"Better."

"Well, don't be a stranger. Put down the gun, and I'll fix us a drink. What's your poi—"

Shea put a forty-caliber slug through his right eye. He dropped like a sack of potatoes.

"That's enough outta you."

She slipped out of the cabin and began the long drive home.

ALSO BY DHARMA KELLEHER

ABOUT THE AUTHOR

Dharma Kelleher writes gritty crime thrillers including the Jinx Ballou Bounty Hunter series and the Shea Stevens Outlaw Biker series.

She is one of the only openly transgender authors in the crime fiction genre. Her action-driven thrillers explore the complexities of social and criminal justice in a world where the legal system favors the privileged.

Dharma is a member of Sisters in Crime, the International Thriller Writers, and the Alliance of Independent Authors.

She lives in Arizona with her wife and a black cat named Mouse. Learn more about Dharma and her work at https://dharmakelleher.com.